beneath this
MASK

MEGHAN MARCH

contents

charlotte

I stepped off the witness stand feeling like I'd been skinned and gutted, my insides laid out for public viewing. I refused to meet my father's piercing aqua stare—the same one I saw every time I looked in the mirror. Instead, I focused on the sleeves of his navy pinstripe Armani suit jacket and his gaudy diamond cufflinks winking in the buzzing fluorescent light of the courtroom. My father was a general, flanked by his army of thousand dollar an hour defense attorneys. Not that they could save him. The disgust on the jurors' faces spoke louder than any convoluted defense they could mount. I slipped through the swinging wooden gate and glanced at my mother, sitting primly, ankles crossed and hands folded, in her favorite Chanel suit and tasteful gold jewelry. Lisette Agoston was the quintessential picture of a woman standing by her man. She expected me to take the seat next to her. The seat I'd vacated hours before, hands sweating and stomach churning, to give my testimony and endure the brutal cross-examination. But I couldn't do it. I couldn't sit down and be the supportive, naïve daughter anymore. So I kept walking. I didn't look at the gawking members of the press or the scornful sneers of the victims. I pushed open the heavy, carved wooden door and took my first deep breath of air that wasn't laced with lies.

I was done.

With them.

With this life.

With all of it.

It had all been a meticulously constructed fairy tale, and I'd been too blind and trusting to see through the façade. *I was done.* Burning shame swamped me. The Assistant U.S. Attorney's words rang in my ears:

How does it feel to realize your privileged life has been paid for with other people's dreams?

The objection came too late to prevent the cutting words. But no objection could erase the fact that he was right. My life had been paid for with money diverted from the hard-earned savings of tens of thousands of innocent victims. Move over Bernie Madoff. Alistair Agoston figured out a better way. Exponentially more complex and devastating, because the moment the scheme started to topple, $125 billion disappeared into thin air. Or hundreds of offshore accounts. No one was really sure. My father refused to admit anything, but the dozens of charges leveled by the Securities and Exchange Commission and the Department of Justice would ensure he spent the rest of his life in federal prison.

And after the cross I'd just been subjected to, it was clear the Assistant U.S. Attorney thought I should be joining him in an orange jumpsuit. If trusting your father was a crime, he'd be right about that, too.

I exited the courthouse, running down the marble stairs through the gauntlet of shouting reporters, dodging the microphones and cameras they shoved in my face.

"Charlotte, did you know—"

"Charlotte, where's the money?"

"Charlotte, are you being charged? Did you cut a deal?"

They battered me with questions until I dove into a waiting cab and slammed the door.

"East 60th and 3rd, please." My plan was simple: have the cabbie drop me off a couple blocks away from home and sneak into the service entrance of our building without being seen or recognized. My strawberry blonde hair— heavy on the strawberry—was too distinctive. That would be the first thing to go as soon as I got out of this town. I clutched my purse to my chest. My future, a one-way ticket to Atlanta, where I could disappear to my final destination, was tucked inside. I was flying coach for the first time in my life—a fact I wasn't proud of. I bundled my hair into a low bun and fished a giant pair of sunglasses and a scarf out of my purse. Somewhat disguised, I kept my head down until the car slowed to a stop. Tossing some bills at the cabbie, I slid out of the taxi.

The service elevator trundled its way up fifty-one floors, stopping at the penthouse. My hand shook as I typed in the code required to enter. Pushing the door open, I stepped into the cavernous, ultra-modern space that was my family's Manhattan home. After the inevitable guilty verdict came down, it'd become the property of the federal government along with the rest of the meager assets that the FBI had managed to find and freeze. To finance my escape, I'd cashed in $20,000 worth of savings bonds I'd found tucked into my First Communion bible. I tried not to dwell on the irony of my salvation being found in the good book.

My one bag was already packed, but a casual observer would never know I had taken anything from my walk-in closet. The racks of designer suits and couture my mother insisted I wear were untouched. The shelves of Manolos and Louboutins were intact. They had no place in my future. I'd never put on another suit and walk into Agoston Investments, or any other reputable company. Never apply to Wharton and get my MBA. I'd naively thought I could somehow atone for the sins of my father by throwing myself into charity work. Put my newly earned finance degree to work for a good cause. I'd been laughed out of every organization I'd visited over the last two months. No one wanted me. And I couldn't blame them. I wouldn't trust anyone with my last name either.

After the last rejection, I'd come to a decision: I would never use my degree for my own benefit. Ever. I didn't deserve it. I might have earned it myself, but how could I profit from it with good conscience? Along with that decision came a stark realization: I had no future in this

3

city, where I'd forever be watched under a cloud of suspicion. So I started planning my escape.

I stripped out of my black Saint Laurent wool blazer and V-neck dress and hung them up in their appropriate places. I pulled on a pair of black skinny jeans, an American Apparel tank and hoody, and the contraband pair of black Chucks I'd kept hidden in the bottom of my closet. This was the new me. This was the me who would never set foot in this penthouse again. After I dressed, I left my cell phone on the dresser, hefted a black duffle bag over my shoulder, and headed through the kitchen to the staff entrance. It seemed fitting. Come in the front door one way and leave out the back a different person.

Juanita, the housekeeper who had been part of my life for all of my twenty-two years, blocked the doorway. She looked pointedly at my attire and the duffle. "And where do you think you're going, hmmm?"

"Somewhere else." As much as I wanted to tell her where, I couldn't. I wanted her to have plausible deniability.

She wrapped me in her soft, familiar arms and hugged me. Lisette Agoston didn't hug. And she would cringe to see me hugging *the help*. For the daughter of a plumber from upstate New York, she'd had no problem becoming a classist bitch.

"You can't run from this, sweetheart."

I drew back, loathing releasing her for what might be the last time, and met her kind brown eyes. "I know. But I can try."

I took a sealed envelope from the pocket of my duffle and held it out. "Could you make sure my mother gets this?"

She gave me a sad smile. I threw myself into her arms one more time. I kissed her papery cheek and blinked back the gathering tears. "Thank you. For … everything."

She stepped back, and her chapped hands cupped my face. "Charlotte, just because you are your father's daughter does not make you like him."

I nodded. Because she would argue with me until the end of time to prove her point. But she was wrong about this one. I *was* my father's daughter. His blood. Raised in his image to follow in his footsteps. If he was capable of that kind of evil, what was I capable of? I never wanted to find out. I kissed her cheek one more time and opened the door, leaving behind the only life I'd ever known.

simon

One year later.

New Orleans, Louisiana.

"Getting Mandy's name tattooed on your ass is the worst fucking idea you've ever had. And that's saying something." A metallic ding sounded, and a rush of cold air hit me as Nate and I followed Derek into Voodoo Ink, hoping to hell I could talk him out of it. Not only would I be the worst best man in the history of the planet, but Mandy would have my ass. There was no way this wouldn't end up being my fault.

Flash drawings papered the black walls. Tiny pinpricks of light twinkled in the ceiling, which was swirled with white, red, and black paint. They looked like a million stars in an apocalyptic sky. The place was creepy, but it had a phenomenal reputation.

"She's gonna fuckin' love it, man. I know my woman," Derek said, his words slurring. I shrugged, hoping this place would refuse to tattoo his drunken ass.

A petite woman dressed in skinny jeans and a tight white tank top strolled out from a hallway to stand behind the counter. Her hair hung in waves that stopped midway down her back. The tangles of black were interspersed with sections dyed deep red and purple. Tattoos started at her shoulders and continued down to her wrists. Some were words, others intricate black and gray drawings. Even more were brilliantly colored, swirling designs. She narrowed her eyes, sizing us up. I pictured us from her perspective: three guys, dressed in jeans and partially unbuttoned dress shirts—courtesy of the strippers we'd barely escaped. We probably looked like douchebags. And one of us wanted his ass tattooed. Yeah. Total fucking douchebags.

"What can I do for you, gentlemen?" She tilted her head and watched as Derek stumbled into one of the waiting room chairs. I yanked him back and steadied him.

"I want a tattoo right here." Derek slapped the right side of his ass. "Of my bride's name." The woman tilted her head the other direction.

"What about that seems like a good idea to you?" she asked.

"She'll fuckin' love it."

She pursed her lips. "Doubtful." She looked at me for the first time. "Bachelor party?"

I nodded, tongue gone thick. Her aqua eyes speared me. I'd never seen eyes that color. Her features were delicate, with high cheekbones and a slightly turned-up nose. Her dark and vibrant hair seemed at odds with her creamy, pale skin. The combination of the hair, eyes, and tattoos was striking, more intoxicating than the dozen or so drinks I'd already consumed. She was the polar opposite of the perfectly coifed and manicured women my parents pushed at me. She was … I couldn't think of a word that didn't sound stupid, even in my head.

"I'm afraid we can't help you. We have a strict 'no dumb fucking idea' tattoo policy for drunk people."

"Come on … don't be like that," Derek said.

Nate added, "You're like two blocks off Bourbon. You gotta tattoo drunk people all the time."

She pointed to the sign on the wall. It read: *NOLA To Do List: 1. Get tattoo. 2. Get wasted.*

"We're sticklers. Come back tomorrow after you're done puking. If you still want your future wife's name on your ass, Delilah or Con will be happy to do it. Have a good night." She faked a smile and nodded to the door. We'd been dismissed.

Derek whined, but followed as Nate led him outside. My feet were rooted to the black-and-white checkered linoleum floor. Even through the haze of alcohol, one thought stuck out: I couldn't leave without getting her name.

"What's your name?" I asked.

Her narrowed gaze landed on me, and she started to turn away. *No.* I couldn't let her leave without finding out her name. It might've been a drunken compulsion, but it was a compulsion all the same. I reached across the counter and grabbed her wrist. She froze.

"We have a problem here, Lee?" A tall blond man dressed in a faded Jimi Hendrix T-shirt and ripped jeans, tattooed from neck to wrists, sauntered out of the back room. He stopped next to *Lee* and wrapped an arm around her, pulling her into him. The gesture was so possessive that even my drunk ass couldn't miss it. I dropped her wrist.

"No problem. Just wanted to know her name."

He raised an eyebrow. Under the ink, he was still the punk who'd gotten expelled from our prep school for hot-boxing the athletic director's office. If I recalled correctly, he'd ended up in military school after that stunt. Constantine Leahy. Well, fuck.

"It's fine, Con. I'm good. He was just leaving." A second dismissal. And it blew.

Con looked at me, his eyes not giving anything away. He glanced down to the tattoo on the inside of my forearm. "We touch up work for vets for free. Come on back anytime—before you start tipping 'em back." He jerked a chin toward the sign. I stared at his hand curling around her waist. It was too familiar to be an act. They looked like a perfect couple. All ink and fuck you attitudes.

"Thanks. I'll keep that in mind." I turned and walked away. I told myself it was for the best. She wasn't for me. But those eyes…

charlie

"Was the caveman act really necessary?" I asked Con, my boss, friend, and sometimes fuck buddy, as I stepped out of his hold.

"You can't tell me he wasn't trying to pick you up and take you home."

"Maybe I wanted him to." Our arrangement was completely open. The only rule: if you were with someone else, you had to get tested before we got together again. Well, I guess it was really my rule for Con. I hadn't yet needed to get tested, but he regularly went home with other women. I felt no jealousy. I used Con to feel close to someone occasionally, and it didn't hurt that he was a stellar lay. He was the only guy who'd touched me in more than a casual way since I'd left New York. I shoved the thought of home to the back of my brain. After all, it wasn't home any more. I'd gone days without thinking about my old life. It was a game I played. How long could I go without remembering? I was getting better at it. Sex, booze, and tattoos helped. Although, I was a little light on the sex portion of the equation lately; it'd been over two months since I'd been with Con.

"Yeah, right. He wasn't exactly your type."

"Really?" I pointed at the door. "Did you see the same guy I did? Because he was every woman's type." Tall, broad shouldered, with dark hair styled in that artfully messy way, a little stubble on his jaw, and flashing hazel eyes. The military ink on the inside of his corded forearm was pretty hot too.

"A little straight-edge for you, Lee. Trust me. Plus, you shouldn't even be thinking about leaving here with some

guy you just met. I thought you were smarter than that."
Con frowned down at me.

I winced, feeling guilty, and knowing he was right. In my quest to lie as little as possible about my past, I let people assume whatever they wanted about my motives for keeping a low profile. Con's assumption: I was running from an abusive boyfriend. Some days I wished that was the truth, and then I wanted to kick my own ass for feeling sorry for myself and thinking my messed up situation was anywhere near as bad as a battered woman's. Besides, I didn't deserve pity. Even from myself.

I looked at the clock. "You care if I head out? I'm working an early shift tomorrow."

He smoothed my hair back from my face. "You work too damn hard. I wish you'd just let me…" His statement trailed off when I looked away. It was a conversation we'd had too many times to count. "Get your mutt, and get out of here, Lee." Con was the only person who called me Lee. He claimed I was too sexy to call by a guy's name. *Whatever*. Thankfully, given what he assumed to be my *situation*, he paid me under the table and had never asked to see my ID. So I'd let him call me whatever the hell he wanted.

I grinned. "Thanks, boss." I whistled shrilly, and he clamped his hands over his ears.

"Jesus, fuck. Was that necessary?"

"That's for cock-blocking me."

Con rolled his eyes as my brindle mutt trotted out of the back room. His head came up past the counter, and he stood thirty inches tall at his haunches. Huck and I had arrived in New Orleans on the same day one year earlier, or so I'd been told. I'd met him on my third day in the Crescent City. He was the newest resident of the Humane Society of New Orleans, and I was their newest volunteer. I took one look at the thirty pounds of roly-poly bear-cub-looking pup and begged Harriet, my honorary grandmother and landlord, if she'd allow a pet. She'd agreed. When I'd learned that he'd been found floating down the Mississippi on a pile of plywood and old tires, I'd realized that he was my very own Huckleberry Finn. Fast forward one year, and another 130 pounds, and Huck and I were inseparable. The best I could figure, he was a cross between an English Mastiff and a Great Dane. I wasn't sure what other combination would produce such a monster. He was my baby, my guardian, and an irreplaceable part of the new family I'd built. Unfortunately, my volunteering had been curtailed by my crazy work schedule.

Con smacked my ass, and Huck growled softly. "Stow it, mutt. I let you sleep on my goddamn couch." Con held out a hand, and Huck head-butted it. I wondered if Con had been someone Huck didn't know, whether he might have lost that hand. It was a theory I didn't want to test.

"Get out of here then, girl. I'll see you tomorrow." Con leaned down and brushed a kiss across my temple.

I snagged my bag from the break room and headed out the back door. I unchained my pale blue Schwinn and hooked a leash to Huck's collar. He tolerated the indignity for appearance—and leash law's—sake. Given the thick Friday night crowd, I opted to walk my bike instead of ride. Jimmy, my favorite hot dog vendor, was set up on the corner of Bourbon and St. Louis. He grinned and waved his tongs as I slipped through the mass of people.

"You want the usual, Ms. Charlie?"

"Yes, sir. One with everything and one plain."

He handed me one hotdog wrapped and the other one unwrapped. Huck sat at my feet, licking his chops; he knew how this worked. He downed his in two head-jerking bites.

I shook my head. "Someday you'll learn to savor your food, I swear." I looked up at Jimmy. "Have a good night. I'll see you tomorrow."

"It's a date, Ms. Charlie. To be sure, it's a date."

I pushed my bike, and the drunken revelers parted like the Red Sea. It was a common occurrence when traveling with Huck. His rangy stride was pure king of the beasts, and he looked mean as fuck, so no one bothered us.

A half-mile later I dug out my keys and unlocked the narrow wrought iron gate that blocked off the passage leading to my secret garden oasis. Okay, Harriet's secret garden oasis, but she let me use it. Locking the gate behind me, I unclipped Huck's leash, and he trotted over to his designated grassy section. After he'd taken care of business, we ascended the wrought iron spiral staircase that led to my 500 square foot apartment. It had hardwood floors, a space that could loosely be called a kitchen, an itty-bitty bathroom, and skylights dotting the ceiling throughout. It might be tiny and humble, but it was mine. Well, again, it was Harriet's, but she leased it to me. The woman was my very own fairy godmother. She was the grandmother of my crazy best friend from college. The one who my mother begged me not to befriend because she had *tattoos*, and even worse, she was a *Democrat*. Lena Zwiers was actually more of a socialist, but I didn't tell my mother that. After college, she'd opted for a stint in the Peace Corps and was now living in Madagascar. Beyond being a fantastic—though long distance—friend, Lena had begged Harriet to let me rent the place. So when I showed up, fresh off the Greyhound from Atlanta, with my newly black hair still reeking of cheap dye, she'd taken me in with open arms. I paid fair rent, but Harriet treated me like more than a tenant. A shrewd businesswoman who owned several shops in the Quarter, Harriet preferred to spend her time painting and traveling the country showing off her art. She'd farmed out management of the shops to trusted employees, one of whom had agreed to hire me— *despite* the fact that Harriet was my landlord. Which was the reason I had an early shift tomorrow morning at the Dirty Dog, a vintage clothing and novelty shop. I looked at the clock and sighed. It'd be another night of too little sleep.

I scrubbed the heavy black eyeliner from around my lids and slathered on face cream before curling up in my bed. I reached out a hand to ruffle Huck's fur where he slept on the rug. With my other hand, I traced the ink on my arm revealed by the dim glow from the skylight. With each line the needle buzzed into my skin, I was another step removed from my former life. The tattoos had become more than camouflage to hide the girl I'd once been; they were a declaration that I was never going back. I'd permanently marked myself to ensure that I could never again fit into the life I'd previously led. The life I'd run from rather than face every day as my father's daughter. Rather than face constant questioning by the FBI and the chance that the Department of Justice would eventually decide that despite the truth I'd spoken on the stand, I was somehow culpable for my father's crimes. I could freely admit it had been cowardly to run, but at least by running I gave myself a shot at having some sort of future. A future where my every breath wouldn't be scrutinized and dissected. Each tat was a conscious, deliberate choice to move toward the new me. I'd taken the tiny spark that had always burned to rebel against my mother's directives as she groomed me into a perfect society princess, and I'd fanned the flames. The irony of it was, even though I had assumed a false identity, I was finally discovering the real me. All it took was ripping off the blinders I'd worn for twenty-two years.

simon

I pushed open the door of Voodoo Ink at four o'clock on Saturday afternoon. I'd spent the morning hung over and pathetic, with one thought from the night before bothering the shit out of me—there was no way that girl was as stunning as I'd remembered. I mean, I had on beer goggles, tequila goggles, Hurricane goggles, and every other kind of goggles out there. But my curiosity had gotten the better of me. It was a thread of my drunken compulsion from the night before that my brain wouldn't let go of. I had to know.

Just like last night, the bell dinged and a cool rush of air conditioning hit me as I stepped inside. The place was deserted, and, even sober, it was still creepy looking. A glance at the door told me they'd just opened and would stay open until 2 AM. I couldn't figure out how the rule about not tattooing drunks gave them enough customers to stay open that late. Not my business or my problem. A woman with chin-length blond and pink hair, wearing a '50s style pink and orange polka dot dress, was sitting at the counter.

No Lee.

And yes, I remembered her name, even after the last two bars we hit.

"Hey, handsome. How can I help you?"

I looked around, but I didn't see anyone else. Disappointing, but it'd been worth a shot. I glanced down at my faded tattoo. Might as well make the trip a useful one.

"Con mentioned something about doing touch-ups for veterans." I held out my forearm where the trident and anchor I'd gotten shortly after graduation from the Naval Academy were now a dull gray.

The woman flipped open the appointment book on the counter and then extended a hand with orange-tipped nails. "I'm Delilah, and I'd be happy to do that for you. Thank you for your service." I shook her hand and followed her to one of the small rooms where she pushed aside the black curtain. "I'm the only one here right now," she explained. "We may get interrupted with walk-ins, but you picked a good time, because things don't usually pick up until later."

I almost asked about Lee, but held my tongue.

Delilah's eyes narrowed at my silence. "Don't think that means I won't fuck you up if you try to make a move on me. You don't have the kind of equipment I like."

I held back a smile at her serious expression. "Duly noted, ma'am."

She got to work.

Just over an hour later, I was pretty fucking happy with the touched-up tattoo. It looked better than it had when I'd originally gotten it. I'd shot the shit with Delilah, and she'd drawn up another tattoo for me. One that I'd been thinking about getting for years, but had never made time to actually do it. It was a memorial. A list of dates I knew by heart and the call signs of the brothers I'd lost. Simple script. Nothing fancy. But long overdue. I was pulling my T-shirt off so she could place the transfer paper on my left shoulder blade when I heard a door shutting and what sounded like nails clicking on the linoleum floor. And then I heard *her* voice.

"Sorry I'm late, Delilah! Huck chased after one of the horse-drawn carriages and yanked me off my bike. I ripped my damn jeans, and I need the freaking first aid kit."

Delilah jumped into action, but I remained in place.

"Oh sweetie, look at your knee. And your hands. Ouch. Clean yourself up. I've got this covered. Just doing a walk-in." Delilah's voice lowered. "And if I were into guys … let me tell you…"

Someone snorted. "As many times as I've heard you say that … don't you think you might be bi-curious?"

My attention was wrenched away from their conversation when the clicking nails materialized in the doorway of the tiny room as a massive fucking dog. His black and brown swirled fur was short, thick, and dense. He stared me down with giant, dark brown eyes.

"Huck! C'mere, baby. Get outta there." Lee's voice was a smoky alto and sexy as hell.

She peeked a head into the room. "Sorry—" She jerked back. "It's you."

I couldn't help the smirk that tugged at the corners of my mouth. I wasn't just a faceless customer. Good to know.

"And it's you. Lee, right?"

She nodded slowly. "Charlie, actually. Con's the only one who calls me Lee."

I held out my hand. "Simon."

She reached out to reciprocate the gesture, but I saw the angry red scrapes on the base of her palm, and turned her small hand over in mine. "You should probably take care of that."

She scrunched her nose. "I know. But it's going to hurt like hell when I pour that stinging stuff on it. I'm trying to psych myself up first." She looked down at the dog that had moved to place himself directly between us. "And I need to get Huck into the back room. I don't like to let him wander. He scares the shit out of customers."

"Since he's roughly the size of a pony, I can see why." The dog was eyeballing me as I held his mistress's hand in mine. "Is he going to rip me to pieces for touching you?"

She smiled down at the furry giant. "If he thought you were a threat, probably. If he knew you, maybe not. But I don't know you, so I'm not introducing you to my dog.

19

For all I know, you could be some creepy stalker." She eyed me up and down, and it occurred to me that I was shirtless. And she was studying the tattoo over my left pectoral muscle ... and the rest of my chest ... and my abs ... before she dragged her gaze back up to my face. If I knew anything about women, which was debatable for any man, I would've said she looked interested.

I released her hand and flipped over my forearm. "Came back for my touch up. And Delilah's going to hook me up with another."

"She does great work. I'm sure you'll be pleased." Charlie inhaled and let out a long breath. "I guess I better go clean myself up. Come on, Huck."

She turned away, and the dog followed close on her heels.

Well, I had my answer.

She was every bit as gorgeous as I remembered.

charlie

I pulled the giant first aid kit out from under the sink in the employee bathroom. I hadn't lied to the guy. *Simon.* I really didn't want to pour that shit on my hands and knee. It would hurt like hell, and Juanita wasn't here to blow on it and lessen the sting like she had when I was a kid. *Dammit. Two days in a row.* But I couldn't push the thought of Juanita aside. I missed her. I kept up with her life as best I could with my infrequent stops at the public library. There, at least, my searches and internet browsing couldn't be tracked back to me. But since the library wasn't Huck-friendly, and I pretty much took him everywhere, I didn't get to keep as close of tabs on her as I would have liked. Huck's presence had deterred a close call about six months ago, and after that he'd become sort of a security blanket. Without him, I might have … I shivered, remembering the scrape of the brick across my cheek as some tweaker asshole had shoved me up against the public restroom at the NOLA City Bark—the off-leash dog park downtown.

Huck and I had stayed until closing one night, and I'd ducked into the restroom for a pit stop before starting our trek home. I was kicking myself for not leashing him while I stepped away, because when I came out of the bathroom, he was off exploring the other side of the four and a half acre park. Before I could even open my mouth to call him back, I was slammed face first into the brick wall. I'd been paralyzed with shock for a beat before I'd started struggling against his hold. Sour breath wafted over my shoulder as cruel hands roamed my body, tearing at my clothes. His garbled words didn't register; all I could hear was the blood pounding in my ears. I pushed against the wall, scraping up the skin of my hands, and found my voice. I have no idea what I'd yelled, but Huck had come barreling toward us, his puppy bark transforming into something deep and vicious. The man had stumbled back, seeing the hundred pound monster heading for him, teeth-bared, and run for the fence, scrambling over it before Huck's snapping jaws could reach him. I'd dropped to my knees, adrenaline pumping, lungs heaving. Huck had barked at the fence for only a few moments before racing back to my side and guarding me against any other potential threats. He'd shown his loyalty before, but that day … I let out a long breath and shook off the memory, grateful to my pup that a close call was all I had to remember.

Back to happier thoughts—Juanita. She was living with her daughter and son-in-law in New Jersey. She was now a full-time stay-at-home grandma. I was glad she got to spend as much time with her family as she wanted, rather than the limited amount she'd been able to take before. Her social network accounts were splashed with pictures of her beloved grandkids and all of the fun they were having together. It made me think back to my childhood. She'd been the one to take me on nature hikes through the woods at our country house, and take me swimming during the summers at the Hamptons. She played a central role in all of my best memories. I swallowed the lump in my throat. It was better this way. I'd give it a few years—let the dust settle—and then I'd contact her.

The other person I kept tabs on was my mother. Not that there were many tabs to keep. She'd basically gone into hiding, although not nearly as successfully as me. She had, I'm sure, much to her horror, gone back upstate to live with my grandparents. It seemed that her stable of wealthy friends had turned their backs on her. Not surprising considering most had lost millions investing with my father. They might have recovered easier from the losses than the people who'd lost their whole lifesavings, but it didn't make them any happier about it. According to every article I'd read, my father still hadn't given up a single sliver of information as to where the money went. His sentence had equated to multiple lifetimes in federal prison. Unless there was an upside for him, he'd never talk. Then there were the news articles I avoided—the ones that speculated on my whereabouts. It seemed that the leading hypothesis was that I was living off my father's ill-gotten gains in Switzerland. Every time I accidentally ran across one of those articles, I'd take a deep breath and remind myself that they wouldn't be speculating if they knew my actual whereabouts. And then I'd head back to Voodoo and get another tattoo. More camouflage. Another mask to hide behind. I hadn't quite moved into the facial piercing phase, but depending on what the news said, I could be headed that way. I also kicked myself for not thinking of getting colored contacts. My eyes were too damn distinctive not to attract attention. But it was too late now. People would ask way more questions if I suddenly showed up with brown eyes.

I shimmied my black skinny jeans off and scrubbed the grit from my knee and hands. After patting the raw skin dry with paper towel, I hissed as I poured the antiseptic over the scrapes.

"Fuck, that hurts," I murmured through clenched teeth.

The door cracked open. I stilled. Was Simon checking out my thong-clad ass at this very moment? Surprisingly, the thought didn't bother me. The man was built, and I wouldn't kick him out of my bed for eating crackers.

"Damn, Lee. Now that's what I like to see when I get to work." A rough hand cupped my right ass cheek, and Con's head bent low over my shoulder. "It's been too long, babe. Need to get you home." He kissed my neck. "Get you in my—what the fuck?"

He spun me around and grabbed my hand. "What the hell happened? Did someone put their hands on you? Push you around? Was it like last—"

"No! Nothing like that." Con, Delilah, and Yvonne "Yve" Santos, my boss at the Dirty Dog, were the only ones who knew about my near miss at becoming a sexual assault statistic. Harriet would worry too much. And beyond those four, I didn't really have anyone else to tell. Depressing thought to some maybe, but it was my choice. The fewer people I let in, the fewer people I had to lie to. They'd become dearer than my actual family, and they deserved better than the half-truths and outright lies I fed them. I met Con's concerned blue gaze. "Huck decided he wanted to chase a carriage. I fell off my bike."

Con looked out the bathroom door to where Huck snored, taking up the entire break room couch. "Damn dog."

"Yeah."

"Well, maybe you should go home." My spine stiffened.

"It's just a couple of scrapes. I'm fine. Besides, you know I need the money."

"Because you're stubborn and won't let me pay you more so you don't have to work so damn much."

"That's because I'd feel like a whore." We'd had this conversation a hundred times. If he paid me more than he did before we'd slept together, I'd feel like I was getting paid for services rendered. You know, above and beyond.

"Like I said, stubborn." He smacked my ass. "But I like that thong. What do you say? Come home with me tonight if you're up to it?"

Inexplicably, my mind snapped to the man only a few walls away. I stalled. "Umm … I don't know … Ask me later?"

He gave me a chin jerk before heading toward the corner of the break room and his makeshift office. Con may look like a tatted-up bad boy, but from what I could tell, he was actually a fairly astute businessman.

An hour later, Simon came around to the register to pay for his new tattoo. I'd been stealing what I'd hoped had been covert glances over my shoulder the entire time he'd sat, shirtless, in Delilah's room. But every time I glanced his way, his eyes had flicked to mine. Intense, assessing hazel eyes that I wanted to see up close so I could figure out how the green, brown, gold, and gray swirled together. I didn't understand my attraction to him. Yeah, he was pretty to look at. But so were lots of guys. He had the cut muscles and banging six-pack that said he took care of himself. But again, so did a lot of guys. Con, for one. But, for me, Con was about comfort, being close to someone for a night because I missed the feeling of being touched. With Simon … it was burning curiosity and flaring lust. I wanted to know how his hands would feel against my skin. If he'd strip me naked and trace the lines of ink with his fingers … and then his tongue. If he'd like the little surprises I had tucked beneath my clothes. Con had never even seen them, and I'd sworn Delilah to secrecy after I'd accepted her dare. When Simon stopped in front of the counter I was shifting on my cushioned stool, trying to relieve the ache my wandering thoughts had produced.

He didn't speak for a moment, just studied me. He pulled his wallet from the back pocket of his worn jeans without breaking eye contact.

"Do you get a break?"

His question jolted me back to reality. "What?" I asked.

He pressed both palms against the scarred, graffiti-covered surface and leaned toward me. "Have dinner with me. Tonight."

25

I opened my mouth to speak, but Con, who seemed to have the shittiest timing on the planet, stepped out of the break room and came to stand behind me. "Councilman, I didn't realize you'd come back." Con's voice held a note of something I couldn't identify. It wasn't jealousy. It was something … else. He must have glanced down at Simon's forearm, because he said, "Glad to see you got your touch up. No charge for that. Feel free to be on your way."

I glanced back at Con, giving him a *what the fuck* look. His behavior was completely off. He might not be unfailingly polite to every customer who walked in the door, but he didn't usually try to throw anyone out.

"I got a new one, too. I'll settle up with Charlie, Constantine." Simon's tone carried a stubborn edge.

Clearly there was history here I wasn't privy to. And then Con's words solidified in my brain. Councilman?

"Seems strange that someone rumored to be kicking off a campaign for daddy's old congressional seat would be getting more ink." Con wrapped an arm around my waist and pulled me against him. "Or is it something—or someone—else that brings you back?"

I jabbed an elbow into Con's gut. He dropped his arm. I spun and whisper-yelled at him. "Quit being a dick, and drop this whole junkyard dog pissing on your territory act. That shit doesn't fly with us, and you know it."

"Lee … I just…"

"Just what?"

He sighed. "He's not the kind of guy you should be getting mixed up with." Con bent close and whispered in my ear, "I know you keep a low profile for a reason, and being seen with Simon Duchesne might not be the best idea."

The heat that had been thrumming through my veins turned to ice. Con was right. He had no idea why he was so right, but he was. Regardless, I didn't need him to run interference for me. I'd been taking care of myself for the last year, and I'd keep on doing it.

I pressed a hand against his chest. "It's cool. I got this, Con." He stared me down for a moment and then turned and left.

I spun back around and faced Simon Duchesne. Councilman. Son of a congressman. Rumored congressional candidate. The kind of man my mother would have salivated over having me date when I was Charlotte Agoston. The kind of man who was off limits and straight up dangerous to the continued anonymity of Charlie Stone. The potential consequences of being seen with him—and recognized—played through my mind at hyper speed. I'd have to leave New Orleans and this makeshift family I'd fallen in love with. It just wasn't worth the risk.

"I'm sorry, I can't."

His eyes narrowed. "Because of Con? You're with him."

It wasn't any of Simon Duchesne's business who I was with, but I told him anyway. "No. It's not that. We're not … together, together."

He continued to study me. "Then why? Because I'm not going to pretend like I didn't see you every time you stopped and stared at me over the past hour."

Well and truly busted. Conceited ass. "You're pretty to look at, that's all. Doesn't mean I want to have dinner with you."

"Fine. I won't waste my breath then." He handed over four hundred-dollar bills. "Tell Delilah to keep the change."

He turned to walk away, and my ridiculous heart sank. Before I could berate myself for my ludicrous reaction, he turned back around and pulled something out of his pocket. A business card. He dropped it on the counter. "If you ever change your mind, Charlie."

charlie

I turned down Con last Saturday night. It was the first time
I'd ever done that. Given the awkward tension that had
lingered between us all week, I was even more grateful to
have the rest of the weekend off. Besides, I hadn't had a
Saturday night to myself in three weeks. And followed by
an entire Sunday off? It'd been forever. Now I just needed
my shift at the Dirty Dog to *end* already.

I looked at the clock. Twenty minutes to go. I sighed,
reorganizing a rack of vintage concert T-shirts for the
seventh time. My paycheck was going to take a hit this
week because there was a Black Sabbath Heaven + Hell
Tour T-shirt I needed to own. I didn't splurge often, never
really, but this shirt was so perfectly ironic because of the
lyrics on the back. The part about blinded eyes and stolen
dreams sent my thoughts back to Manhattan. The song
summed up so much of my former life. Wearing it would
be another little rebellion. I checked the time again. Five
o'clock couldn't come fast enough.

A slobbery tennis ball hit me in the side of the head.
"What the hell?" I grabbed it off the floor and looked
around for Huck. But all I saw was Yve rolling her eyes at
me.

"What's your deal, girl? You've been dragging ass all
day and staring at the clock. Got a hot date?"

My breath caught in my chest. A hot date was exactly
what I didn't have. I thought about the business card
buried in the bottom of my junk drawer. I still wasn't sure
why I'd kept it, but now it was dog-eared from all the
times I'd dug it out only to shove it back in the drawer just
as quickly. I hated the indecision Simon dredged up in me.

"Earth to Charlie…"

Shit. I hadn't answered her question. "No—no hot date." I decided, against my better judgment, to share. Maybe Yve would just kick my ass, and I could move on and stop thinking about him. I took a deep breath and added, "But … there is this guy…"

Yve rested her elbows on the glass case that served as a checkout counter and steepled her fingers. "Tell Yve all about it."

So I did. I told her about both times he'd come to Voodoo, how he'd asked me out, and how Con had reacted.

"So, a hot piece of man asked you to dinner and you turned him down, why? Because Constantine was having a jealous moment?"

"It wasn't jealousy really. It was more protectiveness … I think."

"Call it what you want, but I've always thought your fuck buddy thing with Con was going to end with one of you gettin' your heart broken."

My eyebrows shot up to my hairline. "Umm … what? No. It's not like that between Con and me. So, just no."

"Whatever you say. So what's the real reason you're not calling this guy?"

I cringed, because I couldn't tell her the *real* reason. But I could give her at least part of the truth. "Because Simon is Simon Duchesne. Current city councilman, son of a former congressman, probably going to run for Congress?"

She tapped one perfectly manicured nail on the glass. "And?"

"And—well, look at me." I gestured to my tattoos. They started at the tops of my shoulders and swirled down my arms and sides, stopping at my wrists and hips. I didn't have a chest piece, or any on my hands, but still. I was a walking work of art. Not exactly prime arm candy material for a politician, even if I could risk the cameras. But it wasn't like I wanted to be, or would ever allow myself to be, someone's arm candy. "I'm not exactly his type."

"He asked *you* out. So *he* thinks you *are* his type. Besides, that old rule about good girls liking bad boys—it cuts both ways, sugar. He's a good boy, and you're a pretty bad ass bad girl." She paused. "I notice you didn't say anything about not wanting to take him up on his offer because you weren't attracted to him."

I skimmed my hand along the rack of hanging shirts. "How could I not be? I mean, the man is gorgeous. I thought I was going to have to find a new pair of panties after he left."

Yve shrugged. "So take him for a ride. Doesn't mean you have to keep him. You get off, he gets his bad girl fix, and no one gets hurt."

Goddammit. "I hate it when you make sense."

"Then get out of here, girl. Go get your booty call. I'll close up. It's been a slow night anyway."

So Huck and I went.

My hands were sweaty as I sifted through my junk drawer for his card. *I can't believe I'm even considering this.* If it had just been about scratching an itch, I could've gone to Con. But it was more than that. It was *something* unique to Simon—he exuded this innate confidence, this *I'm strong enough to handle anything you can throw at me* vibe—and it drew me in.

Finding the crumpled piece of white cardstock, I scanned it for what seemed like the millionth time. I punched his cell number into my prepaid phone and buried a hand in Huck's fur as it rang. I hadn't been this nervous to call a guy since middle school. My stomach churned as it rang a second time, then a third, and a fourth. And then, Simon's voice asked me to leave a message. *Shit.* I didn't know what to say, but for some stupid reason I didn't hang up. I mumbled something about being Charlie from Voodoo wanting to take him up on his offer and rattled off my number. I dropped my phone on the kitchen counter and scrubbed both hands over my face. How very anti-climactic.

Huck head-butted my thigh and padded to the door. He was right. It was a gorgeous late-May evening and perfect for sitting in the garden oasis. I uncorked a bottle of cheap red wine and grabbed a glass.

Setting myself up at the bistro table, I poured a generous serving, and cracked open the book I'd brought down.

Huck rolled in the grass, all four long legs in the air. His head arched to the side as he tried to bite his tail. Crazy mutt. I shoved the book aside and dropped onto the ground beside him, scratching his chest and belly as I polished off my first glass of wine.

I was lying next to Huck when I heard one of my most favorite sounds of the Quarter—the sousaphone, drums, and brass band that signaled a wedding parade. It was quiet at first, the beats rumbling through the still evening, and it grew louder and louder. I actually felt giddy when I realized they were coming down my street. I pushed off the ground and ran up to my apartment to get my keys for the gate. Pausing by the table, I splashed more wine in my glass.

I wanted to watch like a goddamn tourist.

I slipped down the narrow brick walkway that led to the gate with Huck on my heels. I squeezed out, locking him inside. He growled his displeasure, but I was already entranced by the large crowd of wedding guests marching and dancing down the street toward me. Neighbors and tourists lined the sidewalks, snapping pictures and cheering on the crowd. The bride's parasol bounced in the air, delicate white feathers floating from the edges. The band stopped and broke into a raucous tune. The wedding party and guests grabbed partners and danced with abandon, handkerchiefs flying. The groom swept the bride up in his arms and spun her in dizzying circles.

It was my own secret fantasy—one that I'd never admit. I swallowed back the regret for what would never be and focused on the happy couple. The groom ... he looked familiar, but I couldn't place him. I sipped my wine and tried to recall where I'd seen him before. It hit me as soon as I saw *him*.

Simon.

He was leading a gray-haired woman in a jaunty waltz in the middle of the street, dressed in a black tux tailored to perfection. Gone were the jeans and simple T-shirt that he'd worn the last time I'd seen him. He looked every inch the Southern gentlemen-politician in black tie. Several women in matching seafoam green dresses watched him like he was last Versace dress in creation designed by Gianni himself. *Bridesmaids.* A surge of jealousy ripped through me to think about Simon as the stereotypical groomsman who would, by the end of the night, undoubtedly have the opportunity to nail one—or more— of them. I suddenly felt ridiculous. I looked down at the nine dollar wine in my glass, my wife beater, tight, pale gray skinny jeans, and two dollar flip-flops. For a split second I wished I still had some of the wardrobe that would put those bitches to shame. I gave myself a mental shake. *No. That's not me. And it'll never be me again.*

I shouldn't have called him. Shouldn't have left that stupid message. I'd never belong in his world. And what's more, I didn't want to belong there. *I didn't.*

I turned away from the parade, spirits doused, and struggled to fit my key into the lock. My hand shook, and I kept missing the tiny keyhole. A large, tanned hand closed over mine. A second hand gripped the bars and trapped me in the circle of his arms.

I stared down at the white dress shirt and monogrammed silver cufflink peeking out from the sleeve of his black jacket.

He spoke into my ear, his voice low and gravelly. "If I keep seeing you, I'm going to take it as a sign."

I swallowed and squeezed my eyes shut. Huck growled, but I reached out a hand and patted his head through the bars. He quieted and lay down against the gate. I turned in Simon's arms, careful to avoid spilling my wine, and stared up at him. At five-four, I wasn't exactly *short*, but he dwarfed me, especially when we were this close. He had to be almost a foot taller than me, and with his broad shoulders filling my view, I couldn't see anything but him.

Rather than his face, I focused on the black studs in his pristine white tux shirt, and cleared my throat.

"A sign of what exactly?"

He released the bars of the gate and tilted my chin up so I was forced to meet his eyes.

"I'm not sure. Maybe just my own good luck because I wanted to see you again." He paused before adding, "Have dinner with me."

I forced a humorless laugh. "I think you're a little busy right now." The crowd had started to move again, although slowly, but he was going to be left behind if he didn't rejoin the wedding party.

He glanced over his shoulder and nodded. "Later. After the reception. Meet me somewhere."

I shook my head. "I don't think that's a good idea."

"Charlie—"

His words were cut off when someone yelled, "Duchesne, let's go!"

I spun and shoved my key into the lock. Simon's heat melted away as he stepped back.

"I'm guessing, based on the monster dog, this is where you live?"

I didn't reply. I pulled the gate open and slipped inside. Simon didn't try to stop me as I maneuvered around Huck and shut the gate in his face.

From behind the safety of my iron bars, I finally found the courage to look up at him again. His hazel eyes burned into me.

"I want to see you again. Just dinner. Or drinks. Your choice."

"I think you should go. You're losing your friends."

"I'll catch up. Just give me your number. Please, Charlie."

I shook my head. He made me want things I couldn't have. "Maybe I'll see you around, Simon." I turned and walked down my narrow corridor back to the safety of my garden oasis.

simon

I thought about getting hammered at the reception, but I didn't want to be that guy. Besides, there were too many flashing cameras to catch any missteps I might make. So I gave my toast. Tasteful, heartfelt. Derek and I had been friends since we were old enough to climb through the fence that separated my parents' Garden District home from his. Given the close connection between our families, my parents had attended the wedding, though not the parade. My father was two weeks out from a knee replacement and would be recuperating through the summer at the house in Bar Harbor. Which meant I'd be saved from their meddling in my love life—or lack thereof—for two months. I loved them to death, but they were relentless in their quest to see me settle down. My father's lectures about finding a woman who would be an asset to my political career were enough to make me want to find the nearest bottle of scotch. I didn't want an asset; I wanted a best friend, a lover, a partner, someone I could depend on and raise a family with. At thirty-one, my friends were pairing off, and it occurred to me that I wanted that too. Not today, or maybe even this year, but sometime in the foreseeable future. Except I certainly wasn't settling until I found *the one*. It was corny and cliché, but I was only planning on doing the marriage thing once. So I'd wait until I found her.

I pictured the woman who'd effectively shut me out earlier today. *Charlie*. I didn't know her, or know anything about her, but I wanted to have the chance to get to know her. It was a nebulous feeling, but it seemed imperative. I didn't want to let her walk away, but I wasn't the kind of guy to keep going back where I clearly wasn't welcome. She was just so damn different from every other woman I'd ever met. She wore her attitude like armor, daring someone to challenge her so she could tell him to fuck off. I shouldn't have found it so appealing, especially because I was the one she'd most recently told to fuck off. But it was. She made no apologies for who she was, and it was sexy as hell. *And I needed to move on.*

I sighed and headed to the bar in search of that scotch.

As the bartender poured my three fingers, I pulled my phone from my jacket pocket and noticed I had a missed call and voicemail from a number I didn't recognize. Tossing a tip in the jar, I grabbed my drink and headed out into the lobby, away from the noise of the reception. As soon as I heard her voice on the message, I damn near dropped my glass. I looked at the time of the missed call. *Before the parade.*

A surge of excitement rushed through me, followed closely by confusion. She'd called me *before* I'd seen her today. I dropped onto a bench near the door. It didn't add up. It'd been less than an hour between the time she'd left the message and the parade. Something had obviously happened to cause her complete one-eighty. I looked down at my watch. I had to stay for at least another hour, but then I'd track her down and get my answers. I'd been ready to let go of my fascination with her, but she'd smashed the ball back into my court. This wasn't over yet.

charlie

I'd finished the bottle of wine and changed into a pair of threadbare lilac cotton pajama pants to go with my wife beater. The bra had been tossed to the top of the bureau. If I could go the rest of my life without wearing one, I would. But with boobs that topped out just under double D, it wasn't an option. I envied those B-cup girls some days. My hair was up in a ratty bun, and I was debating whether or not I wanted to open a second bottle. I'd be hung over in the morning, but I didn't have to work, so why the hell not? I'd toast Simon Duchesne goodbye. *Why am I still thinking about him?* I gave myself a mental kick. *Enough.*

My buzzer rang as I reached for the corkscrew. I looked at the clock. It was 11:30 on a Saturday night. Who the hell? It rang again, and I crossed the tiny space to the ancient intercom on my wall.

"Yes?"

"It's Simon." As if my very thoughts had conjured him. Damn the juju in this town.

I inhaled sharply, my nipples perking up at his dark, rumbling voice. *No, body, the brain has already made this decision.* But the reprimand was pointless. I clearly couldn't trust myself around him. Or his voice.

I pressed the button on the intercom again. "Go away, Simon."

"I got your message."

Oh shit. Of course he had. Finishing off the wine had helped me forget my earlier lapse in judgment. And now I supposed I owed him an in-person blow off. After all, I was sending off more mixed signals than a drunken air traffic controller.

"Hold on." I slipped on my flip-flops and left Huck inside.

In the dim glow of the street lamps I could see him leaning against the gate, bowtie, jacket, and the top four studs of his shirt missing. His sleeves were rolled up, and I could see the anchor and trident on his inner forearm. I was all set to tell him to go the hell home, but that peek of his ink combined with the casually confident way he held himself had the words clogging in my throat. I couldn't help but think that even though his public persona was hazardous to my very existence, it might be worth flirting with danger to steal a taste of the man beneath it. I stared up at the sky for a beat, seeking divine guidance. Finding none, I looked back to Simon.

"What are you doing here?" I asked. My tone was less than welcoming. If he let me run him off, then I'd be saved from the temptation that was Simon Duchesne.

"You called me."

"I shouldn't have."

"I'm glad you did." He shifted, as though annoyed by the bars between us. *Sorry, Simon,* I thought, *even without the bars, there will always be impenetrable walls.*

A thought struck me. "Are you drunk?"

"No," Simon replied with a laugh. "Are you?"

"A little." At least I could be honest about that.

A provocative smile spread over his face, and I caught a flash of dimples. *Damn. Come on world, throw me a bone.*

"Are you going to ask me in?" He punctuated the question with a raised eyebrow.

"I shouldn't." To myself I added, *I really, really shouldn't.*

"You don't look like the kind of girl who doesn't do things just because she thinks she shouldn't."

I looked down at the uneven cobblestones beneath my feet. "Don't pretend like you know me."

"I want to."

"Why?" It was a question I desperately wanted answered. I was still trying to sort out all of the reasons for my attraction to him. Maybe he could articulate whatever this crazy *thing* was between us, and solve the mystery for me.

He reached through the bars and tucked a flyaway strand of hair behind my ear.

"Honestly, I have no idea. You're just ... there's something about you."

Dammit. I took a deep breath and exhaled slowly, giving myself a moment to think. Ultimately, it was his honesty that decided it. We were equally off balance here. I was probably going to regret this, but ... what the hell. I twisted the lock and opened the gate. For some reason, it didn't feel wrong. I thought of Yve's advice. One night. Get him out of my system. I never had to see him again. I could steal this night and emerge unscathed.

My heart hammered as my plan formed. I forced myself to walk slowly as I led Simon to the inner courtyard, and he paused to take in the garden oasis. It was magical. A hidden gem in the middle of the Quarter. The brick walls enclosed a huge live oak, draped with thick blankets of Spanish moss and resurrection fern. Fairy lights and solar-powered Chinese lanterns dangled from the branches. The tinkle of the fountains and the koi pond were the only sounds beyond the noise of the city. The blue water of the small splash pool reflected the lights and the stars.

"This place is amazing." Simon spun in a slow circle, taking in the oasis and the spiral staircase that led up to my apartment.

My plan was crazy, but I had the privacy I needed; Harriet was at an art showing in San Francisco. Simon was going to think I was insane, but in my messed up mind, this was the only way I could make it work. I wanted us on a level playing field, and his shiny black dress shoes, pressed white shirt, and tux pants did nothing but remind me of my past and the light years between our current situations in life.

My hands trembled as I reached for the hem of my tank and tugged it up and over my head. I let it dangle from my fingertips and float to the ground. My courage faltered as Simon turned to face me, but I kept going. I stepped out of my flip-flops and caught the waist of my pajama pants with my thumbs and tugged them down. His eyes widened comically, and his jaw slackened as he took in my nakedness. I pulled the elastic from my hair and let the waves fall around my shoulders. The black, red, and purple tresses covered my breasts and hid the gold rings that pierced my nipples. I tried to picture myself from his point of view. Inked from shoulders to wrists. Script down my left side, along my ribs. An abstract phoenix down my other side. My legs were pale white, yet untouched by the needle. I was offering him everything I was, stripped down to the core of me—albeit temporarily. I turned and stepped into the splash pool, the warm water rising up to my chest. My hair floated on the surface before sinking down and clinging to me.

"Are you coming in?" I was proud that my voice didn't shake. He hadn't moved, and I couldn't read his expression. But I wanted him to be as naked as I was—all evidence of his status and position left outside the little bubble I was creating. For tonight, I wanted there to be no past, no future. I just wanted right now. This moment. With him.

"Charlie—"

I leaned back and let my body float to the surface as I treaded water with my hands. I never thought the synchronized swimming lessons I'd been forced to take would ever come in handy, but the gracefulness with which I floated proved me wrong.

"Don't think, Simon. Just strip."

He tugged his bottom lip between even white teeth and hesitated a moment before reaching for his belt and unbuckling it. He unbuttoned his pants and drew down his zipper. I watched, fascinated by his efficient movements. He pushed his pants to the ground, revealing snug black boxer briefs stretched by his thick erection. *Well, it's good to know I'm not the only one who thinks this is a good idea.*

He plucked the remaining studs from his shirt and shrugged it off, letting it drop to the ground, before gripping a handful of the back of his white undershirt and pulling it over his head. Underneath it he was all broad shoulders and defined muscles. I let my eyes wander down his rippling abs to the trail of dark hair that began at his navel and disappeared into the gray band of his underwear. He obscured the perfect V of his hips when he hooked his thumbs in the top of his boxer briefs, and my eyes snapped up to his. He was grinning at my unabashed ogling of him. As much as I wanted to look down, I held his stare. He bent slightly, and I knew he was stepping out of his briefs. He crossed the last few feet to the pool, stepped into the water, and came toward me. I paddled toward the far end and he followed.

"What game are you playing, Charlie?"

"No game. Just … this." I spread my arms out wide, gesturing to … everything. Because I couldn't explain myself any other way without exposing too much.

Backing me into a corner, he trapped me in the circle of his arms, much like he had earlier at the gate. I reached up and laid my palms against his chest, tracing the compass inked on his pectoral muscle with my index finger. Our skin didn't touch anywhere else, but mine prickled with the need to feel him against me. I leaned closer, but he grasped my shoulders, effectively holding me back.

I looked up questioningly.

"You left me a message, then slammed a gate in my face, then you strip in front of me, and invite me to go skinny dipping. I can't keep up with you. I need to know what the hell is going on here before it goes any further."

I sagged back against the edge of the pool, letting the concrete lip dig into my spine. So much for my hastily constructed plan. An experienced seductress I was not. He must have read the defeat in my expression because he said, "I'm not saying I'm not interested. Hell, I'm buck ass naked, and I can't exactly hide that I want you. But I need to know … why now? What changed?"

I stared down at the water, wishing fleetingly that the pool lights were on so I'd know for certain that he still did, in fact, want me. But given the leap I'd taken by stripping naked in front of him, I suppose I owed him at least some sort of an explanation.

"I decided that, for tonight, I didn't care that you're you and I'm me. I decided to take a risk and see what happened." My answer was vague and without substance, but I hoped it would be enough. Heat pulsed between my legs and my nipples beaded almost painfully. I wanted him. Now.

But he didn't relent. "It doesn't matter who I am or who you are. Tonight or any other night. We're just people."

I held in a snort. Barely. He wouldn't be in this pool if he knew who I really was. I was poison to someone like him. To everyone.

Simon tilted my chin up, forcing me to meet his eyes. "If I fuck you tonight, are you going to throw me out on my ass as soon as we're done and never call me again?"

I bit my lip. Damn. He should be a freaking interrogator instead of a politician. But I wasn't going to lie to him. At least not about this. "Probably."

He released my chin and backed away. "Then, no." He shook his head. "This isn't happening. Not tonight." He turned and made his way to the stairs. I caught a flash of his pale, muscular ass as he climbed out of the pool. I looked down at the water, hot humiliation filling me. *What the hell am I doing?* I sank farther beneath the surface, up to my chin. I needed to be covered. I heard the rustle of clothes and wondered how he was drying off without a towel. But I didn't look up to assuage my curiosity. I'd given in to curiosity once already tonight, and *this* was where it landed me. In a pool of my own shame.

He cleared his throat, and I finally looked up. He was wearing his tux pants, and the shirt was partially buttoned. He held his soaked white undershirt in his hand. *One question answered.*

His hazel eyes drilled into me. "You have my number. Call me when you want more than a quick fuck."

And then he was gone.

charlie

I spent all day Sunday ricocheting between being pissed and embarrassed. My hangover didn't help matters. After Simon left, I'd uncorked that second bottle of wine and drowned both my shame and my desire. When Monday rolled around, I'd decided that I'd dodged a bullet. It was a moment of weakness. I wanted to hate him for walking away, but for some reason, it made me respect him. It gave me a glimpse of his true character. I had to assume that most guys would have taken what I had offered and been happy to get laid and then bail without guilt. But not Simon Duchesne. He wanted more than a quick fuck. But I wasn't capable of more. Not now, and not for the foreseeable future. Or was I?

If I was giving off mixed signals before, now my emotions were spinning like the weathervane at our country estate. Former country estate, actually. Since it had been auctioned off by the feds. *Dammit.* Wasn't thinking about that today.

I glided up to the Dirty Dog, parked my bike, and chained it to the drainpipe next to the back door. I was seriously contemplating taking Huck to obedience school. He was getting bolder when it came to the horse-drawn carriages. So my choices included: obedience school, not riding my bike while holding his leash, or leaving him at home to laze around in the oasis all day. But I liked to think that he preferred to be where I was. It hadn't helped that I'd seen a dark-haired guy in a suit and ended up distracted by thoughts of Simon.

The store was quiet when I unlocked the back door, and Huck trotted inside. Usually Yve beat me to work every day. Maybe she'd taken her own advice and gone out and gotten herself a man for the night. She was cagey about her past, but I had a feeling that her last relationship hadn't ended well. She referred to the guy as only the 'ex' so I didn't even know his name. I calculated it had ended around the time I showed up in New Orleans, because she was distant during our first few months of working together. We hadn't really become close until last September when we'd discovered our mutual love of classic rock and punk bands. In a city that revered jazz and partied to zydeco, classic rock and punk weren't exactly at the top of the play list. After she'd let her guard down some, we'd gone barhopping with the tourists down Bourbon Street. Our friendship had been cemented while holding each other's hair back at Pat O'Brien's. As a Crescent City native, Yve would never admit to the indignity, and I was sworn to secrecy.

She strolled in fifteen minutes late with a wide, satisfied smile.

"You totally got laid this morning, didn't you?" I asked.

Her smile, if possible, got wider. "Oh, hell yes I did. You never told me that Con was a stallion in the sack."

Ummm. What the fuck?

I gaped. "Seriously? I mean … what the hell?"

When she registered my look of shock, her feline smile faded. "Oh shit. I thought you were … done with your friends with bennies thing with him. I never would have if I'd thought you were…"

I held up a hand. "It's fine. I'm not jealous. I'm just … surprised." And I wasn't jealous. I didn't even feel a pang. It was like my body had moved on from Con Leahy and wanted someone new. He who would remain unnamed.

"So what happened with Simon Duchesne?" Yve asked.

Okay, maybe he wouldn't remain unnamed.

"Nothing. Nothing happened. Nothing at all." To myself I added, *Except I sort of threw myself at him and saw him naked. And good God…*

Yve leaned back against the counter. "That's too many 'nothings' in one sentence for that to be the truth. Spill, girl."

"Do I have to?" I winced at my whiny tone. It was not attractive.

"After that answer, hell yes, you do." She crossed her arms and pinned me with her amber stare. I took in her golden brown skin and curly dark locks. She had on a teal halter dress with pink and teal platforms.

"You look really cute today, by the way."

She narrowed her eyes. "Spill. Now."

I rolled my eyes and spilled. Her mouth was hanging open by the time I finished recounting the events of Saturday night.

"So you see, it was a humiliating mess. And I'm better off having dodged that bullet."

She closed her gaping mouth and tapped a finger to her lips. "Dayum. Only you, Charlie. Only you would find a guy who won't let you 'one night' him. I gotta see this man who's got your wet panties in a twist." She moved behind the counter and started typing. I could only assume she was Googling him. I forced myself to stay where I was.

"Holy shit. Now that's a man. Damn, can he wear black tie. And in a uniform…" She fanned herself. I clenched my fists, embracing the sting of my nails digging into my palms. She started to read. "Simon Jefferson Duchesne. Age thirty-one. Highly decorated fighter pilot honorably discharged from the Navy two years ago, after he spent a year teaching at his alma mater, the United States Naval Academy in Annapolis. Only son of Jefferson Duchesne and Margaret LeBlanc Duchesne. The senior Mr. Duchesne served sixteen years as a congressman for

Louisiana's 2nd Congressional District, leaving his seat to run for governor. After he was defeated in his gubernatorial bid, he purchased a small Mississippi River shipping company, Southern Cross Logistics, which he has grown over the past decade to the ranks of the Fortune 500. Currently, the younger Mr. Duchesne is serving as vice president of Southern Cross, in addition to being a councilman for District A of the NOLA City Council. It is rumored he will be announcing his candidacy this fall to challenge the incumbent for his father's congressional seat."

I'd known the bare bones of this information, but hearing the details just highlighted our differences, once again reminding me why it was better I avoided him. I tried to tell myself this was a good thing. Then she continued.

"Simon Duchesne is frequently accompanied to charity events by long-time friend Vanessa Frost. Rumors abound as to the couple's status, and all are speculating whether Mr. Duchesne will pop the question prior to hitting the campaign trail. Ms. Frost is the daughter of Royce Frost, CEO of Louisiana Steel Products, and the late Amelia Bennett Frost, heiress to the Bennett textile empire…"

The roar of blood rushing in my ears drowned out whatever Yve said next. I exhaled, feeling like someone had punched me in the gut. Long-time friend? Pop the question? A fucking heiress? What the hell? So why the fuck was he naked in my backyard on Saturday night? *And why am I so pissed?*

I pushed the anger and disappointment away. I told myself that now I *knew* I'd dodged a bullet. I didn't screw around with guys who were taken. But if he were the cheating asshole I wanted to paint him as, why wouldn't he have jumped at the opportunity to nail and bail? Nothing about Simon Duchesne added up.

"Charlie." My attention snapped back to Yve. "Calm the hell down. It's all gossip from the society pages. Who knows the truth? I'd say actions speak louder than this trash." She gestured to the monitor.

"It doesn't matter. I mean, whatever happened Saturday night was an anomaly. Not to be repeated. I'll probably never see him again anyway." Why had I felt the need to tack on that last sentence? Like I wanted to see him again? Ugh.

The rest of my shift passed slowly, and I was gearing up to head out when we closed at five o'clock. Mondays weren't busy, so we'd been able to get ready for closing while the store was still open. Huck was bouncing on his paws, eager to get outside when I clipped the leash to his collar. I was pretty excited too, because I had the rest of the night free. Cognizant of Huck's excess energy, I decided to walk my bike rather than risk another encounter that would require first aid. We were seven blocks away from the store and three blocks away from home when all hell broke loose.

I was distracted, thinking about everything Yve had read to me earlier. And then I turned my head and watched the whole scene unfold in slow motion: the carriage turning the corner, Huck tugging the leash from my negligent grip and darting into the street after it, the street sweeper careening down the narrow road.

I screamed as the truck clipped Huck's torso and rear legs, sending him spinning toward the sidewalk on the other side of the street. I dropped my bike and ran into the road, barely missing getting hit myself. His broken body was sprawled in the gutter, his chest heaving, and a pool of blood was forming and running into the street. I dropped to my knees beside him and held back my vomit as I saw one of his rear leg bones protruding from beneath the skin and a gash along his side. I flipped the fur back over the wound, not able to stomach looking inside him. The truck hadn't stopped, nor had the car behind it. The carriage was gone. The streets of the Quarter were rarely empty, but of course now … when I desperately needed someone, it was deserted. Tears streamed down my face, and I fumbled with my bag, where it still hung across my body. I pulled out my phone and pressed buttons. I had four numbers. One of them had to answer. It rang. Once. Twice. And then someone picked up.

"Charlie?"

It was not a voice I'd expected to hear. But I didn't fucking care. "Charlie? I can hear you breathing."

"I need you. Now. Please. Help me." The words were disjointed syllables strangled by my sobs.

I could almost feel a change in Simon's demeanor through the phone.

"Where are you? What happened? I'm getting in my car. Tell me where I'm going."

I looked up. "Corner of Toulouse and Dauphine. Huck got hit by a car. I need…" My words broke off when Huck's eyes blinked open at his name. "Please. Hurry."

"I'm on my way. I'm not far. I'll be there in five minutes. Just breathe, Charlie."

Huck yelped, and I dropped the phone back into my bag.

I stroked Huck's head and spoke to him in low, soothing tones. He tried to move his back legs and yelped again, and his panting breaths sped up. I tried to hold him steady. His big brown eyes stared into mine. "It's going to be okay, baby. I promise. You're going to be fine. I swear."

Simon lied. He was there in less than five minutes, but it still seemed like an eternity. My face was buried in Huck's neck, trying to keep him still, listening to his pained whimpers. I heard the roar of an engine before a vehicle jerked to a stop on the street next to me. The door flew open, but I didn't look up. I kept my eyes locked on Huck's. A hand on my shoulder snapped me out of my stupor.

"Charlie, step back for a second." Simon was holding a gray cargo blanket. "We need to get the blanket under him to lift him into the back. We're going to do it together, okay?"

I moved toward Huck's head and Simon lay the blanket down. "Fuck," he breathed. "Need to wrap up his wounds before we can move him." Simon was all business, ripping off his suit coat and wrapping it around Huck. His dress shirt and tie became a tourniquet around Huck's hindquarters. "Never done a field dressing on a dog, but this is the best I can do." He worked the blanket under Huck's body, trying to jostle him as little as possible. Huck whimpered and tried to move. "Hold still, buddy."

Simon stood and spun to hit a button in the car. The tailgate of his BMW X5 rose. Wearing only a white T-shirt and suit pants, Simon crouched next to me. He nodded toward Huck's head. "You get his head. It's going to be a tight fit, but the back seat is down. As soon as we've got him in, climb over the seat and try to keep him calm. I'll get us there as fast as I can without bouncing him around too much. Got it?" When I didn't reply, he grabbed my shoulder and shook me. "Charlie, you with me?"

"Yeah." I nodded.

"Okay. Let's do this."

We awkwardly maneuvered Huck into the SUV, and my heart clenched at every whimper and whine. Once he was settled, I scrambled onto the back of the seat so I could sit next to him. Simon put the car in drive and activated his Bluetooth system. I only half listened to his call, but it seemed he was relaying Huck's condition to someone. He made another call, but I was deaf to everything but Huck's whimpers. Long minutes later we pulled up to a large white and tan building, and three women and a man in scrubs scurried out, carrying a doggy stretcher. Simon popped the tailgate, and the man started calling out orders to the others. A strong arm wrapped around my middle as I tried to follow them as they maneuvered Huck out of the car.

"Come on, let's go," he said, pulling me back and out the side door.

When we entered the building, my eyes darted around, but Huck was already gone. I tugged at Simon's arm, which was still wrapped around my waist, holding me upright.

"Where is he? Where did they take him?"

A woman at the reception desk responded. "They've taken him back to surgery. He's in good hands, ma'am." She slid a clipboard across the counter. "I'll need you to fill out some forms for him and," she hesitated, "I'll need a credit card."

I bit my lip. "I don't have a credit card." I looked down at the forms. *Shit.* It was like going to the fucking emergency room. Something I'd been happy to avoid for a year because I worked too damn hard to stay off the radar.

Simon shoved the clipboard away. "I've already instructed Jack—Dr. Richelieu—to add him to the Duchesne account."

Her eyes went wide. "Oh, of course, Mr. Duchesne. I apologize."

Simon nodded at her and led me to a bathroom where we both washed the blood from our hands. The gravity of the situation was further highlighted by the swirling red water running down the drain. My breathing accelerated, and I started to feel lightheaded. Simon once again wrapped an arm around me as he directed me into the waiting area and pushed me down into a chair. He crouched in front of me, pulling my hands into his. "Charlie, you need to breathe. You're going to hyperventilate, and I don't want to have to take you to the ER too."

I looked down at our joined hands. His were big, tanned, with little white scars on the knuckles. They didn't look like a politician's hands. Mine appeared childlike in his grasp. My nails were short ovals painted black. His thumbs brushed back and forth over my wrists, where the ink stopped and unmarked skin started.

I matched my breathing to his, slow and rhythmic. He squeezed my hands, and I looked up to meet his eyes. I said the first thing that came into my head.

"I'm sorry. I didn't mean to bother you. I wasn't even trying to call you. I mean—I don't even know how I called you. I was—" He squeezed my hands again, and I went silent.

"It's okay. I get it. I wouldn't have been your first call if you'd had your shit together."

"No—I didn't mean ... I just meant I shouldn't have troubled you." I gave him what I hoped was a heartfelt stare. "But I'm really glad you came. I ... I don't know what I would do without him. He's just a baby." A fresh wave of tears spilled over, and Simon released my hands to wipe them away with his thumbs.

"Jack's going to do everything he can for Huck. I promise. He's one of the best; I wouldn't have brought him here otherwise." He paused, catching another tear on his thumb. "I'm glad you called me. You scared the hell out of me, but I'm glad it was me you called. Even if you didn't mean to."

"I'll pay you back for everything. I promise. I ... don't do credit cards, but I have cash. At my place. I'll pay you back every dime, I swear." I hoped I wasn't lying. Because I knew this wasn't going to be cheap. It'd probably wipe out my emergency fund. But I didn't care. I'd do whatever I had to do to make sure Huck was okay.

"Let's not worry about it right now. Jack's an old friend; we'll work it out." He stood, stretched, and sat in the chair beside me, threading his arm around my shoulders. "We're going to be waiting a while, so why don't you try to chill, okay?" It was so easy to let my head rest against his solid shoulder. I felt some of my tension drain away, but I couldn't get the picture of Huck lying in the street out of my head.

Two hours later I was pacing the waiting room. I'd already flipped through damn near every magazine without reading a single word. The door to the back of the clinic opened, and a man in black scrubs stepped out. He looked to be in his early thirties and was classically handsome—blond hair with striking green eyes. But I didn't give a shit what he looked like—all I cared about was the name embroidered in red above his pocket. *Dr. Richelieu.*

Simon rose and reached out a hand. The vet shook it. "How's Huck?"

I crossed the room, barreling into Simon's side in an attempt to get closer to the vet. "Please. How is he?"

"Why don't you come in here for a moment." He gestured to a small private room connected to the waiting room.

"Why? What's wrong? Please—" My words died, and dread spread through me as I followed Simon inside.

"Just let Jack tell us. Okay, Charlie?"

I refused to sit, so Simon stood beside me, and the vet leaned against the closed door. "He made it through the surgery. He's in recovery."

Relief momentarily smothered the dread, but I needed more information. 'Made it through surgery' didn't sound promising. "And?"

"His leg was severely broken, and I had to screw a stainless steel plate directly into the bone. Because of his size, it was really the only option we had. The upside is he'll be able to walk a little sooner than he would otherwise. He also had extensive internal bleeding, but we were able to stop it. I'd like to keep him here for at least a week so we can monitor the initial stage of his recovery. It was a hard hit. He's very lucky."

I stumbled to a chair and dropped my head into my hands. I was thrilled he was going to be okay, but the hours of waiting had sapped my energy.

"He's really going to be okay?" I felt like I had to ask one more time, just to make sure I hadn't superimposed the words I wanted to hear over his.

The vet nodded. "He's young, otherwise healthy, and a fighter. Barring any unforeseen complications, he should be just fine."

"Can I see him?" I asked.

Dr. Richelieu nodded. "Just for a few minutes. We're keeping him sedated so he doesn't further injure himself."

He led us back through the clinic to a wide room containing what looked like horse stalls. Huck was laid out on his side on a thick stack of blankets covering the floor, an oxygen cannula in his nose. The vet opened the chain link gate, and I knelt and stroked Huck's silky ear. I whispered nonsense to him for several minutes before kissing his furry forehead and standing.

"Can I come back in the morning?"

"Anytime you want. And if you have any questions, Simon has my cell number. Feel free to call me. If I'm in a procedure, I'll call you as soon as I'm finished."

"And you'll call us if anything changes?" Simon asked.

"Absolutely, man. He's in good hands. We'll watch him all night and call you immediately if there's any change in his condition."

I shuddered at the thought and hoped we were through the worst of it. I dejectedly thought about going home to my empty apartment. Harriet was still gone, so there'd be no crashing with her for company. As good as I'd gotten at being a loner, I really didn't want to be alone tonight.

My mind was whirling, trying to figure out who I was going to call and beg to sleep on their couch. Things were still awkward with Con, so that left Delilah or Yve. Delilah lived with her brother, and Yve lived alone. But for all I knew, Yve might still be with Con. *Dammit.* Simon helped me into his SUV before rounding the hood and climbing into the driver's seat. I was still contemplating my limited possibilities when I realized we weren't driving back toward the French Quarter.

"I live that way." I pointed toward the rear of the vehicle.

"I know." Simon didn't turn the car around; he just continued to St. Charles Avenue.

"Where are we going?"

He didn't answer. We headed down Third Street and slowed as we entered the heart of the Garden District. He hit a button on the rearview mirror and turned into a driveway where a section of elegant green fence topped with fleur de lis was sliding open.

"Where the hell are we?" Simon hit the button again, and the fence closed behind us. He hit another button as we pulled up to a garage around the side of one of the most gorgeous homes I'd ever seen. It was easily as large as many of the homes in the Hamptons, and was built in a similar Neoclassical Italianate style, but that was beside the point.

"My house. Well, to be fair, it's my parents' home. But I live here as well."

I didn't know which fact to take issue with first, so I tackled them both. "You still live with your parents? Why didn't you take me home?"

He opened the driver's door and exited the vehicle, ignoring both of my questions. I was still sputtering when he opened the passenger door and unbuckled my seat belt. I smacked his hands away. "What the hell, Simon?"

He frowned, his features turning dark in the dim light of the garage. "You don't need to be alone tonight. And for some inexplicable reason, I want to help you. So stop being so prickly and independent for a goddamn minute and let me."

I glared at him. "Don't tell me what to do. And don't freaking kidnap me without asking first."

He scrubbed a hand across his face. "Fine. I'll take you home." He walked back around the car and opened the driver's door again. But I'd already gotten out. He was dead on; I didn't want to be alone tonight.

Simon slapped both hands on the roof of the car before peering through the cabin to where I stood outside the open passenger door. "Are you always this stubborn?"

I shrugged. "I don't know. I can't help it." He slammed the driver's door shut a second time and came around the hood and grabbed me by the hand.

"Come on, woman." He led me out of the garage, and when we didn't go toward the main house, I looked up at him, confused.

"Where are we going?"

"I live in the guesthouse."

I smirked. "So you only sort of live with your parents? Aren't you a little old for that?"

He tugged on my hand. "Trust me, I was going to buy my own place when I got out of the Navy. You would have thought I told my parents I was taking a vow of silence. To say they were horrified is putting it mildly. When I refused to move home, my father had the guesthouse renovated, and my mother guilted me into it. It would make them feel 'so much better to have someone on the property when they're traveling. And they'd missed out on so much time with me while I was in the service.' It was easier just to give in."

"You're a momma's boy, aren't you?"

"As much as any good ole Southern boy. I like sports, huntin', fishin', fast cars, and faster women, but I love my momma."

I smiled slightly, but my heart wasn't in it. His statement made me think about my relationship with my own mother, which was much too screwed up for such a pure sentiment.

We walked through the front door of a house a fraction of the size of the mansion, and Simon turned to face me. "Hey, Huck's going to be all right. Jack's one of the best."

He'd mistaken my silence as concern for Huck, and guilt flooded me; I'd spent two minutes not worrying about my pup. I was a bad daughter and a bad dog mom.

"Thank you. Again. For everything." I looked away and took in the dark paneled interior of the foyer and the crystal chandelier hanging overhead. A wide, gleaming wooden staircase curved up to the second floor. I stood dumbly. I didn't want to get the grime of my person on the pristine furnishings.

"How about a shower?" Simon asked.

"That would be great," I started, but paused to look down at my blood-smeared shirt. "But I don't have any other clothes."

"I'll find something for you. Might be a little big, but they'll work for tonight."

"Umm … okay. Thanks."

I followed as Simon led the way up the stairs, lost in my own thoughts. He seemed to understand that I needed the silence and didn't fill it with inane chatter. He gestured to a bathroom and opened the glass enclosure to flip on the water and adjust the temperature.

"Wait just a minute."

He left and returned with a fluffy white robe, a T-shirt, and boxers. He stacked them on the counter.

"Thanks," I whispered again. He closed the door as he left me alone in the white and gold bathroom that was quickly filling with steam. I stripped and stepped into the shower. I let the water cascade over me, soaking my hair and skin. Whatever strength had been holding me together was washed away with the grime and remaining traces of Huck's blood. I lowered myself to the tiled floor, wrapped my arms around my knees, and let myself fall apart.

simon

I paused outside the bathroom door, listening to Charlie's gut-wrenching sobs. I gripped the back of my neck with both hands and stepped away, not wanting to invade her privacy any more than I already had. I hated seeing the stooped set of her shoulders. I much preferred her with her chin held high, blowing me off. Wanting to do something, anything, I called Jack. He assured me that Huck was doing fine, and although the recovery was going to be long, he'd likely come through it as good as new. For Charlie's sake, I hoped he was right. She treated the dog like most people did a child. For a non-dog person, that might seem strange, but given the way my mother coddled her Pekinese and my father had babied his retrievers until they'd passed, it was nothing new to me. Hell, even the homeless folks in the Quarter twisted the sentiment to their advantage, using pathetic looking dogs to pry dollars from the hands of softhearted tourists.

But for Charlie, it seemed to be something more. She was a mystery, a standoffish enigma. In the age of Google, everything about my life was available for public consumption with a few keystrokes. I didn't know her last name, but I wondered what I would find if I did. Honestly, though, I'd rather learn about her *from* her. But that seemed unlikely to happen. She freely admitted she was only interested in one night—or less. But something about her made me want to explore this ... whatever this was between us.

I'd almost come in my pants like a teenager the night she'd casually stripped in front of me. She was willing to show me her body, but I wanted more. It was an uncomfortable feeling. Normally I was the one pushing women away. Charlie had shut me down more times in a handful of days than I'd been shot down in years. I wasn't trying to be arrogant—it was just the truth. First, I was the son of a congressman, then a Navy pilot in a strike fighter, which was a straight up pussy magnet. Most recently, I was the decorated vet returning home to take his place in the family dynasty. The former debutantes my parents pushed at me wilted into my arms. I carefully extricated myself from those situations, because the daughters of the city's leading families would expect a ring, when I wouldn't even stay the night.

So why was I so pissed when Charlie turned my very own M.O. on me?

Probably because I had my own reasons for not staying the night, and they had nothing to do with not wanting to do so on occasion. I headed to one of the guestrooms and turned down the bed. Given her worry about Huck, I hoped my actions would seem gentlemanly and not strange.

I met Charlie in the hallway as she came out of the bathroom drowning in the white terry cloth robe. Her clothes were rolled up in a bundle under her arm, and my shirt and boxers dangled from her other hand. Damn. That meant she was naked under the robe. I pushed the thought away and gestured to the guestroom with the two glasses of bourbon I held.

She followed me into the room, and I set one glass on the nightstand. Charlie placed her bundle of clothes on the dresser. She laid out the T-shirt and boxers on the end of the bed.

"Thought you might want a drink to help you sleep," I said.

"Thank you." She took the glass and sipped. She surveyed the room, lingering on the artwork. "This isn't your room."

"No. Guestroom."

She turned to face me. "Good to know my instincts aren't completely off. Cezanne's fruit doesn't really seem like your style." She gestured to the still life painting on the wall with her glass.

My eyes narrowed, and once again I was struck by the feeling that this woman was much more than she pretended to be. She drank the rest of her bourbon, and I cast about for something to say; I hit on the most pertinent fact.

"I called Jack and checked on Huck. He's still doing fine."

Her shoulders tensed for a beat before relaxing. "Thank you, again. I was going to ask you for his number so I could do that."

"I'll make sure you have it." The silence stretched between us, heavy and awkward. "I guess I'll let you get some sleep then. I'll be down the hall if you need something."

She watched as I pulled the door shut, but said nothing about my abrupt departure.

I walked down the hallway to my own room, wishing I wasn't so fucked up that I couldn't have a woman spend the night in my bed. Because that's where I wanted Charlie, even if all I was doing was holding her close to take away some of her worry and replacing it with peace of mind. Not that she'd let me. Yet.

I sucked in a deep breath and exhaled slowly as I shut my door. In the morning, I'd make a call I'd been putting off for years. It was time.

charlie

The night was endless. Bouts of sleep interrupted by flashes of Huck's collision with the street sweeper and everything that came after. Then my disordered mind would insert snippets of my parents and the angry faces of my father's victims into my dreams, and I'd jolt awake. I was exhausted and staring at the blank white ceiling, trying to clear my thoughts, when I heard a shout followed by a loud groan.

Simon.

He sounded like he was in pain.

I threw back the covers, and dressed in his T-shirt and boxers, I padded down the hall to his bedroom. The door was closed.

"Simon?" I whispered. Another pained moan and garbled words. Fear gripped me. I didn't think; I opened the door and slipped inside. A shaft of early morning light cutting through the open drapes highlighted his contorted face. He thrashed against the covers, hands clenching the sheets.

"No. Fuck. No."

A nightmare. That was something I could understand. I crossed to the side of the bed, my only thought to wake him up and free him from whatever horrors were haunting his sleep. I shook his shoulder.

"Simon, wake up." His hands released the sheets and grasped my shoulders, yanking me onto the bed and rolling us both until I was pinned beneath him. I cringed at the pain of his hold. His muscles were flexing and clenching. Fear bubbled up inside me.

"Simon."

When he didn't respond and his grip tightened, I acted on pure instinct—I reached up and slapped him across the face. His eyes snapped open, and he looked down at me, blinking and confused. I wiggled to get out from under him, and as he realized he was holding me down, his eyes went wide. His chest heaved with ragged breaths.

"Holy fuck. Charlie. What the hell are you doing in here?"

"Get off me," I said.

Simon rolled and flopped onto his back.

His chest continued to rise and fall, and he buried his fingers into his hair. "Jesus, fuck. I can't believe…" He glanced over at me, eyes wild. "Did I … did I hurt you?"

I didn't respond, only rubbed my shoulders where he had grabbed me. "I'll be fine."

"Jesus. That means—fuck. I did hurt you." He sat up and reached for me. Reflexively, I flinched. "My God. I'm so sorry. I'm—"

I sat up and slid off the bed, legs a little shaky. "It's fine. I should've left you alone. It's my own fault."

Simon sprang off the mattress, scrubbing both hands over his face. "I'm so sorry. I…" He looked up at the ceiling, fists clenching. "I … fuck. I'll take you home."

I shook my head. "It's okay." I sidestepped toward the door. "I'm just going to go back to bed."

"Charlie, wait. Let me explain—"

"You don't owe me an explanation. It's fine."

He crossed the room, and I felt behind me for the door handle.

"Christ. You're fucking terrified of me. Because I hurt you."

I shook my head again. "It's okay, Simon."

"Fuck. Please, just let me explain." He glanced at the clock. "It's almost six, and I'm not going back to bed. If it's okay with you, I'll make some coffee and tell you what the fuck just happened." He paused. "It's about time I told someone."

Well, that was cryptic.

He reached for a pair of USNA sweatpants and shoved his muscled legs into them. My eyes were riveted to him even as I told myself to look away and give him privacy to dress, but it was a losing battle. Although he'd scared the shit out of me, I was still drawn to him. Simon's outward appearance screamed perfection, but the idea that maybe he wasn't quite so perfect on the inside intrigued me even more.

I followed him down to the kitchen and took a seat at the table in the breakfast nook. I watched as he ground the beans and set the coffeemaker up to brew. He leaned back against the counter and crossed his arms over his chest. "How much do you know about me?" he asked without preamble.

"Enough," I said, even as I thought, *not nearly enough*.

"So you know I was in the Navy. I flew Super Hornets in Operation Enduring Freedom. I spent six years in the cockpit on missions. Almost all highly classified." He rubbed the heels of his hands into his eyes. "I was young, cocky, and thought I was invincible. Until I saw the first one of my brothers get shot down. That's a lesson in human fragility you never forget. I lost six more over the years, and I should have been one of them."

I wasn't sure how I was supposed to respond. So I didn't.

He continued, voice haunted. "I can't tell you the whole story, but I can tell you that a man I considered a brother picked up on a surface-to-air missile locked on me before I could even react. Kingman flew into it, trying to catch it on one of his tail fins so he'd at least have time to eject, but he miscalculated. We'd been flying missions non-stop for days, and we were all dog-tired and off our game. I watched him explode in a ball of fire. And I can't stop seeing it happen. It was my fault—a misread of my instruments—that we were even there, where they could get a clear shot at us, and he was the one who paid the price. He had a daughter he never got to meet, and I made his wife a widow."

His hazel eyes were shining with unshed tears when he finished. He turned to fumble with the carafe, hand shaking as he poured two cups. He reached into the fridge and pulled out cream. "How do you take your coffee?"

It was such a mundane question after the emotionally wrought confession. But I rolled with it.

"Black, please."

He fixed his coffee with cream and sugar, sat both mugs on the table, and dropped into the chair across from me.

I decided to ask the obvious question.

"Do you have PTSD?"

"Not officially."

"So ... what does that mean exactly?"

"It means I gave all the right answers to every shrink the Navy made me see."

"So you..."

"Lied? Yes." He took a sip of his coffee.

I was stunned, holding my mug to my lips, unable to drink. Yes, stunned by the confession, but more so stunned by how open and honest he was with me. Someone he barely knew. *Someone who could never be so honest with him.*

My next question made me feel like a complete hypocrite. "Why weren't you honest about it? Why didn't you let them get you some help?"

He closed his eyes for a beat before answering. "Because of the black mark it would leave on my record. And the stigma. I didn't want anyone to know that I was broken."

I set my mug down on the table with a loud thump. Goddamn. His honesty tore through me. Staggered me.

"Oh." It was a ridiculously useless word, but I didn't have anything else.

"And now, it's time I did something about it. Because I haven't spent a full night with a woman in four years. I haven't let myself fall asleep holding someone for fear that I would scare the shit out of her when a nightmare hit. Like this morning."

"Why now?" I asked.

Simon looked up, and his stare trapped me with its intensity. "Because I want to spend an entire night with you."

My eyes went wide.

"More than one night," he added.

"Oh," I said again.

I felt a pang in my chest where my heart was thumping double time. His brutal honesty did what legions of charm couldn't—it broke through my walls. Demolished my better judgment. I tried to appear unaffected, squeezing my mug to hide my trembling hands. He continued drinking his coffee as though he hadn't just rocked me to the core. One thought echoed through my head: Things were about to get complicated.

charlie

Three sharp raps sounded on the door, and a woman called out, "Simon, I saw your light on. I hope you have coffee!"

"Shit," Simon mumbled, standing and moving to the coffeemaker.

A petite, dark-haired tornado blew into the kitchen. She looked to be in her fifties and was wearing black yoga pants, a black zip-up jacket, and hot pink sneakers. Her sleek hair hung to her chin in a flattering bob. Her hazel eyes and the angle of her nose gave her away immediately as Simon's mother.

"Oh. Hello there! Didn't mean to interrupt," she said as Simon handed her a mug.

I pictured us from her point of view and winced. This looked like an intimate morning after. Simon was shirtless, wearing only sweatpants hanging low on his hips. I was dressed in his shirt and boxer shorts. Awkward, to say the least. But Mrs. Duchesne acted as though nothing was amiss.

She held out a small hand with perfectly manicured nails. "I'm Margaret Duchesne."

"Ch-Charlie Stone." I shook it, choking a little when I realized I had almost given her my real name in response to her formal greeting. *What is this family doing to me?*

"It's a pleasure to meet you. We get to meet so few of Simon's—"

"Mother," Simon interrupted.

She smiled warmly before releasing my hand and speaking to Simon. "I just wanted to stop in and say hello. I'm headed to my yoga class, and I haven't seen you in a few days. We need to have dinner sometime soon. Time is running short before we leave for Maine. So much to do before we go." She turned to face me again. "So Charlie, tell me, who are your people? What do you do?"

"Ummm ... I ... uh..." I stuttered.

"Mother, it's too damn early for that. You can interrogate Charlie some other time. I'm sure you'll be seeing her again soon."

Whoa. When I thought things were going to get complicated, I hadn't even considered a meet-the-parents scenario and the questions they'd have.

"That's lovely, Simon." Her smile was sincere and welcoming, and not strained and fake like my mother's would have been if I'd introduced her to a guy covered in tats with crazy bedhead. "I'll leave you two alone then."

"We have to get back to Jack Richelieu's office anyway. Charlie's dog had surgery yesterday."

Her eyes turned huge and sympathetic. "Oh, you poor dear. I'm so sorry for keeping you. I know you must be anxious to see your baby."

My heart clenched at the thought of Huck. I'd been counting down the minutes until I could call the clinic while I'd lain awake in bed. I glanced at the clock. Still too early. My plan was to get a verbal update, run home to change, and then peddle my ass over there. *Shit, my bike.* I left it on the side of the road. *Fuck.* It was history.

Margaret balanced on her tiptoes to kiss Simon's cheek. "Have a good morning. Tell Jack I said hello and that we'll be bringing Minka to see him before we leave town." And then she was gone. A dark-haired tornado indeed.

I dressed in my jeans from the day before and put on my bra, but I wore Simon's T-shirt, as mine was headed for the rag bin. When I'd mentioned that I was an idiot and had forgotten about my bike, Simon had shocked me by telling me he'd called Voodoo and asked Delilah to get it. Apparently she'd texted him while we were in the waiting room to let him know my bike was waiting for me at work.

Simon dropped me off in front of my place and drove around the block to find a parking spot. By the time he'd walked back to Harriet's, I was ready to go. He'd called Jack on the way, and Jack had informed us that Huck was doing well, but they wanted to keep him sedated for another day or so to give his body additional time to recover. It broke my heart to think of Huck still knocked out in his stall, but Simon trusted Jack implicitly. And I was learning that I trusted Simon. It was yet another foundation-rocking discovery.

"You all right?" Simon asked as we drove to Jack's clinic.

"Fine, just lots to think about."

"Huck's going to be okay."

"I know." I pulled a stack of hundred dollar bills from my purse, wrapped with a paper band with '$10,000' printed on it. The money was a huge chunk of what remained from the cash I'd run with. I dropped it on the center console. "This is for yesterday and hopefully will cover some of the bill for this week. I'm sure I'll owe you more though."

Simon nearly swerved into a parked car when he looked down at the money. "What the fuck, Charlie? Put your money away. I told you we'd figure it out."

"No. I pay my debts. And I know Huck's surgery had to cost a small fortune. Not to mention a week in doggy post-op. He's my responsibility. My family. And I'll pay for it."

Simon shot me an annoyed glare. "I haven't even gotten the bill, so at least keep it until we know how much we're talking about." His frown deepened. "I really don't like the idea of you carrying around that much cash."

I stuck the bills in my purse. "Well, I tried to give it to you, but you wouldn't take it. So I guess that's your problem."

"You are so damn stubborn."

"I'm not the one who won't take the money."

Simon growled. Like, actually growled. I laughed, thankful for the distraction.

"What am I going to do with you, woman?"

"I'm sure you'll think of something."

"Oh, I know what I want to do with you. But you'd go running for the hills if I told you."

After this morning, that was doubtful. "Try me."

He shifted in his seat. "I'd rather show you." He gave me a meaningful look. One full of seductive promise.

Heat rushed through me and took up residence low in my belly and between my thighs, only to be doused when we pulled into a parking spot in front of the clinic. Jesus. My libido was inappropriate and schizophrenic.

As if he knew what I was thinking, Simon added, "We're going to continue this conversation later."

simon

"Mr. Duchesne, it's a pleasure to meet you. Please, have a seat."

I supposed that my sitting down on the plush leather couch meant Dr. Carlson was officially my new psychiatrist. I also supposed I should be grateful that he'd agreed to see me on such short notice.

The session started as I imagined most sessions with a shrink did.

"Tell me what brings you here today, Mr. Duchesne."

"It's Simon, please."

"Of course, Simon." He waited with his pen poised over a manila file filled with sheets of paper. It was somehow comforting to know that he was still old school. The sound of someone tapping away on a keyboard while I spilled my darkest secrets would have annoyed the shit out of me.

"I have nightmares. Trouble sleeping," I admitted.

"How long has this been going on?"

"Just over four years."

He flipped a page, probably looking at the life story I'd been required to commit to paper before my appointment. "You were a pilot in the Navy?"

"Yes."

"And the source of the nightmares?"

I told him much the same story that I'd told Charlie a few days before. It was easier the second time. Probably because she hadn't judged me. Hadn't responded with platitudes. She'd just let me get it out. I also told him about how I'd pinned her to the bed when she'd woken me in the midst of a nightmare. My stomach still knotted when I remembered how she'd carefully backed away from me afterward.

"I understand, given the high profile nature of your family, why you've opted not to seek treatment at the VA."

This part made me feel like a hypocrite. Because most veterans didn't have the financial means that I did—and would have no choice but to seek treatment at the VA. But I also didn't want them to just write me a script for psychotropic drugs and send me on my way. I explained my reasoning, and he only nodded and continued with his questions.

"Have you told anyone this before?"

"Yes, just recently."

"And how did you sleep after that?"

I thought about the last couple of nights, both of which I'd slept through without nightmares.

"Better."

"I'm not saying you're going to be healed just by talking about this with someone a time or two, but it does help. And making the decision to come here today was a big step."

I continued to answer the questions he posed, and Dr. Carlson jotted down more notes. When the session was almost over, he laid his folder aside and studied me.

"While it is my opinion that you have PTSD, I think it's a relatively minor case. From what you've told me, you function very well, and I believe the biggest block you've been facing is that you've refused to discuss your experience until recently. I'd like to see you twice a week to start, and then we'll see how it goes from there."

"What about what happened with my … girlfriend?" I liked referring to Charlie that way. Too much. It was way too soon, but that was where this relationship was headed, if I had anything to say about it.

"I don't have any concern that you'd hurt someone, including her. I would suggest she not try to wake you from your nightmares, however."

We shook hands, and I left, feeling lighter than I had in years. Hope was a heady thing. Now I just needed to track down one mouthy, tatted-up girl who'd been MIA since Tuesday.

charlie

On Friday afternoon, fifteen minutes before closing, the door to the Dirty Dog swung open with a *whoosh*. I looked up and almost dropped the stack of jeans I was holding.

Simon filled the doorway, his big body blocking out most of the late-afternoon sunlight.

"Well hello there, handsome," Yve said. And he did look good. The light gray suit, crisp white shirt, and navy tie were understated yet sexy.

Simon nodded in response and looked pointedly at me. "You avoiding me?" he asked.

"What are you talking about?"

"You haven't been answering my calls or texts."

Oh. I'd called the clinic so many times over the last few days that I was burning through my small, monthly allotment of minutes way too fast. To conserve them, I'd kept my phone off the rest of the time. It was a double-edged sword, because with my phone off, the clinic couldn't reach me—so I overcompensated by calling every few hours for an update. I'm pretty sure the woman who answered the phones was ready to strangle me.

"Sorry, I haven't been keeping my phone on."

Simon took it in stride. "Got it. I was starting to wonder what was up."

I set the jeans down on the shelf where they belonged and arranged them into a neat stack. I had to keep my hands busy or else I might twirl my hair or something stupid like that.

He came closer, and I could smell the woodsy scent of his ... cologne? Aftershave? Deodorant? Whatever it was, it made me want to rub up against the five o'clock shadow shading his jaw.

"I was hoping I could give you a ride to go visit Huck. I hear he'll be coming home in a few days." Warmth bloomed in my chest. He'd been checking on my dog.

I looked up at the Kit-Cat clock on the wall. It was quarter to five, and I had a shift at Voodoo starting at seven. Without a ride, I'd be cutting it close to see Huck. I'd been pedaling my ass over to the clinic every day after work, but riding through the somewhat sketchy area without Huck by my side freaked me out, especially when it started to get dark.

"That'd be great." I met his intense stare. "I'll be done here in a little bit."

"You can clock out now. It's cool," Yve said, leaning up against the counter and shamelessly listening in. I glanced her way, but her attention was fixed on Simon. "Take that girl out to get some food. She ain't eatin' enough to keep a ghost alive lately."

Finally, Yve looked at me, and I glared back, giving her a *seriously, bitch?* look. She crossed her arms and raised an eyebrow.

"Done." Simon tucked a flyaway piece of hair behind my ear. "Anything you need before we go?"

"Just my bag," I said, as Yve pulled it out from the cabinet beneath the counter. "And my bike."

"We can put your bike in my car. I'll meet you around back?"

"Okay. Thanks." He smiled and headed for the door, pushing it open with as much gusto as when he'd come in. I looked at Yve.

"Seriously? Ain't eating enough to keep a ghost alive? What the hell? Don't even think about meddling." Yve fancied herself a *matchmaker*. Her disastrous efforts to date hadn't stopped her from trying.

She smiled a smug smile. "I don't think I need to meddle. That man is hung up on you. I nearly swooned when he did that thing with your hair. Damn, I need a man who looks at me like that."

"Just leave it alone, okay? More likely than not, this isn't going anywhere," I said, at the same time hoping I might be wrong. After Simon's raw honesty on Tuesday morning, I'd been thinking about my own situation. An idea had taken root, but given my crazy work schedule, huffing and puffing halfway across town to see Huck, and then falling into bed at night, I hadn't had much time to consider the implementation, let alone the ramifications of it. But the idea was germinating. I just wasn't sure I had the courage—or the skill—to see it through.

Yve gave me a quick hug as I picked up my bag off the counter. "Later, girly. See you tomorrow morning. You better come ready to dish the dirty details."

I rolled my eyes as I slipped out the back door.

Simon was leaning against the door of his X5. It was idling with the tailgate already open.

Within moments, Simon had my bike loaded, and classic rock was quietly thumping through the sound system. Spotting the volume control, I turned the song up, because "Hotel California" deserved to be more than background noise. He shot me a crooked smile, his dimples peeking out, and I had the urge to lean over and kiss him.

"Dinner before or after we see Huck?"

"After." He pulled away from the curb.

"I figured you'd say that. Seafood okay?"

"Of course." I gestured to myself. "But nothing fancy, obviously."

"You look beautiful. And I have just the place."

Simon drummed on the steering wheel as we headed to Jack's clinic. The silence was companionable rather than awkward. But I had questions that I wanted answered.

"I tried to pay Dr. Richelieu. He wouldn't take my money. Want to tell me why that is?"

Simon stopped at a red light, expression darkening. "Please tell me you did not ride your bike through this part of town with ten grand in cash."

I looked down at the fancy tan floor mats embroidered with the BMW logo.

"Charlie…" His tone wouldn't allow for anything but the truth.

"Okay, in hindsight, it wasn't the best idea. But I only would've had to carry it one way if he would've taken the money. So really, it's kind of your fault." I glanced back up.

Simon's knuckles whitened as he gripped the steering wheel. He may have whispered something about a prayer for patience. After a long pause, he said, "Let's make a deal. You want to go see Huck, you call me. I'll make sure I'm available."

"You can't just drop everything…"

"Just call me. *Please.* It would give me peace of mind. Otherwise I'm just going to wait outside the Dirty Dog for the next few days after closing and pick you up and put you in the car anyway."

"That's kind of stalkerish. And sort of kidnapping."

"Exactly. So please spare me the disgrace."

I tapped my finger on my lips.

"So do we have a deal?" Simon asked.

We were pulling into the clinic. It was the look of sincere concern on his face that made me cave.

"Fine. Deal."

He reached out a hand, and I shook it. When I went to pull my hand back, he held on for a beat. "Thank you."

Dr. Richelieu confirmed the good news: Huck would be well enough to come home on Sunday. I guess one of the perks of being friends with the vet was that he was willing to come in on his day off and give me all of the care instructions I'd need. I already knew that Huck's recovery wasn't going to be easy. I'd be moving downstairs into Harriet's guest bedroom, because there was no way Huck would be able to tackle the stairs up to my place for at least a month, if not longer. He'd have to stay in his crate almost all the time, except for short trips outside to do his business. I scratched his ear, and Huck licked my hand and rested his giant head on my lap, his heavy tail thumping on the ground. I didn't care about the inconvenience; I was just so damn glad that my big mutt was going to be okay.

Dinner was boiled crawfish served in a bucket and all the fixings. It was absolutely not what I expected. Which was turning out to be a theme when it came to Simon.

When I questioned his dinner choice, he explained, "What you don't realize, is that I've got some bayou in my blood. My momma was raised in a house on stilts in Jean LaFitte, and crawfish was a regular Sunday dinner. My granddad captained his own commercial fishing boat until he died at age seventy-eight."

"And here I thought you were as silver spoon as they come."

"Maybe some, but this," he flicked his tie, "is only one part of me. It's just the surface." He picked up my hand and traced the tattoos up my arm. "Just like you're more than the sum of your ink. I want to know who you are beneath all this." I shivered. Whether from his words or his touch, I'm not sure. But when he looked at me like that, it was like he was seeing inside me. There was no way in hell I'd hold up under his scrutiny.

I pulled my hand away and shattered the moment. "I'm going to be late for work if we don't go soon."

He flagged down our waiter and paid the bill, giving me a decidedly dirty look when I reached for my purse. I guess bayou manners precluded going Dutch. I was already five minutes late when we pulled up in front of Voodoo and Simon put the SUV in park.

"Thanks for dinner. Would you mind opening the back? I need to grab my bike." I didn't want to cut and run, but I was already late and wasn't sure what to say after Simon's statement at dinner.

My body was angled toward the door, fingers wrapped around the handle.

Simon scrubbed a hand across his five o'clock shadow. "Just leave it. I'll pick you up."

Umm, what? I smiled. "That's not necessary."

"Charlie, you can't think riding your bike home at two o'clock in the morning, by yourself, is a smart idea. Maybe once Huck is back on his feet, but without him…"

He was right. I couldn't argue the point and not sound like a moron. "I'll get Con to take me home. It'll be fine." I didn't want to put Simon out more than I already had today.

He frowned, jaw clenching. "Are you still sleeping with him?"

I bristled. *What the hell?* I was just trying to save Simon an extra trip. "That's none of your damn business."

"It sure as hell is." His tone was begging for a fight.

I yanked the door open and climbed out. I was struggling with the tailgate when Simon slammed his door shut and strode toward me.

He pressed both hands against the rear window, trapping me against the car. "Open this stupid thing," I demanded.

Simon's voice was low, his breath hot against my neck. "It's my business because I want you in my bed. No one else's."

I spun in his arms, his words sending a bolt of lust straight through me. I should not find his high-handed behavior attractive. At all. I lifted my chin and countered, "What about what I want? Doesn't that mean anything?"

He leaned down, resting his forehead against mine. "It means everything. And I think you want exactly the same thing I do." He pulled away. "I'll be here at two. Don't let Con take you home, Charlie."

I took a deep breath and let it out slowly, trying to give the impression that I was considering telling him to fuck off when all I wanted was for him to take me home *now*.

"Fine. But just know, I'm not always going to give in this easily."

He grinned. "I can live with that."

He pushed a lock of hair behind my ear, the same move that made Yve swoon, and I decided he'd waited way too damn long to kiss me. I leaned up and slid my arms around his neck, pulling him down until our lips met. Simon didn't resist, but my control over the kiss vanished the instant he angled his head and sought entrance to my mouth. I opened, and his tongue slid inside, tangling with mine. He wrapped both arms around me, hauling me up against him. His woodsy scent surrounded me, and I tasted peppermint, beer, and something uniquely Simon.

I barely registered the sound of the door chime and a throat clearing. "You coming in, Lee? Or you gonna make out like a teenager with the prom king?"

I pulled back, swiveling my head to look at Con. He looked … bored. Which was his go-to expression when he didn't want anyone to know he was pissed. I pressed another quick kiss against Simon's lips, refusing to let Con dictate how this scene ended.

"Were you really the prom king?" I asked, hoping to erase the scowl that had formed on Simon's face.

He looked away from Con and back to me. "Maybe." He bent to kiss my cheek, his lips brushing lightly across mine once more. "I'll see you at two."

He nodded to Con. "Leahy."

"Councilman."

I followed Con into the shop, and swore the temperature dropped about twenty degrees.

"Seriously? Simon Duchesne? Jesus, that's fucked up, Lee. Fucked up." The buzzing of Delilah's tattoo gun quieted.

"Why? What exactly is so fucked up about it?"

Con paced. He wouldn't look at me. "It just is. You don't get it. He always gets what he wants. And the rest of us poor fucks have to watch it happen."

I planted my hands on my hips and stared at him. "I don't know what's between you two, but I don't think it has anything to do with me. And don't pretend like I'm breaking your heart, Con. We had fun. That was it. I know you slept with Yve. So, you're certainly not pining away for me."

Con stopped his pacing, finally facing me. "I don't want to see you get hurt, babe. And what we had was more than just fun, at least to me. You're important. I care about you. I ... don't want you to be surprised when this doesn't turn out how you're hoping."

"I don't even know what I'm hoping for. I've got no expectations. All I'm doing is enjoying it while it lasts."

"Just keep your eyes open, okay? You're worth way more than being some politician's sidepiece."

The door swung open, and we both turned to see three giggling young women stagger in, each dressed in short shorts, halter-tops, Mardi Gras beads, and mile-high heels. I took the opportunity to step behind the counter and end the conversation.

charlie

Simon's X5 was idling at the curb when I walked out the front door at two o'clock. He was already out of the car and smiling when I hit the sidewalk. He'd changed into worn jeans and a plain black T-shirt. He followed me around the front and opened my door for me. His mother, the tiny, dark-haired tornado, had definitely raised him right. Or maybe it was just a Southern thing. The guys I'd dated in New York had always let valets and drivers get my door, never bothering to do it themselves.

"I have to admit, the Southern gentleman thing is growing on me." I was about to climb in when Simon put a hand on my arm.

"Where are you fr—"

Oh shit. Not wanting him to ask me something I'd have to lie about, I stood on my tiptoes and pressed my lips against his, cutting off the question. One of his arms wrapped around me, pulling me against his body, and his other hand delved into my loose waves. I could feel him harden against me, and my body heated. Damn. The man could kiss.

He pulled away but didn't let go.

"Hi," I said. It was the only word I could latch on to. After a few breaths, Simon released me.

"Hello to you too."

Knowing that I was standing next to the car looking like a slack-jawed idiot, I climbed inside and shut the door. A grin tugged at the corners of my mouth when I realized Simon was still standing next to the passenger door, staring at me through the window. Apparently the kiss had made idiots of us both.

I was still trying to rein my body's reaction in when Simon finally pulled the SUV away from the curb in the direction of Harriet's home. The silence between us was comfortable, but I needed music to distract me from where my thoughts were headed. I reached out to turn up the radio, and Simon slowed to let a group of pedestrians cross the road. He looked at me, brows drawn, and grabbed my right wrist.

"What the hell happened?"

I looked at him, confused. "I was just turning up…"

"No—your arm. Did you hurt yourself?"

I followed his gaze to where it rested on the gauze on the inside of my right bicep.

"Oh. Just adding to my collection."

His brows shot up. "Another tat?"

My smile died as I studied his expression. *Do not tell me he disapproves.* Because I'd tell him where to get off. No one told me how to dress, how to wear my hair, or anything else any more. *No one.*

"Yeah, what's it to you?" My tone took on a *don't fuck with me* edge that I'd acquired shortly after I stepped onto the Greyhound in Atlanta just over a year ago and some asshole had decided I looked like easy prey. I'd kneed his balls up into his lungs when he'd tried to feel me up after I fell asleep on the bus. The memory fueled my temper.

"Nothing … I was just surprised."

"One more tat put me too far over the bad girl edge for you, councilman?" The words felt like ground glass in my throat.

"Hey—that's not fair. It's not like that. I saw the bandage and … anyway, I think the ink is hot, so don't get your back up."

My quick rush of anger dissipated at his words. I relaxed into the seat as we started moving again. I felt like a bitch for overreacting and being so defensive. Especially after he'd just kissed the hell out of me. Just the thought of the kiss had heat starting to gather low in my belly.

"So what is it?" he asked.

He turned down my road and pulled into a rare empty parking spot across the street.

My answer came easily. "Why don't you come up and I'll show you?"

His hands flexed on the steering wheel, and he stared directly out the windshield. He nodded, as if deciding something. "I'll get your door."

Simon pushed my bike into the garden oasis and followed me up the spiral staircase to my apartment. I unlocked the door and held it open. When I flipped on the light, I tried to see my place through his eyes. It was tiny. Not much bigger than the bedroom I'd stayed in at his house. The living room was furnished with a love seat angled toward a small fireplace, a side table, and a lamp. The door to my bedroom was ajar, and my double bed looked like it barely fit inside. Calling one corner a "kitchen" was a bit of a stretch. There was a sink, a foot of counter space, a dorm-size fridge, and a microwave. A small table and two chairs were tucked into what I grandly referred to as the "breakfast nook." In actuality, it was a corner behind the door.

"It's not much, but I don't need much. And I kind of love it." Simon finished his visual tour, and focused on me, his hazel eyes burning with heat. He seemed even bigger in the small space, and the moment became undeniably intimate.

"This is probably too forward," he started. "But I'm going to come right out and say it. I want you under me in that bed." He nodded toward my room, as if the statement needed any clarification.

Whoa. That *was* forward. I swallowed, feeling heat rise to my cheeks. Well, hell. I wanted the same thing. I wasn't denying it. I toed off my Chucks. "I guess if you play your cards right—"

He reached for one of my hands and cut me off. "But that's not happening tonight."

What the hell? Although this rejection didn't sting as much as him leaving me floating naked in the pool, it still felt like rejection.

"Way to let a girl down easy, Simon." I rubbed my hand over my face and tugged at the one in his grip. "Why did you come up then?"

He wouldn't release my hand, instead using it to pull me closer. "You were going to show me your new tat. And you know why I can't stay. It's not because I don't want to. Not because I don't want you."

The pieces clicked together in my brain. Damn. Sometimes I really was dense. My face heated again, this time with shame. "Oh, shit. I didn't even think … I mean … Jesus, I'm such a bitch."

"No, you're not." He twined his fingers with mine. "I'm glad you forgot."

"I just … wasn't thinking."

"Then I'm glad I can make you stop thinking." He rubbed his thumb over the back of my hand. "I'm seeing someone—a shrink. So believe me when I say, I will be spending the night with you in that bed, but not quite yet."

My gaze shot up to his. "Seriously? That's good, right? I mean, I thought you didn't want to talk to anyone about it."

He brought our joined hands to his lips and pressed a kiss to my knuckles. "I didn't, but then I found something I wanted even more."

"Oh." It was the best I could do. I didn't know how to respond to that. It was sort of huge. He wanted me enough to bare his soul to a perfect stranger in hopes of sorting out his issues? It was good to know I wasn't the only one who was feeling something. Even if that feeling was dangerous to my very existence.

He nodded down at my arm. "Can I see the new tat?"

I untangled my hand from his and peeled away the gauze to uncover a black and gray Lady Justice, blindfolded, holding out her sword and balanced scales.

Simon studied it and then met my anxious gaze. "Why that?"

I gently skimmed the outline of the ink with a fingertip. It was a physical manifestation of the idea that had been percolating within me for days, and his confession about the shrink made me even more determined to go after it. He was facing his demons. It was time I did something to face mine.

One of his long, blunt-tipped fingers followed mine, tracing the lines, and I could tell he was waiting for my answer. I could only give him a vague one, as usual. "Truth. Justice. Balancing what's owed. All good things to remember."

His next question caught me off guard. "Where are you from? Because I know you're not from here."

I pulled away and headed toward the fridge. Not going there. "You want a beer?"

"Not so fast. You're going to have to tell me eventually, Ms. Stone." He cornered me against my sliver of counter space and cupped my jaw. "But I'll wait until you're ready. Right now, I'll settle for a taste of you." He pressed against me, and my nipples hardened. I met him halfway, twining my arms around his neck and pulling his head down. I was throwing myself wholeheartedly into this change of subject.

"You're so damn tall." I pushed up on my tiptoes again, trying to reach his lips. But Simon crouched, wrapped one arm around my back and one under my ass, and swept me up into his arms. I couldn't hold in my girly squeak of surprise. He crossed my miniscule living room and sat on the love seat. I resituated myself so I was straddling him. The position rubbed the center seam of my jeans directly over the growing bulge in his pants. The pressure against my clit had me rocking slightly against him. He didn't know it, but my hood piercing ratcheted up the 'holy shit that feels amazing' feeling several notches. My head dipped backward, and he took advantage, his full lips kissing along the line of my jaw and down to my neck. His fingers dug into my hips and all I could think was that I wanted him naked, inside me. I reached for the hem of my tank, pulling away so I could get it over my head.

"Goddamn, you're beautiful," he breathed.

I reached around my back to unhook my bra, but he stopped me with his words. "Let me." He deftly unhooked it, and I drew it forward, off my arms. His hands were cupping my breasts as soon as they were unbound.

"I stand corrected. You're fucking gorgeous." His eyes were riveted on my gold hoops. "Are they ... can I?" I smiled, glad that he was as turned on by them as I was.

"It's okay. They're a couple months old. You can ... play. You're the first person besides Delilah who's seen them."

"I'm fucking honored." He bent his head and circled one ring with his tongue before tugging on it gently with his teeth.

Bursts of pleasure streaked through me, straight from my nipples to my clit. I groaned and rocked against his erection.

He lifted his head momentarily. "Could you come from just this?"

"I don't know ... maybe?" My words were breathy and didn't sound like they'd come from my mouth.

He chuckled, and the low rumbling sound made me rock harder against him. I felt shameless, but it was too damn good to stop. I was so freaking glad I'd taken the leap on the piercings. Best. Idea. Ever.

"Then let's see what we can do."

Simon cupped my breasts, lifting them to his mouth again. Between his fingers and his mouth, I was bucking against him and coming apart in under a minute. I dropped my head forward, muffling my unintelligible sounds against his shirt.

I shuddered, letting the waves wash over me. Holy hell. I didn't know that was possible.

When the shivers finally subsided, I realized that in my quest to stay quiet, I might have accidentally used my teeth against his shoulder.

"Omigod. I'm so sorry."

I started to pull away, intent on climbing off him, but Simon's hands cupped my ass and held me in place.

"That might be the hottest thing I've ever seen. Jesus, Charlie."

He pulled me back down against his cock, and the spirals of pleasure started to twine around me once more. If he didn't stop, I was going to come again.

"It's ... the ... piercing," I breathed.

His eyes dropped to my nipples, so I elaborated, "My hood. It's pierced too." I couldn't slow my rocking hips. "So when ... you ... do that..." I dropped my head back and let the second orgasm roll over me.

simon

Holy. Fuck.

Watching Charlie rock against me to get herself off was one of the sexiest things I'd ever seen. So damn sexy that I thought my dick might bust right through the zipper of my jeans. I had to try to think of something else. Anything else. Anything but the fact that she had another piercing that I was dying to see. When she slumped against me for the second time, I stood, wrapped her legs around me, and headed to her bedroom. Just because I wasn't planning to stay tonight didn't mean that I couldn't make her come a few more times before I tucked her into bed and went home and jacked off to the memory of how fucking amazing she was.

As I laid her on the bed, she reached out and flipped a switch. The lamp on the bedside table illuminated the room with a soft glow. She unwrapped her legs from around my waist, and her smile turned sultry. I knew she could read my mind.

The thought was confirmed when she said, "You want to see it, don't you?"

"Fuck yeah. Are you joking?"

She bit her lip, whether out of shyness or because she was trying to keep herself from laughing at me, I didn't know. I didn't care. I was barely restraining myself from ripping her pants off.

"I've never quite had this experience before."

"Oh … well then." She looked down meaningfully and reached for the button of her pants. I brushed her hands away and unbuttoned and unzipped them myself. When she lifted her hips, I peeled them down her legs.

Laid out on the bed, she looked like a goddamn fantasy come to life. Her legs pale and unmarked, her arms covered in works of art, the glinting gold tipping the pink nipples of her fantastic rack, her wild red, purple, and black waves spilling across the quilt. I paused to appreciate the sight. I was even more dumbstruck than I had been the night she'd stripped by the pool, because tonight I had enough light to see everything I'd missed then. She was more than a fucking goddess. "You're so goddamn beautiful … there aren't words…"

"I don't need words. Just you."

I knelt and hooked my fingers in her panties and slid them down, unveiling the rest of her, inch by inch. Once I'd dropped the black lace to the floor, I bent to drag my tongue along her slit until I bumped her hood piercing. It was gold, matching her nipple rings, and it was the hottest fucking thing I'd ever seen. I tongued it, flicking it against her clit, and she writhed on the bed, her fingers gripping my hair and tugging.

"Holy … Simon … don't stop." Her words were breathy, and my dick pulsed in my jeans. I ignored my hard-on and continued devouring the sweetest pussy I'd ever tasted. Jesus Christ. This woman would own me.

She bucked against my mouth, and I flicked her piercing again. When she screamed my name, I'm pretty sure everyone in a four-block radius heard it. I fucking loved it. Her hips jerked and she sank deeper into the mattress, pulling away from my mouth. She pushed my head away, and I looked up at her. Her features were languid, sated. I wanted to make her look like that every day for the rest of my life.

The thought slammed into me with the subtly of a two-by-four to the face. I knew I wanted to see where this could go between us, but I hadn't stopped to consider exactly what that could mean.

As she reclined against the bed, I considered what I knew about her: she had attitude and ink in spades and constantly kept me guessing. I knew her name, where she worked, where she lived, that she had only a few friends, and she loved her dog. That was the sum total of my factual knowledge of Charlie Stone. Before I let myself get any deeper into whatever this was becoming, I needed to know more.

She propped herself upon her elbows, eyes raking over me. "Are you going to let me return the favor?"

All coherent thought fled my brain except for *hell yes*.

charlie

I locked the door behind Simon and sagged against the wood. Sweet baby Jesus. The man had rocked my world. Both in bed and out. Because of him, I was going to potentially put my safe and anonymous existence at risk. I crossed into my bedroom and punched in the code to the small, hotel-type safe bolted into my closet. Harriet's last tenant had left it behind, and I used it to hoard my cash and the reminders of my past. My license, passport, and old credit cards were stacked inside. It was strange to see my real name again. Only Harriet knew it, and I was confident she'd never reveal my secret. I'd stopped thinking of myself as Charlotte Agoston about three months after I'd left Manhattan. By that time I'd embraced my new identity. All it took was 1,300 miles and a fake name to finally discover the real me.

Under the false bottom built into the safe, there was a nondescript composition book. It was deceiving in its simplicity, but the pages were filled with a gibberish mess of letters and numbers. It was the one thing of my father's I had taken from the penthouse, although I probably shouldn't have. But I'd run across it by chance and taken it as a sign. I didn't know what it contained, but I did know that my father wouldn't go to the trouble to encode something unless it was pretty damn important. It was my insurance policy. Although, it could just as easily be my ticket to facing an obstruction of justice charge. Either way, I'd known that my disappearance wouldn't go over well, and there was a chance the Department of Justice might still decide I belonged in prison with my father. If that happened, information would be my only bargaining chip. I just didn't know what kind of information I had. I hadn't touched the book since the day I'd stashed it in the safe. And I didn't want to be touching it now. It was an irrational fear—that my father's evil would somehow seep under my skin if I handled his dirty secrets. Honestly, I'd planned to do nothing with it unless and until I needed to use it as a defensive weapon. But Simon had unknowingly convinced me to be proactive. The only way I'd ever be able to stop looking over my shoulder was to find the money.

The FBI had all of the computers, servers, files, and records from Agoston Investments, and with all that information and the resources at their disposal, I assumed they would have found something by now. Tens of thousands of people were counting on them. But nothing in the news mentioned even a dollar being located. If I could decipher the notebook, and it actually contained information that would prove useful in the search, I could feed the feds anonymous tips while retaining my ace in the hole. Once all of the money had been recovered, I could emerge from hiding on my own terms. It was an idealistic plan, but it might be my only shot at exploring something real with Simon.

That was, if Simon could stand to be near me after he knew the truth. My hopes deflated at the thought, but I wouldn't let it deter me. It was a long shot on both fronts, but it was the only shot I had. So I'd take it.

I thought about tonight. Simon was unlike anyone I'd ever met before. He seemed to just want me ... for me. That was a novel experience. As the daughter of a billionaire, I'd always questioned people's motives for befriending me. As a child, parents had encouraged their kids to get close to me in order to be invited into my parents' social circle. Imagine being fourteen years old and being grilled for investment advice by a friend's dad. Seriously.

I know, poor little rich girl syndrome. But you could
never know what someone else's life was like until you'd
walked that metaphorical mile in her designer pumps. Pre-
scandal Charlotte Agoston would have been the perfect
match for someone like Simon. Well-bred, poised, not to
mention wealthy and well-connected. But he seemed to
like the simple, rough-around-the-edges, poor, loner
version of me just fine. His political ambitions and
upcoming campaign were the biggest wildcards right now.
He'd never discussed them with me.

Would Simon still want to be with me when I refused
to accompany him to fundraisers and public events? Or
would he grow frustrated and lose interest? At this point,
there was nothing to do but wait and see. The most
startling realization was that I *wanted* to find some way to
fit into his life.

I flipped open the notebook and delved into the wily
depths of my father's twisted mind. I stared at the words,
letters, and numbers for hours, hoping a pattern would
emerge.

It was his own shorthand encrypted with some sort of
code—that much was clear. But without the key to the
cipher, I could stare it for years and never break it.

The boldly scrawled numbers and letters were blurring
together when I flipped the book shut hours later. The sun
was already shining through my skylight, and I was no
closer to figuring it out than I had been when I started.

The book went back into the safe, and I took a quick
shower before dressing and heading out for coffee and my
Saturday morning beignet. I had to be at the Dirty Dog by
nine to help Yve sort through a new shipment of inventory
she'd bought online. I opted to leave my bike at home and
walked up Dauphine to St. Philip and my favorite café. A
hotspot frequented by locals more than tourists, it was
already jam-packed with the early crowd. While I waited in
line, I noticed *The New York Times* on one of the tables.

The headline snagged my attention:

MONEY TRAIL COLDER THAN EVER

More than one year after his devastating fraud was uncovered, sources say federal authorities are no closer to locating the billions stolen by Alistair Agoston. Victims are demanding progress, and those demands have been met with silence.

The article went on to detail the arrest, the trial, my father's 175-year sentence, my mother's activities, and then: *Charlotte Agoston, only child of Alistair and Lisette Agoston, has been in seclusion in an undisclosed location since giving her testimony just over one year ago. Sources indicate that while she's not thought to be complicit in her father's scheme, she's considered a person of interest by the FBI, which has been unable to locate her for further questioning. When asked, Lisette Agoston denied having any knowledge about where her daughter was currently living. Anyone with information concerning the whereabouts of Charlotte Agoston is asked to contact the FBI.*

At the bottom of the page was a picture of me. Well, the old me. I looked around to make certain no one was watching as I folded that section of the paper and stuffed it in my bag. It wasn't like I could hide all the copies, but why leave it where someone might make the connection? The line was barely moving, so I picked up the local paper that was tucked under *The New York Times* and flipped through to find the entertainment section. It'd been a while since I'd been to a good show, and I wanted to see who was coming to town. I froze when I saw Simon's face staring up from the society section. He was once again dressed in black tie, but this time his arm was wrapped around a gorgeous blonde in a sleek gray designer gown. She was tucked in close to his side, hand pressing against his chest. I read the headline:

NOLA'S FAVORITE SON SHINES
AT CHARITY GALA

My eyes flicked to the date on the paper. Today. I forgot about the line and dropped into a chair.

Last evening New Orleans's leading citizens gathered at a gala to raise funds for the final stage of construction of the art museum expansion. All eyes were on Simon Duchesne and his lovely companion, Ms. Vanessa Frost, as it is rumored that he is preparing to launch his campaign for the United States House of Representatives in hopes of ousting incumbent, Robert Carter, and reclaiming the seat his father held for sixteen years before his unsuccessful run at the Governor's mansion...

I skimmed the rest of the article, and the words blurred when I saw the same speculation that a marriage proposal was expected to be forthcoming prior to Simon hitting the campaign trail. When I dropped the paper, my sweaty hands were smeared with gray ink from the newsprint. My churning stomach rebelled at the thought of food. A cold detachment settled over me as I realized Simon was apparently a very busy man. Somehow, between taking me out for dinner and picking me up for work, he'd managed to squeeze in a charity event with his ... whatever she was. His girlfriend? I mentally ticked off his schedule for the evening: dinner with me, gala with her, then orgasms with me before calling it a night. Fucking over-achiever.

Hot anger burned through the detachment when I recalled my thoughts from the wee hours of the morning, about how I wanted to try to find a way to fit into his life, and about how Simon's honesty had inspired me to find a way to unbury the secrets I'd been hiding. I didn't care that my reaction was hypocritical. My reason for hiding the truth from Simon was to preserve the life I'd built in New Orleans. His was ... what? The quick fuck he'd claimed not to want? *What a joke.* He was just as bad as any of the people who'd used me before, except this time, I wasn't being used for financial gain. I was just a toy to be played with when it was convenient for him. Con's harsh words from last night came back to me: *You're worth way more than being some politician's sidepiece.*

Con knew. And he'd tried to tell me. But I wouldn't listen. I didn't know why I was so shocked. Yve had mentioned the speculation about their relationship in the online gossip columns. Except dumbass me had assumed it was just that—speculation. Because a good guy like Simon wouldn't keep a lady for his public persona and a tatted-up bad girl on the side, right? I laughed humorlessly. *That's what I get for making assumptions.*

Again, maybe I wasn't being fair, because even if he'd asked me to go to an event like last night's gala, I would have turned him down cold. There was no way I could brave the cameras to stand by his side. Someone would figure it out, my anonymity would evaporate, and then the FBI would swoop in. *But he didn't ask me—he hadn't even mentioned it—so fuck being fair.*

I walked out of the café without getting coffee or my damn beignet.

charlie

I stalked into the shop, but didn't make it more than three steps past the door before Yve pounced.

"Who pissed in your Cheerios?"

"Not talking about it." The incriminating section of the local paper was shoved in my bag with the section of *The New York Times*. I wasn't sure why I took that one too. Maybe so I could pull it out and look at it for a reality check every time I remembered how amazing last night had been.

Yve frowned. "Seriously, Charlie. You look ... sad. Is Huck still coming home tomorrow?"

"Yeah." Which was one more kink I had to iron out. I was sure Simon would be showing up to help me get Huck home, and no way in hell was I accepting any more help from him. Harriet would just have to haul out her old diesel Mercedes station wagon. And then the bill ... I'd pay the whole freaking thing. If it was more than I had, I would swallow my pride and ask either Harriet or Con for a loan. I was not going to be further indebted to Simon or his friend.

"Then what gives?"

Yve wasn't going to let it go. She was almost as bad as Juanita when it came to needling you until you confessed. I reached into my bag and pulled out one of the sections of newspaper, checking first to make certain it was the right one. I slapped it on the counter in front of her.

"Went for coffee. Found this instead."

Yve looked down and studied the picture. "Same blond bitch from the society pages online."

"Yeah, well, I thought whatever they had was history. Especially because last night he was at my house. And I was naked. And orgasms were involved."

Yve scanned the paper, presumably doing what I had done first—looking for the date. "But he was at the gala last night."

"After he picked me up from here, but before he picked me up from Voodoo at two. Busy guy."

Yve's eyebrows shot up to her hairline. "Damn. I'm sorry, girl. That sucks. You better believe if he shows up here, I'll run his ass out."

"Thanks. You mind if I leave a little early today? I have a feeling he's going to be coming by." I hated to ask, especially because I needed the money now more than ever, and I'd been leaving early way too often already.

"Do what you need to do. You need some help tomorrow getting your pup home?"

I shook my head, a new plan already forming. I would skip Harriet's Mercedes and get Con to help me. He had a beat up Tahoe that he drove when he wasn't on his Harley. And he wouldn't let Simon get near me if I didn't want him to. Con wasn't the type to say 'I told you so,' but I still wasn't looking forward to telling him I'd learned my lesson the hard way despite his warnings. I felt so … stupid. Which was just one more strike against Simon.

I ducked out of the Dirty Dog before closing and went straight to Voodoo. I didn't want to run the risk that Simon would stop by the parlor before I had a chance to tell Con that I was unavailable if Simon Duchesne was doing the asking.

Con wasn't in yet, so I took the opportunity to call Jack Richelieu's cell number from the shop phone.

When Jack answered, I explained that since I was so excited to come get Huck—which was no exaggeration—I was hoping we could do it earlier on Sunday morning than we'd planned. He agreed without question, clearly assuming that 'we' meant Simon and me. I hoped his assumption would stop him from calling Simon to confirm. I would owe Con an even bigger favor for getting his ass out of bed at eight o'clock on a Sunday morning, but hopefully it would be worth it.

When Con finally showed his face, he looked like he'd partied until noon and still hadn't slept at all. Our conversation went much the way I expected: he was happy to help me out and told me I owed him one. Then he sent me home, telling me to lay low tonight. Between disconnecting my intercom and keeping my phone off, I had no idea if Simon tried to contact me or not. I told myself I didn't care.

I was all nerves when Sunday morning dawned, and Con rolled up in his Tahoe.

"Thanks for this," I said as I climbed in the passenger side.

He nodded. "No problem. You know I'm always here if you need something, Lee. No matter what."

His loyalty was more than I deserved.

We rode in silence to the clinic, The Steve Miller Band jamming on the stereo.

My stomach dropped to the floor mat at the sight of Simon's blue BMW in the parking lot. *Shit. Shit. Shit.*

Con backed into a spot next to the door, the same way Simon had parked. At my panicked expression, Con reached over and squeezed my shoulder. "Don't worry, babe. He won't cause a scene. Wouldn't be proper Duchesne behavior."

Simon shoved open the clinic door as soon as I stepped down from the Tahoe, and proved Con's theory wrong.

"What the hell is going on, Charlie? I tried to get in touch with you all day yesterday, and you were a goddamn ghost. I get stonewalled by Yve, Delilah, and this jackass." He jerked his chin toward Con. "Is there something you want to tell me? Because I thought we were past this hot and cold bullshit."

Con stepped in front of me. "Back off, Duchesne. And don't you fucking talk to her like that."

Simon halted in his stride toward me. "You back off, Leahy. This has nothing to do with you."

"I disagree." They squared off, and for a minute I thought they were going to start brawling in the parking lot.

I inched around Con and looked at Simon. He broke Con's stare to look at me. Anger, confusion, and hurt were reflected in equal measure on his face.

Seriously? Did he really have no idea why I might not want to see him? Did he think I was stupid? That I wouldn't find out? Or worse, that I wouldn't care? I had to know.

I pulled the folded newsprint from my bag. I'd continued to carry it with me just in case I was tempted to forget. "How's this for hot and cold bullshit?" I held it out, and our hands brushed as he took it. I jerked mine back like I'd been burned. Simon unfolded the paper, and his eyes darted back up to my face. Understanding dawned.

"Charlie, it's not what it looks like." He stepped toward me, but Con blocked him with an outstretched arm and a fierce glare.

I held up a hand and choked out a bitter laugh. "You, the politician, telling your dirty little secret, 'it's not what it looks like,' might be the most clichéd thing I've ever heard. Is that what you were going to tell the blonde when she caught you with me?" I swallowed, trying to compose myself. "Just go, Simon. I don't screw around with guys who are taken."

The muscle in his jaw ticked. "Don't you dare call yourself a dirty little secret. I'm not fucking taken by anyone but you. She's a friend. That's it. That's all."

I crossed my arms over my chest. "Did you or did you not attend a charity gala with her after you dropped me off at work?"

His lips compressed. "Yes. I did."

"Then this conversation is over." I turned away.

"I never lied to you." Simon's tone was resolute. I snapped back around to stare at him.

"No, you just gave me selected pieces of the truth. An omission is still a lie, Simon." *I should know*, I thought; *omissions are my specialty*. But if, and when, the truth came out about me, I wasn't going to split hairs over it. I'd own up to that shit.

"Just hear me out. Please."

"What could you possibly say that would change anything?"

"She's not my girlfriend, but her dad backs off when she goes to events with me. As long as he thinks she has a chance at being Mrs. Duchesne, he doesn't hound her about finding a suitable husband. I let people believe it because she's an old friend, and it's my way of helping her out."

I raised one eyebrow, skepticism branded on my features. "Look," he continued, "there's nothing between us like that. I can't say for certain, but I'm pretty damn sure she's hung up on a guy she thinks her dad won't approve of. He's old school and a control freak, and being seen with me just buys her time while she figures out her own shit and keeps her dad off her back."

The steel reinforcing my spine dissolved in time with my fading anger. His explanation was too candid and random to be anything but the truth. I was fairly confident on that point. But still, there was something else I needed to know.

"Why didn't you at least tell me about the event?"

He rubbed a hand over his face before gripping the back of his neck. "Because, honestly, Charlie, I forgot. My head is so damn full of you that I can barely think about anything else. Vanessa called me after I'd dropped you off at work, wondering where the hell I was, because the first course was already being served. I ran home, threw on a suit, made it there in time for the main course. I shook some hands and posed for a picture. That's it. That was everything."

"And later?"

Simon stepped around Con, and Con didn't try to block him this time. He'd backed down and was leaning against the Tahoe. He looked like his mind was a million miles away.

Simon framed my face between his hands. "When I see you, it all falls away. The expectations, the politics, everyone else's plans for me. Everything. Nothing matters but soaking up every moment with you." He skimmed a thumb across my cheekbone. "I don't know what else I can tell you to make you believe me. You can talk to Vanessa. She knows all about you because you're all I talked about the whole time we were together. She also knows Friday was the last time I'd be taking her to an event, because you're the only one I want by my side."

I looked down at the tattoos covering my arms. I needed to give him fair warning. "If what you're looking for is a woman to stand next to you looking poised and perfect for the cameras, I'm not her, Simon. I'm never going to be her."

"I wouldn't ask you to be anyone but who you are. And if people have a problem with you, then they can go to hell."

Con pushed off the bumper of his SUV, finally rejoining the conversation. "Lee has her own reasons for keeping a low profile. The kind of publicity that comes along with you isn't something she needs."

Simon's attention flicked to Con and then back to me. "Are you in trouble? Running from someone?" His voice was low, and his forehead was lined with worry.

I grimaced, not wanting to lie to him again after I'd just raked him over the coals for it, and so I answered as honestly as I could manage.

"Not in trouble, exactly, but I'm also not broadcasting my whereabouts." Okay, so maybe being wanted for questioning by the FBI counted as trouble.

"Why didn't you tell me?" Simon asked.

"It's not your problem. I just prefer to fly under the radar."

Simon started to ask another question, but Jack opened the clinic door. "Anyone coming in? Huck's getting antsy."

"Yes. Right now. Sorry to keep you waiting," I replied.

I took a step toward the door, happy to leave the conversation behind, but Simon's grip on my hand tugged me back.

"This conversation isn't over, Charlie. We have some shit to get straight. If you ever find out something that bothers you, come talk to me. Don't shut me out. I've always tried to be completely honest with you. And I'd never do anything to intentionally hurt you."

I nodded. "That's fair." And it was. Beyond being fair, it was a hell of a lot more than I could say to him. Complete honesty wasn't something I'd be trying anytime soon, and I may not intentionally hurt him, but it seemed inevitable that I would.

Simon pulled me into his side. "Let's go get Huck and take him home."

charlie

My relationship with Simon was recovering from the newspaper incident. He was unfailingly polite and didn't hesitate to reach for my hand whenever we were driving or walking somewhere, but he was reserved in most other ways. It was clear that my lack of trust and choice to shut him out had hurt him. When he looked at me, the questions he wanted to ask were all over his face, but he never voiced them. Part of me felt guilty for being happy that he didn't—happy that I wouldn't have to lie to him. Another small part of me wanted to come clean and tell him everything. And finally, a third, bigger, part of me wanted to bitch slap that small part for even thinking it was a possibility. But it was that small part that had me up at three in the morning after a full day of work at both of my jobs, studying an old book on cryptography I'd picked up from the library.

I had the composition book open, and I was trying to identify patterns so I could attempt to apply the code-breaking methods to the mess inside. So far, I was failing miserably. After further study of the notebook, I realized that my father had probably been using it for years, if not decades. His handwriting changed over time. It was subtle when you flipped through a page at a time, but when you compared the initial notes to those toward the back, it was obvious. This discovery confirmed my suspicions: this scheme had been going on for much longer than anyone had guessed. It was likely my father had spent more time covering his tracks and hiding the money than he ever had on legitimate investments. Once again, I was ashamed to be his daughter.

I looked back down at the notebook, thinking of all the lies I'd been fed since childhood. For several years, I'd been pulled out of school so much that my parents had hired a tutor to travel with us. We'd spend time at the house in Switzerland, the yacht in Monaco, the villa in the Caymans. And then back to New York for a few weeks before jetting off to more exotic locales: Mauritius, Seychelles, Singapore, and the Cook Islands. It had been equally frustrating and exciting to me. Frustrating because I'd just wanted to go to school like a regular kid. But exciting … well, for the obvious reasons.

Holy shit. I was such an idiot. I flipped through the pages to a series of letters and numbers that kept drawing my eye. My heart raced and my breathing accelerated as I skipped to the pages in the back.

Holy fucking shit.

I'd assumed the book held valuable information, because otherwise it wouldn't be in code, but this … I shook my head. If I was right, I wasn't just holding some of the clues to the puzzle; I had the keys to the kingdom.

I let out a long, slow breath.

My technophobe father had recorded the dates and locations of his illicit deposits in a *fucking composition notebook* that he'd hidden under the tissue paper in the shoebox of my Chucks. And the FBI had missed it in their search of the penthouse. *Holy shit.*

I still had to crack the code, but at least now I was pretty damn sure what I was looking at: the first two numbers in each of the sequences, when decoded, would most likely give the country code where the account was located. And I had to believe some of those accounts would be located in tax havens like Switzerland, Monaco, the Caymans, Singapore, Mauritius, Seychelles, and the Cook Islands. Places where my father could have easily made physical, untraceable deposits for years—all under the guise of a family fucking vacation.

The only one of those country codes I knew for sure was Switzerland: CH. We'd learned about International Bank Account Numbers, or IBANs, in one of my international finance classes. All of the examples in our textbook had involved Swiss numbered accounts. I needed to get back to the library tomorrow, so I could do more research. I needed the other country codes. There was no telling what kind of encryption my father's twisted mind might have deemed necessary, but at least I had a clue about some of the contents of the book. There were several paragraphs of letters and numbers that had way too many characters to be account numbers, but those could wait.

Hope blossomed within me. *I might really be able to figure this out.* And if I didn't … well, the stakes just got higher, and the consequences of taking the book became severer. I was withholding real, vital evidence. I should have turned the damn thing over to the FBI as soon as I'd found it. But I couldn't change that now. My year of silence would equate to a year of guilt in the eyes of the feds. So I had to be smart. I had to get the information where it needed to go without letting them figure out it was coming from me. Anything less, and I'd probably either find myself in prison or protective custody—neither of which worked for me.

But I wasn't going to borrow trouble just yet. First, I needed to solve the cipher, and then I'd worry about how to deliver the information.

If I could pull this off—*really* pull this off—I might have a chance at a semi-normal life. And that life could possibly include Simon. Except, even if I were able to wash away the worst of my father's sins, when the dust all settled, did we really have a shot at a future? One that was out in the open, in front of cameras and God and everyone? I didn't see how that was possible. I'd still be a liability to his political ambitions.

But there had to be some middle ground.
And I would find it.
I just had to break the damn code first.

simon

When my mother asked why Charlie hadn't joined us for our family dinner on Friday night, I'd told her the truth: Charlie had to work. What I didn't mention was I hadn't invited her. I hadn't wanted Charlie to be subjected to my parents' interrogation tactics and spend the entire evening helping her awkwardly dodge every question. Because I knew her well enough to know she wouldn't give a straight answer to any of them.

It was starting to piss me off. How could I ever really get to know someone who wouldn't share even the most basic information? I didn't know how old Charlie was, where she was from, if she'd gone to college, why she was keeping a low profile, or any of the hundred other things I wanted to know about her. The discussion that had started in the parking lot of Jack's clinic had never been finished.

I hadn't pushed it for the same reason I hadn't invited her to dinner.

The most screwed up part: I didn't need to know any of those things to start to fall for her. The little I did know was enough. I'd kept our interactions over the last week fairly casual, but even with all of the unknowns, one thing had become very clear: I wanted her. I wanted whatever it was we were still figuring out. And I was done with casual.

I'd had six solid nights of sleep without nightmares. I was far from "cured," but I was taking those six nights as a victory. I was being selfish, but I didn't want to sleep alone tonight. Spending the night with Charlie would be taking a huge risk, and I hoped it didn't burn me. Or her. I knew I should wait, but the urge to try was stronger. If she showed any hesitation though, I'd back off.

Forks clinked against china as I tuned back into the dinner conversation my parents were having. I was happy my active participation was not required.

"You absolutely will not be trying to climb on the boat until at least a month after your surgery! I forbid it."

"Don't be absurd, Maggie. I'll be fine."

I added my two cents to give the appearance of paying attention. "Why don't you just wait and see how you're feeling? I'm sure your body is going to tell you what you can and can't do."

"Nice of you to join the discussion, Simon. But you can stay out of it if you're not on my side." My mother shot me an annoyed glare as she reached for her wine.

My father chuckled. "Gotta love a woman with spirit. Speaking of which, your mother mentioned that she met a young lady in your kitchen the other morning. I understand she's working this evening, but I'd like to know when I'll have the pleasure of meeting her as well."

I curbed the urge to shove a giant forkful of poached salmon into my mouth. "Probably not until after you're back from Maine. She's very busy."

"What does she do?"

"She's a receptionist and works as part of the sales staff at a boutique." I cringed inwardly. I didn't know why I'd felt the sudden need to pretty up what Charlie did. Because I didn't give a shit. I cleared my throat and clarified. "At a tattoo parlor and a vintage clothing store in the Quarter."

My father's fork clanked loudly on his plate as it slid from his grip.

"I could have guessed the tattoo parlor part. She does have quite the collection. And her hair was quite fun as well. Black and red and purple, wasn't it?" My mother kept eating as if this revelation was as mundane as the weather. I could've kissed her.

"I thought we talked about this, Simon. You need a woman who is going to be an asset—"

I cut him off, not wanting him to finish the sentence I'd heard too many times before. "Is that why you picked Mom? Because she'd be an asset to your career?"

My father's expression turned sharp. "I married your mother because I was so crazy about her I couldn't see straight. The second she said yes, I dragged her down to the courthouse so she wouldn't have a chance to change her mind."

My mother dabbed the corners of her mouth with her linen napkin. "Yes, it was all very scandalous. Your grandmother and grandfather threatened to disown him for marrying beneath him, but your father told them to go to hell. Which is exactly what you should tell your father." She sent my father a warning look before turning back to me. "I just want you to settle down with someone you can't live without. But sooner rather than later would be fabulous. I want grandchildren while I'm still young enough to enjoy them. And if Charlie makes you happy, then I'm rooting for her."

My father opened his mouth to speak, but then thought better of it and took a bite of rice pilaf instead. I seized the moment to bring up another subject that had been weighing on my mind. I gripped the edge of the linen-covered table with both hands.

"I've been seeing a psychiatrist to … discuss some things that happened while I was in the service. I've been diagnosed with PTSD."

My mother laid her hand over mine. "Is this about the nightmares?"

I shot her a look. "You knew?"

"I'm your mother. Of course I knew."

In response to my obvious confusion, she explained, "It was the month you stayed in your old room before the guesthouse renovations were finished. Did you think I couldn't hear you pacing the halls every night? I didn't want to push you, but hoped you'd find some help when you were ready."

"Well, I did, and actually ... I've been looking into starting a nonprofit to help people like me. Vets, who, for whatever reason, don't want to go to the VA for treatment. Who don't want to be medicated and sent home to wonder if that's their only option. There are a couple in other states, and I've been talking to some people about what I need to do to start one here."

My father reached for his wine. "I think that's an excellent idea. Voters will love it. It would also set you up well to become a member of the Armed Services Committee. Southern Cross will make the first donation."

I forced a smile to mask my disappointment. I'd wanted my father to understand that this was a personal mission, not something to be exploited for political gain. But lately it felt like he scrutinized everything for that purpose. I suppose that was what years in politics did to you. Always had you looking for an angle. The thought made me lose my appetite. I pushed away my plate.

"Now about this girl—" my father started.

"Why don't you save your opinion until you actually meet her, Dad?" I fought to keep my tone even, but I wasn't sure my temper would hold if he said something negative about Charlie.

Before he could respond, my mother jumped in with some amusing anecdote about the neighbor's escape artist of a dog, and my father's attention was successfully diverted.

I looked down at my watch. It would be hours before Con or Delilah would drop Charlie off at home. She'd promised that there would be no more walking alone at night, but only after I'd buried my inner caveman and at least gave the appearance of letting go of my issue with Con Leahy. Knowing that Con was nailing Charlie's other boss helped me become guardedly confident that he wasn't going to steal my girl. To Charlie's point, if she wanted to be with Con, she would be already. It hadn't been an outright declaration that she wanted a relationship with me, but for now, I'd take what I could get from her.

The remainder of the evening's conversation was filled with my father grandly reminiscing about his days in Washington. I stayed silent, drank another glass of wine, and started to wonder if the only reason he wanted me to run for office was so he'd have a chance to move back into the circles that he'd slowly faded out of over the years. I hated to attribute a motive like that to him, but couldn't help but consider it. If I officially threw my hat in the ring this fall and decided to campaign, it would be because it was my decision. Not my father's.

charlie

Harriet's artistic eccentricities easily made her one of the most fascinating women I'd ever met. Her big heart and open-armed welcome made it impossible not to fall in love with her instantly. She was the grandmother I'd never been allowed to have, and she'd filled the hole in my life previously occupied by Juanita. My mother had pretended her own parents were dead until she'd found herself homeless, and my father's address had become the federal penitentiary. My paternal grandparents had both passed away before I was born, so grandmotherly figures were few and far between in my life.

Harriet had emerged from her studio shortly after Con had dropped me off, and she'd uncorked a bottle of champagne. When I asked why we were celebrating, she'd simply said, "Because we can."

I followed her into the garden oasis, more than ready to fill my glass. I told myself it was because I had a full day off tomorrow, but part of me wanted to get just drunk enough to not miss seeing Simon today. Yesterday we'd grabbed dinner at a little hole in the wall gumbo place, and he'd been charming as hell. Playing with my fingers, feeding me bites of his food, and basically ensuring that I'd need a change of panties after dinner. If it had been the type of restaurant to have tablecloths, I would have considered crawling under it. But it wasn't. And that sneaky bastard knew exactly what he was doing. He gave me a chaste peck on the cheek when he dropped me off at Voodoo; I was ready to maul him in front of God and everyone. When I'd asked him if he'd have time for dinner on Friday during my two-hour break between shifts, he'd said he was busy. No other explanation. Just *busy*.

After the newspaper incident, I didn't think he was going to any kind of event with Vanessa, but I could feel my claws coming out at the thought of all the other things he could be doing. I was off kilter all night. Trying to give change to someone who paid with a credit card. Double booking an appointment and having to call one guy back to reschedule. It was like the Simon Duchesne effect had sucked forty IQ points straight out of my brain. *Sneaky. Bastard.*

All through my Friday shifts at the Dirty Dog and Voodoo, I'd stared at my cheap cell phone and willed it to ring. I checked the balance of my minutes four times. Yep. Had plenty now that I wasn't calling the clinic every five minutes for an update on Huck. No word from Simon. I wanted to text him, but of course, my piece of shit phone was barely capable, and I hadn't been willing to pay the extra fee for that particular feature. So now I was guzzling Harriet's second bottle of good champagne like it was Boone's Farm and ranting about how men were sneaky and manipulative—getting you all wound up and not putting out until you spilled all your deepest, darkest secrets.

Harriet was doubled over laughing at my tirade, paint smeared shirt flapping in the night breeze. Through the cackle of her laughter, I heard a clanking sound coming from the iron gate. *What the hell?* I stumbled out of my chair toward the narrow corridor and saw a large form blocking the light from the street lamp.

"Who is it and what the hell do you want?" I yelled in the direction of the gate, still coming off my rant.

"It's Simon. And I thought I'd made it pretty clear I wanted you. I'll even put out, with or without the secrets."

Fuck. My face heated. I hadn't tried to keep my outburst quiet, but I had no idea that I'd been so loud.

Maybe there was a chance... "I was that loud?" I asked Harriet, hoping I'd misheard him.

"I'm pretty sure they could hear you a block away, dear."

"Shit."

"Who's out there?" Harriet asked me.

"A friend," I replied as I stalked down the corridor to the gate, mumbling to myself. "The sneaky, manipulative guy who won't put out."

"I already said I would, babe."

Fuck. He heard that too?

"Yeah," Simon replied, smile spreading across his face. *Dammit. I hadn't meant to say that out loud.*

"I'm too drunk to deal with you," I said.

"Let me in, Charlie. I missed you today."

I melted against the wall of the narrow passageway, soaking up his words—the exact ones I'd needed to hear. I twisted the lock, and Simon swung the gate open and shut it behind him. He crowded me against the wall and cupped my face with both hands. I barely registered his intent before he bent to kiss me. Not a chaste peck this time. An all-consuming, devastating, soul-stealing kiss. I clung to his shoulders as he slid one hand down to cup my ass and pull me closer.

"Well now," Harriet interrupted. "Seems you might have to retract your complaints, dear."

Simon's head jerked up, and I fell against him. He tucked me into his side and held out a hand to Harriet.

"Simon Duchesne, ma'am. It's a pleasure to meet you."

Harriet clasped Simon's hand with her paint-smudged one. "Likewise. I'm Harriet Sullivan. And I believe this is my cue to head back inside. Charlotte, darling, I'm happy to keep an eye on Huckleberry tonight if you decide to stay upstairs. I'll even let him out in the morning."

I sucked in a breath. I wasn't drunk enough to miss the fact that Harriet had just called me by my real name. Simon stiffened. He hadn't missed it either.

"Umm ... thanks. Good night, Harriet."

She shuffled away, and we didn't speak until we heard the back door close.

"I like Charlotte, but I think Charlie suits you better." In the dark corridor, I couldn't make out Simon's expression, but he didn't sound angry. My drunken self needed to know conclusively.

"Are you mad?"

He pulled away, and I wondered if that was his answer. Maybe he'd leave and I'd never see him again. My heart clenched at the thought. If he couldn't handle something small like this, then I guess it was better to know now. But he didn't leave. Instead, he led me out of the narrow passageway into the garden oasis and swung me up in his arms.

"Do you have the keys for your place?"

"It's unlocked."

He grumbled at that and carried me up the spiral staircase. I buried my head in the crook of his neck and held on tight, praying he wouldn't drop me. "I got you, babe. Don't worry."

He pushed open the door and flipped on the light before carrying me directly into my bedroom and setting me on the bed. He switched on my bedside lamp, and I finally saw his face clearly.

My head was fuzzy from the champagne, but he really didn't look angry. He looked ... thoughtful? Maybe? Dammit. Why did I drink so much?

He reached a hand back and tugged his shirt over his head. I drank in his tanned skin and rippling muscles. He truly was a beautiful man. He kicked off his shoes and knelt at my feet to pull off my Chucks without untying the laces. It was a staggering realization to my champagne-soaked brain that he might have noticed I never untied them. What other details about me had he noticed that no one else would? I was crazy to think he'd never find out the truth. *I never should've let it get this far.* But how could I stop myself? He was so … perfectly imperfect, and I wanted all of him. For every second I could steal.

He reached for his belt and paused. "I'm staying tonight." It wasn't a question.

"Okay." I reached for the hem of my shirt and started to drag it upward. He reached out, covering my hand with his to stop me.

"But if you take that off, I'm not going to be able to stop myself from having you."

"Good." I yanked at his grip, trying to get the shirt off.

He squeezed my hand. "No. Not tonight. The first time we're together, you're going to be stone cold sober, because I want you to remember every single thing I do to you."

My insides turned hot and liquid. A pulse thrummed between my legs. "You already told me you'd put out. No take backs. It's not fair."

He leaned down and brushed his five o'clock shadow against my cheek before saying into my ear, "Tough shit."

He pulled back, and I stuck out my lip and pouted. Simon caught it between his teeth and tugged before releasing it. "So fucking tempting. You have no idea." He spun and looked at my bureau. "Pajama pants? And I know you own them. I distinctly recall a striptease that involved a pair."

I huffed. "Second drawer from the bottom." He opened the drawer, pulled out a silky pink pair, and tossed them at me.

"I'll be right back. You better not be naked."

"You're such a hardass prude, Mr. Duchesne." He took a step toward the doorway and gripped the top of the frame. His tongue swiped across his bottom lip, and his hazel eyes shifted from playful to serious.

"You're worth the wait."

He walked out of the room, and I heard the bathroom door shut.

I clutched the pajama pants in my fist as my heart tumbled further down the path of no return. A single thought crystallized in my head: *Fuck. I could fall in love with this man.*

simon

I awoke as the sun was just starting to rise. But it wasn't a nightmare that woke me. It was the hot, wet suction on my dick. I groaned, burying my hand in Charlie's— Charlotte's—wild hair.

"Jesus, woman. Holy shit." I jerked my hips as she hummed against my cock, and her small, soft hand cupped my balls. "Holy fuck."

My breathing grew labored. The urge to come slammed into me, and I gently tried to tug her away. "Baby, you gotta stop. I—I'm…" She didn't stop. Instead she took me deeper and worked me harder and faster. I couldn't hold back. So I just let go.

After she sat up and wiped the back of her hand across her mouth, she smiled at me. "I'll be right back."

She slipped out of the bedroom, and I heard the bathroom door shut and the water turn on. I tucked myself back into my boxer briefs, laced my hands behind my head, and stared out the skylight in the slanted ceiling above me. She'd already been passed out by the time I'd come out of the bathroom the night before, still in her jeans, pajamas clutched in her hand. I'd been as gentlemanly as possible as I'd swapped out the jeans for her more comfortable sleepwear. I couldn't help but marvel at the pale, un-inked skin of her legs. Next to her arms … they seemed almost … unfinished.

I'd tucked her into bed before slipping beneath the covers and pulling her against me. It was another solid night of uninterrupted sleep. Until Charlie had decided to provide the world's best wake up call. I heard the water turn off, and she walked back into the bedroom. She bit her lip and her hair hung forward, obscuring part of her face. For the first time since I'd met her, she looked … shy.

I grinned. "That was, hands down, the best way I've ever been woken up."

Her smile reappeared. "Yeah?"

"Yeah, babe. Come here." I sat up so I was leaning against the headboard and held out an arm. She climbed back into bed and snuggled into my side. I tucked her under the covers. "Best morning ever." I kissed her hair. "So, tell me about Charlotte."

She froze, and I tightened my grip as she struggled uselessly against me. I spoke slowly, pitching my words so they would resonate in her ear. "I don't care what your name is. I just want you. That's all. I don't care if you're Charlotte or Charlie or Lee or anybody else. I just want to know *you*."

She stopped struggling. I pulled back and looked down at her. "I just want you to let me in. To trust me with a little piece of you." I tucked an unruly lock of purple hair behind her ear. "I'm falling for a girl who won't even tell me where she's from. You'd think I'd care, but it doesn't make a damn bit of difference to me." Her mouth dropped open and her aqua eyes widened. "Nothing you tell me is going to change how I feel."

We stared at each other for several beats before she spoke.

"The East Coast." Her voice was shaky and barely more than a breath. *Finally. Something.*

"Figured you were a Yankee." I leaned down and kissed her. Slowly, reverently, like I was learning her for the first time. And maybe I was. Her fingers gripped the back of my neck as she pressed closer. That fit perfectly with my plans, because we weren't leaving this bed without getting a hell of a lot closer—and not just in the physical sense.

She pulled back from the kiss and asked, "You going to follow through this time or leave me hanging? Because I gotta tell you, I'm not sure I can survive that again."

It was the opening I needed. "What are you willing to give me?"

Charlie pursed her lips before answering, "What do you want?"

"You."

"Done."

"*Information* about you," I clarified.

Her expression turned guarded. I cupped her face and met her eyes. "Simple shit, Charlie. That's all I want. It's not that hard." She broke my stare, and I could almost hear the gears clicking in her head.

"Like what?" she whispered.

"Favorite color."

Her eyes snapped back up to mine, her surprise clear. She dragged her bottom lip between her teeth and let it slide free. The urge to kiss that gorgeous mouth of hers was intense, but I wanted to hear her answer more.

"All of them."

A grin tugged at my lips. Of course. One wasn't enough for her. I rolled and held myself above her. I leaned down and brushed a kiss across her forehead before pulling back to ask my next question.

"Winter or summer?"

"Fall. New England fall." I kissed her nose.

"Baseball or football."

"Neither. Hockey."

I kissed the corner of her mouth before murmuring, "Breaking my heart, babe."

"Don't ask if you can't handle the truth." She turned her head so my lips met hers squarely.

"*Top Gun* or *Die Hard?*"

"Bruce Willis. Definitely." I kissed her jaw.

"Flowers or chocolate?"

"Sex." I chuckled against her neck and dragged my teeth down the tendon. She shuddered.

"Sassy woman."

"Damn straight."

I pulled back again and gripped the neck of her wife beater with both hands.

"Last question." I stretched the fabric to telegraph my intentions. The smile that spread across Charlie's face was pure sin.

"First impression when I walked in the door of Voodoo that night?"

"Preppy douchebag." I shook my head, because … well, I'd figured that's exactly what we'd looked like. And then she added, "And can I take him home?" White-hot need flared in every cell of my body.

I jerked my fists apart and tore her tank top down the middle, leaving it in ragged shreds.

Her high, full breasts—tipped with those sexy as hell piercings—were bared to my gaze. And my mouth. I reached down to draw a nipple into my mouth. She buried her hands in my hair and urged me closer. The time for questions was over.

charlie

Finally. That was my first thought when Simon tore my shirt apart. Followed closely by, *holy shit that was hot.* I arched my back as he tugged on my nipple. I wanted more. More Simon. More everything. Ripples of pleasure zinged from my nipples to my clit. His big hands cupped my breasts, and I reveled in the scrape of his calluses against my skin. He turned the attention of his mouth to my other breast and rolled the nipple he'd just released between two fingers. The piercings added a whole new layer of sensation over anything I'd felt before. Before Simon. At that moment, I couldn't imagine anyone but Simon ever touching me again. My eyes flew open at the thought, but my panic was obliterated when Simon lifted his head and nipped at my lips until I opened to him. His tongue swept inside to duel with mine. I lost myself in the moment and didn't surface until I felt one of his busy hands skim down my body to slide along the waistline of my pajama pants. He pulled away and stared down at me again.

"Are you sure?"

"God, yes." I laughed. "What else do I have to say to get you to believe it?"

He studied me, and I had no idea what he was hoping to find. "You have to know this means something to me."

"I know," I replied.

"Don't break my heart, Charlie."

I slid my hands up through his dark hair, hoping he could see everything I felt for him. Everything I was afraid to put into words. "Not without shattering my own."

He kissed me again. Long, drugging kisses that made me forget who I was and the heartbreak I would inevitably cause us both.

His lips shifted to my jaw, my neck, my collarbone … before moving south. He hooked a finger in the waist of my pants and pulled them down, dragging my underwear off with them. I kicked them to the floor as Simon levered himself off the bed and crossed to where his jeans were lying over my tiny vanity stool. He produced a condom from his front pocket, and I raised an eyebrow.

"Weren't planning to hold out last night?"

"Just wanted to be prepared."

"Boy Scout."

He gave me a lopsided grin and tugged off his boxer briefs. The teasing words on my tongue vanished. A fully nude Simon Duchesne was … awe-inspiring. He stood confidently and let me stare. My survey caught and stopped at his erection, jutting upward, heavy and thick. I'd obviously been up close and personal with it this morning, but there was something insanely sexy about his self-assured stance. Hell, if I looked as good as he did naked, I'd pose too. Simon tore the condom package open with his teeth and rolled it on before striding back to the bed. He knelt and kissed my calf, the curve of my knee, and then the inside of my thigh. All innocuous locations, but my pulse hammered and I could feel myself growing embarrassingly wet. His hooded hazel eyes tracked up my body to my face.

"Wider, baby. I want to see all of you. Gotta taste you again."

I complied, spreading my legs and bending my knees. His broad shoulders forced me wider as he bent to kiss a line from one hipbone to the other. I shifted, needing more, and he responded by darting his tongue out to flick my piercing before dropping down to lick me from bottom to top. My head thumped back against the pillow, and Simon's clever tongue worked me over. I buried my fingers in his hair and urged him on. He slid two fingers inside me and found the spot guaranteed to set me off. I squeezed my eyes shut and bit my lip to keep myself from moaning like a porn star as the orgasm rushed over me.

My lids fluttered open to see Simon holding himself suspended above me. My breaths came in shallow pants as he leaned down to kiss me again. The taste of myself, mixed with his own unique flavor, spiked my need.

"Want you. Now." Complete sentences were beyond me. I just needed him. Inside me. Now. *Right now.*

He shifted to brace himself on one arm, and I felt the broad head of his erection nudge my entrance.

"Good?"

"Just fuck me already, Simon. Jesus." So much for romance.

He grinned and thrust. The porn star moan could not be held back as he stretched me deliciously.

"Holy shit," I gasped.

Simon nuzzled my neck and nipped my ear. "So greedy. Can't a guy take it slow and enjoy the ride?" I writhed against him, already feeling another orgasm building just from the friction of our bodies. But I needed him to move.

"Too much talking. Not enough fucking."

He chuckled and swiveled his hips, and my words disintegrated into breathy whimpers as the pressure on my clit and my piercing sent shards of pleasure shooting through me.

"That. Again. More."

He leaned down to scrape his stubble along my jaw. Withdrawing, he wrapped my legs around his hips and thrust deeply, adjusting his pace from slow to fast and then slow again. My hands shifted to his shoulders and my nails dug into the solid muscles. His alternating, impossible to predict pace, coupled with my piercing had the intensity building until I was on the brink. I held it off, wanting to make this moment last, to memorize this feeling. But the riots of sensation were intensifying, and I couldn't stop myself. I stared up into Simon's hazel eyes as it shattered me.

"So goddamn beautiful," he breathed.

His pace accelerated once more, and I arched up, seeking the friction against my clit and then pulling away when it became too much. "Simon—"

"I got you, babe." And he did. He slid a hand under my ass and angled my pelvis up, relieving the pressure on my clit but shifting his strokes to hit my G-spot. My vision faded as my eyes rolled back. "Holy—" I couldn't get out another word before another climax ripped through me.

I felt Simon jerk and heard his groan. After a few more strokes, he slowed and collapsed onto me. He immediately pushed himself up, trying to save me from his weight, but I snaked my arms around his neck and pulled him back down.

"No, I like feeling you. On me. Inside me. Let me enjoy it for a minute before you crush my lungs."

He kissed my temple. "Now who's a talker? Fucking destroyed me, woman. Jesus. Couldn't stop myself from coming. Can't imagine how good it's going to be to have you raw."

A smug smile formed on my lips, and I couldn't help but think that maybe my dirty, bad girl vibes had rubbed off a little on Mr. Polite-as-Hell Duchesne. Because he was anything but polite in bed.

"I think my dirty mouth is rubbing off on you."

"You can rub your dirty mouth on me any time you want, babe. But I'm afraid I was swearing like a sailor long before you. After all, I *was* a sailor." He lifted his weight off me slightly, but I was still pinned when he asked, "How old are you, Charlie?"

I took a steadying breath. If I could trust Simon with my body, I should at least be able to trust him with the age of that body. "Twenty-three."

His head jerked up, and his eyes went wide.

"Whatever you're thinking, don't say it." I clenched my inner muscles, and the surprise in his eyes turned to searing heat.

"Let me get another condom."

"Good call." He pulled out of me and rolled off the bed to take care of the used one. He was digging in his jeans for his wallet when a loud buzz echoed in the small room. I didn't think my piece of shit cell phone was even capable of vibrating, so it had to be Simon's. Still naked, he pulled the phone out of the pocket and answered it. I listened to his side of the conversation while I shamelessly ogled his tight, naked ass. Damn, the man was comfortable in his own skin. *Thank the Lord.*

"What do you need, Martin?"

Pause.

"You're fucking kidding me. When?"

Pause.

"Shit. Okay. I'll be there in twenty. Call our insurance guy, a retrieval crew, and notify the client."

Pause.

"I know. Twenty minutes."

Simon scrubbed a hand through his hair. He found his boxer briefs and pulled them on before stepping into his jeans. He turned toward me.

"I gotta go, babe." His eyes skimmed over my nude body. "And that blows. I was hoping to stay in bed all day with you."

I arched an eyebrow. "I don't remember inviting you to spend the day in my bed."

"You would have."

"So cocky." I trailed a finger down my chest, between my breasts. "You're lucky I think that's hot."

"You don't play fair."

My smile transformed into an outright grin as he watched my fingers continue down to my belly. "Should I?"

"Never."

He crossed to the bed and leaned down to press a quick kiss to my lips. "Wish I could stay, but I have to take care of something for work. A customer's cargo is currently sitting on the bottom of the Mississippi, and I need to clean up the mess."

I flipped the sheet up and covered myself, suddenly embarrassed that I'd been trying to act the seductress when he had real world problems to deal with. "It's fine. Do what you need to do."

He pulled the sheet away, leaving me naked again. "Like you better this way." He sat on the bed and cupped the side of my face in his big hand. "Dinner tonight?"

I didn't hesitate. "Sure."

"Wear a dress. A short one." My jaw dropped. *He said what?*

"Seriously? You did not just say that."

"Oh, but I did."

I huffed, tugging the sheet from his grip. "Have you ever seen me wear a dress? Let alone a short one?"

He leaned in and brushed his lips over the shell of my ear. "I'm going to see it tonight."

"Cocky bastard," I said, shivering from the contact.

"If it gets you into a dress, I'll be whatever kind of bastard you want me to be."

I won the sheet tug-of-war and tucked it around me before crossing my arms over my chest. "Maybe. No promises."

"I'll pick you up at seven. Short dress. High heels. The same wild, just-been-fucked hair you've got going on right now. That's how I'm going to be picturing you all day while I sort this shit out."

I bit my lip and shook my head at him. "You're crazy."

"Only about you." His lips met mine for one more kiss. This one was long, slow, and full of promise of what was to come. Finally, he pulled away. "See you later, babe."

He left the room, and I heard the door to my apartment open and close. I uncrossed my arms and pressed a palm against either side of my face and rubbed upward. I was in way too deep. I leaned over to snag a T-shirt from the floor and pulled it on. It was one of mine, but I wished it were Simon's. I wanted his woodsy scent surrounding me.

Apparently I now had two tasks for the day: first, flex my code-breaking muscles; and second, find a damn dress.

charlie

I stripped off the dress and threw it on the bed.

"I can't do this," I said to the empty room. I wished
Huck were pacing around my tiny apartment so I didn't
feel like I was talking to myself. But he was downstairs in
his crate in Harriet's guestroom. I'd spent most of the day
down there with him, the composition book, and a stack
of library books. I'd officially made zero progress. I'd
started cycling though the alphabet in the hopes that it was
a basic substitution cipher, but it was a *painstaking* process.

And while my code cracking was going horribly, at
least Huck was doing amazingly well. Dr. Richelieu hadn't
lied about the plate in his leg easing his recovery. He
might've looked a bit like a hobbled horse when he
padded around with his weight unequally distributed, but I
was so damn glad to see him on the mend.

I glanced at the clock on my nightstand. 6:49. I paced
my room, took a deep breath, and exhaled. *Calm*, I
thought. *You can do this.*

"I can't do this." I flopped onto my bed beside the
dress and stared out the skylight to the blue and white
expanse above. My thoughts wandered back to this
morning. Lying on the bed, watching Simon as he stared
me down with desire … and something else. I'd never
wanted anyone more, and I'd never deserved anyone less.
Was I going to humor his simple—albeit caveman-like—
request?

What if he took me to some fancy Michelin Star
restaurant? With the impression I'd given him so far,
Simon would probably think my nerves stemmed from not
knowing which fork to use. Little did he know that if I was

so inclined, I could out-etiquette him any day. The girl who used to dine regularly at Per Se might've been buried, but she was still in there. Somewhere. But letting any hint of her out could put everything I'd built at risk. As it stood, my life might not be much, but it was mine. I looked over at the mini-dress and fingered the deep purple cotton voile. I pictured myself wearing it, walking hand-in-hand through the streets with Simon. I wanted that.

The rationalizations started to filter in: we weren't in New York or L.A., Simon wasn't a celebrity followed by the paparazzi, and unless he was at a public event, it was unlikely that his presence would attract attention.

"I can do this."

I adjusted my strapless bra and matching black, lacy boy shorts and slipped on the dress. My hair hung in huge spiral curls I'd spent the last hour perfecting. Not that I would admit that little detail. I added dangling black and silver chain earrings that almost brushed my shoulders. They gave the outfit just enough 'Charlie' flare to make it acceptable. I slipped on a pair of vintage red leather peep-toe platforms Yve had let me borrow out of the inventory at the Dirty Dog and fastened the straps around my ankles. A check in the mirror, another dab of red lip stain, and I was ready. Which was damn good timing on my part because the intercom—which I'd reconnected—buzzed.

I crossed the room and pushed the button. "I'll be right down."

"Can't wait, babe."

Simon let out a wolf whistle as I strode, hips swinging, toward the gate. If I was going to wear this outfit, I was going to own it.

"Dayum, woman." He slapped a hand over his chest. His white linen shirt was light and airy, and his slacks were much more casual than I'd anticipated. "Step out here so I can see you." Simon moved away as I walked out onto the sidewalk. I spun, giving it a little extra *oomph*, and the skirt of my dress flared. When I stopped my impromptu twirl, I couldn't hold back a ridiculous giggle as I smiled up at Simon.

I expected to see his answering grin, but his expression was serious, almost … solemn. I looked down at my dress. "What?" I asked, confused the abrupt change in his mood.

He shook his head and reached out a hand to trail a finger down my jaw line. "That. That right there. I want to put that smile on your face every day, for as long as you'll let me."

I sucked in a breath and leaned in to his touch. My first instinct was to make some smartass remark to defuse the emotions bubbling up inside me. They were on the verge of spilling out onto the cracked sidewalk at Simon's feet. But I held them down and focused on soaking up this moment. I gift wrapped it and tucked it deep inside so I could take it out later and relive it.

Relive it after I lost him.

Because reality was scraping away at the happiness I was just discovering. The more time I spent studying that damn composition book—the book of lies and ruin—the more I accepted the fact I'd never make it out of this unscathed. I was naïve to think I could escape my past. Losing Simon would be my penance. And when that happened, memories of moments like this would be all I had left.

I opened my eyes, determined to live in the now and not worry about the future. At least not for tonight.

I pulled myself together and asked, "So, where to?"

"You want me to answer that question when all I can think is 'This woman is a goddess, and I can't believe I'm the lucky bastard who gets to take her out'?"

A smile tugged at the corners of my mouth. "You're all charm tonight, Mr. Duchesne."

"Honey, I'll be whatever you want me to be tonight."

This time I trailed my finger down his freshly shaven cheek. "How about just a guy showing his girl a good time."

"Done." He offered his arm, and I took it.

The sun was setting, and I was confused as hell. Simon waved to a guy at a security checkpoint, and we cruised into a large lot surrounded by barbed wire fences. Hundreds, or maybe thousands, of shipping containers— gray, black, tan, red, orange, and blue—were stacked in rows and awaiting transport to their destinations.

"Where the hell are we?"

"Patience."

Simon drove until we reached a seawall holding back the mighty Mississippi and parked in front of a barge. It was secured to the wall with ropes thicker than my arm. Except for a small section toward one end, it was completely covered with shipping containers. I scanned the empty space for a table and chairs. Candles. Champagne on ice. The kind of setup that I expected a guy like Simon to pull together, especially after he ordered me to wear a short dress and high heels. But there was none of that.

Simon climbed out of the car and was opening my door before I could gather my wits to do it myself. He helped me out onto the asphalt.

"Wait here."

He popped the tailgate and retrieved a blanket and a large soft-sided cooler.

My scattered thoughts regrouped, and I realized what he had planned. "A picnic?"

"Yup. Just you and me and the river." I was dumbstruck as he took my hand, led me over the ramp, and onto the barge.

I grabbed a corner, and we spread the thick stadium blanket out over the scarred and rusted steel of the deck. Simon helped me sit before kneeling on the blanket beside me. From the cooler, he produced round aluminum take out containers with inset cardboard lids and a six-pack of Abita.

I shook my head. He *never* did what I expected.

"Do you do this on purpose?"

He looked up from uncurling the aluminum edges of a container. "Do what?"

"The exact opposite of what I expect?"

He grinned and continued, revealing olives, two different kinds of hummus, flatbread, wedges of red and green pepper, slices of cold, rare tenderloin, chunks of cheese, and grapes. "What do you mean?"

"This." I gestured to my dress and the shoes I'd already unbuckled and tossed aside. "You told me to wear a dress. And heels. I expected a fancy restaurant or some trendy club. Not a barge and a picnic and beer."

His grin faded. "Is that what you'd rather do?"

My eyes widened. "No! Not at all. This is … perfect. But … how did you know? I mean … hell, I don't know what I mean."

His smile reappeared, dimples flashing. "You don't give me much to go on, Charlie. I just have to guess. But I like surprising you. You get this look, like you can't believe I'd go out of my way to do something special for you. I get the feeling you haven't had enough special in your life. And the dress … well, I just wanted a chance to stare at those gorgeous legs of yours." He shrugged, as if to say *I'm a guy, deal with it.*

I reflected on his words for a moment. My life had been ruthlessly organized, everything handed to me before I could even think to ask for it. But that was just it. I hadn't asked for any of it. Not the designer clothes or the riding lessons or the schedule cluttered with suitable social engagements. I'd been given, and had done, whatever my parents had deemed appropriate for me. And I had to wonder if they had given those choices remotely as much thought as Simon had in planning this picnic.

I reached for an olive and popped it into my mouth. "How come some smart Southern belle hasn't snapped you up already?"

He smirked. "I'm trying to get a sassy Yankee to, but she's not catching on as quickly as I'd hoped. I'm starting to wonder if she's not as smart as I thought."

I threw an olive at his head, and he caught it in his mouth. He popped the tops off two beers and handed one to me. He held his out, the neck of the bottle angled toward me.

"To an unexpected night," he said. I clinked my bottle with his and nabbed a slice of tenderloin.

I chewed and swallowed it. "Holy crap, that's good. Where did all of this come from?"

"My kitchen."

I was glad I wasn't still chewing because I would've choked. "Are you serious? You cook too?"

"I'd say yes just to keep that look on your face, but it'd mostly be a lie. My parents' housekeeper is jetting off on a two-week vacation tomorrow and asked if there was anything she could do for me before she left. I shamelessly begged her for help."

He reached for a piece of flatbread and scooped up some hummus. I pressed a hand to my chest and made a poor attempt at a Southern drawl. "Well, thank the Lord for that; I almost swooned."

I took a swig of my beer as he finished chewing. "Oh, you'll swoon, I have no doubt. After all, I am devastatingly charming."

We lingered over the food and talked about everything and yet nothing of substance. I loved that he didn't push for more than I was willing to give, but I wondered if it would always be that way or if at some point he would lose his patience with me and demand answers. But I didn't want to think about that right now. Not on such a perfect night.

We'd just popped the tops off the last two beers as fireworks burst over the river. I jumped at the thunderous percussion, and Simon pulled me against him. I followed him down until we lay side by side on the blanket, staring up at the exploding blues and reds and glittering whites against the cloud-covered night sky. This was one more thing I loved about New Orleans. You never knew when there'd be fireworks. The masses of partiers would pause a moment from downing their Hurricanes and stare upward to enjoy the simple pleasure.

Simon threaded his fingers through mine as vibrant colors continued to flare across the sky and the acrid scent of black powder hung in the air. He toyed with my fingers, bringing my hand to his lips to kiss each one. He moved on to my palm and nipped the base with his teeth.

I knew exactly how this picnic was going to end.

simon

I started to sit up as Charlie rolled and threw her leg over my hips. She pinned me, hair blowing in the river breeze, and shoved me back down. Her face was cast in shadows, but I could still make out her determined expression.

"Nope. You're not going anywhere."

I reached up and tucked a curl behind her ear. "That so?"

"Yep." The word popped from her lips. "You're going to pay up on all this teasing hand crap."

I chuckled. I loved her no-bullshit, straight-to-the-point attitude. It was something that was lacking in all other aspects of my life. "Teasing hand crap, is that what that was?"

She shifted against me, and her dress inched up her thighs. "Call it whatever you want, the consequences are still the same."

I raised an eyebrow. "Do tell."

"I'd rather show."

"Even better."

She reached down to the skirt of her dress and began pulling it upward. I was riveted, waiting for all that gorgeous skin to be uncovered, when she paused.

"What? What's wrong?" I looked around, wondering if she'd spotted someone. But that wasn't the cause of her hesitation.

"Why do I feel like I'm always stripping my clothes off in front of you?"

I bit my lip to hold back a grin. "I don't know, but you will *never* hear me complain about you getting naked for me."

"You didn't seem to have a hard time walking away from me that night … in the pool. I distinctly recall being very, very naked."

I cupped her chin, pulling her face down to mine. "What you don't seem to get, is that even then, I was playing the long game. I knew you were something special, and I wasn't going to take the chance that I'd only get a taste. I knew that once I did, I'd be addicted. That I'd have to have more. I needed you to be as off balance as I was." I kissed the corner of her mouth. "And it worked."

She shoved away from me. "You're such a smug bastard." She drew her dress up over her head and let it flutter to the blanket beside us. "Why don't you put that tongue to good use?"

My heart hammered as I took her in. Again, I wished for more light, because I wanted to see her, memorize her. She *was* my addiction. I just hoped she wouldn't be lethal. Regardless, I was in too deep to pull back.

She reached behind her back and unhooked her bra, letting it fall to my chest. She scooted toward my knees and undid my belt buckle and the button and zipper of my slacks. When she shifted, I expected her to pull them off so I'd be as naked as she was, but she only tugged off her panties and resettled herself on top of me. She slipped her hand into my boxer briefs and palmed my dick before pulling it free.

"Are you clean? Because I got tested. I'm good. And I'm protected."

I skimmed my hands from her shoulders down her arms. "I'm clean. But are you sure? We don't have to—"

She didn't wait for my response; she was already sliding the hot, wet heat of her pussy along my length and then lifting up and angling the head toward her entrance.

My words died in my throat as she sank down on me, arching her back and thrusting her breasts outward. With nothing between us, the searing heat and tight clasp of her body sent spikes of sensation straight to my balls.

"Jesus. Charlie—"

"I know." Her words were a breathy moan as she started to ride me. I cupped her ass in both hands, helping her to set a pace that was sure to demolish us both before we were ready. The clouds that had obscured the moon finally drifted away and in the silver light, I watched her take me with pure, unapologetic abandon. It was the sexiest thing I'd ever seen in my life. Knowing that I wouldn't last nearly long enough to call myself a man, I trailed my hand around her waist and thumbed her clit. She moaned and pressed into me, seeking the pressure I offered. She cupped her breasts, tugging at her nipple rings as she flexed her hips and increased her frenetic pace. I attempted to distract myself by promising that one of these days, I'd have her on top of me and force her to go slow and savor the moment. It was a failure as a distraction. It just ramped me up more. Sparks zinged down my spine as my orgasm barreled down on me. Charlie threw her head back and moaned as her body clamped down on me over and over. "Oh shit—I can't—I'm gonna—" Her words were harsh whispers lost in the night.

She slowed, unable to keep up her own rhythm as the climax gripped her. I clutched her hip with one hand and wrapped my other arm around her back. I pulled her down to me. Engulfed in Charlie, I finally let go.

charlie

I laid atop Simon for what felt like hours, but what was in reality probably only minutes. I never wanted to move again. Clouds had covered the moon, and I focused on matching my breathing to Simon's.

A spotlight cutting through the darkness interrupted our afterglow.

"Fuck," Simon whispered, throwing a corner of the blanket over me.

"Time to go?" I asked.

"Unfortunately."

The unfortunate thing was the fact that I had to pull myself away from Simon's fabulous, orgasm factory of a cock. Remembering that we'd gone bare, I felt around for a napkin to clean up the mess. The bouncing spotlight was moving closer, so I hurried into my dress and grabbed my bra and panties. Simon tossed the remains of our picnic into the cooler and bundled up the blanket. I snagged my shoes, opting to leave them off.

"Let's go." He gripped my hand and started to lead me toward the ramp. He stopped abruptly. "Shit. I don't want you walking on this barefoot." He dropped the blanket and the cooler on the deck of the barge and swept me up into his arms. I clung to his neck as he carried me down the ramp and to the car. He'd just shut my door when the security guard reached us. I could hear muffled words, but couldn't make them out. I really hoped Simon was using that silver tongue to talk our way out of this. A cold sweat prickled over my body at the thought of possibly getting arrested. My fake ID wouldn't hold up long under heavy scrutiny. I squeezed my eyes shut. *I'm not ready for this to end. I'm not ready to let him go.* I took a few deep breaths to calm my hammering heart as another thought intruded. *Will I ever be ready to let him go?* It was a stupid question, and I knew the answer before I'd finished thinking it. But it didn't matter. I wouldn't have a choice.

The light turned and headed away from the SUV as Simon opened the driver's side door.

"Sorry about that, babe. It was security. They changed shifts, and my guy forgot to mention it to his replacement." He must have noticed my pale face or my fingers clenching the fabric of my skirt, because his forehead crinkled with lines of concern.

"You okay?"

I nodded, swallowing back my momentary panic. Pasting a smile on my face, I tried to think of something casual to say. I ended up going with, "And here I thought you were finally breaking the rules."

The lines of concern didn't leave his face, leading me to believe that my attempt at masking my freak out had failed. He didn't comment, though, and for that I was thankful. "I'm going to grab the rest of our stuff." Simon flicked on a flashlight I hadn't noticed. Gesturing with it, he said, "Got it from the security guard. Apparently he didn't want to be fishing me out of the river tonight. Be right back."

Simon loaded the blanket and cooler into the back of the SUV, and we drove out what I assumed was the same way we'd entered. Silence stretched between us. I had no idea what he was thinking; I was too busy trying not to think at all.

He reached over to pull my hand away from where it was tangled in the folds of my skirt. "You want to come home with me?"

I studied him in the glow of the streetlights. One hand casually on the wheel, the other holding mine, eyes directed out the windshield as he changed lanes. Of course I wanted to go home with him. But I couldn't.

"I want to, but I can't."

He glanced at me. "Why not?"

"Huck. Harriet helped me out last night and tonight, not to mention letting him out every day while I'm at work. I don't want to take advantage of her. And I also don't want Huck to get lonely. He's already pretty depressed being in his crate most of the time. Although, starting tomorrow, he's allowed to be out for a little bit longer on a short leash." I smiled at the thought of Huck's marked improvement over the last few days.

"Then your place it is."

I raised an eyebrow at his words. "Did I invite you?"

"You were getting around to it."

It was strange waking up next to Simon for the second morning in a row. And it scared the hell out of me how much I liked it. In my full-size bed, we had no choice but to cuddle. And I was not a cuddler by nature, or at least I hadn't been before Simon. I tried not to wonder what that said about me and the other guys I'd been with before. Regardless, I didn't have time to enjoy the heat of his body surrounding me, because in exchange for my Saturday off from the Dirty Dog, I'd agreed to go in and do inventory at nine o'clock today.

I tried to extract myself from Simon's hold, but his arm tightened around my stomach.

"Sleeping, babe. Try it." His voice was grumbly and rough.

I wiggled to get free, but stilled when I felt his morning wood press against the crack of my ass. "I have to go to work. And after that I have to go to my other work."

Simon growled. "You work too much."

"Says the guy who left me naked in bed yesterday to go to work on a *Saturday*."

He sighed and released me. "Fine. When do you have to be there?"

I rolled off the bed. "In twenty minutes."

His eyes popped open, and he looked at the clock. "Shit. You want me to go let Huck out while you get ready?"

My heart warmed at his question. I was leaving him hard up in my bed, and he was offering to help take care of my dog. "That would be awesome." I thought for a moment about warning him that Harriet didn't always wear a robe in the mornings, but figured since we'd heard the sounds of *Madame Butterfly* coming from her studio until shortly after two o'clock, she'd probably sleep until noon.

Simon pulled on his slacks and shirt from the night before and left my apartment as I rushed to get ready for work. I threw on my uniform of choice: black skinny jeans, a hot pink bra, and a white wife beater. My hair went up into a messy bun, and I put on some eyeliner, mascara, and lip-gloss, and called it good. I slipped into my Chucks and was heading down the spiral staircase when Simon was leading Huck back into the house. A few words and a snuggle with my pup to get him settled, and I was about to leave Harriet's guestroom when Simon grabbed something off the bed.

He held up *Breaking the Code with Cryptography*, and I froze. "Harriet breaking codes lately?"

Oh. Shit.

I thought I'd grabbed all of my library books yesterday, but apparently not.

Shit. Shit. Shit.

I snatched it out of his hand before he could flip it open and see the library bar code.

I forced a laugh. "Who knows with Harriet? I'll stick it back in the bookshelf. Otherwise, she'll probably never find it."

My heart pounded and my hands went clammy as I left the room and shoved the book between a Georgia O'Keefe biography and the Kama Sutra.

I jumped when Simon laughed from behind me. "She's got quite the eclectic mix."

Trying to pull my shit together, I rubbed my sweaty palms on my jeans, forced a casual shrug, and turned for the door. "I've really gotta get going."

He followed me out, and I had the feeling I'd just failed some sort of cosmic test. It was an eerily perfect opening to confess all, but every fiber of my being screamed *not yet*.

I regained my composure as we walked toward the Dirty Dog. Simon insisted on accompanying me even though his car was parked in the opposite direction. He even directed me into a little café for coffee and quiche because he didn't like the idea of me skipping meals.

Accepting my coffee from the barista, I finally felt like I was back on even keel. I looked down at my curves and replied, "I could skip a few and be just fine."

His response: "Not without endangering some of my favorite parts."

We walked the rest of the way in companionable silence, his fingers laced through mine. It was like we were a regular couple, living a regular life. Except we weren't. And the close call this morning highlighted once more that we probably never would be.

Simon waved to Yve as I ducked inside the store.

"I don't know what you did to that man, but honey, he is *smitten*," Yve said as she waved back.

"Yeah, well ... I didn't exactly plan this."

"But it's good, right?"

I settled on the stool behind the register and pulled my quiche from the bag. Might as well eat while it was still hot.

"Yeah. I mean, I don't know what the hell I'm doing, and there's no way it could possibly work out, but for now, it's really good."

Yve leaned a hip against a display rack and watched me eat. "I know we haven't talked about what either of us is running from, but I don't think whatever that is should stop you from trying to make something real with him."

My fork halted mid-air at her words and quavered. The bite of quiche landed on the countertop. One thing I had always been able to count on with Yve was no questions. I'd always figured she didn't ask because she didn't want any in return. But she'd just broken that unspoken pact. I thought for a moment before responding.

"It's not that simple."

"Charlie, I'm the queen of 'not that simple,' but even I know you can't let your past dictate your future. That's no life."

She didn't understand the magnitude of the difference between our situations—because I couldn't tell her. Humorlessly, I said, "If I was just running from a bad relationship, I'd agree with you. But this is a whole different level of fucked up."

Yve narrowed her eyes. "Letting a man beat on you for two years because you think you deserve it is a pretty high level of fucked up, I think."

I lost my grip on the plastic fork, and it clattered on the counter. It was what I had suspected, but my stomach still twisted to hear her say it out loud. "Yve—that's ... I ... I don't know what to say."

"You don't need to say anything. But I didn't let that man run me out of my own town. Complicated or simple, some things are worth standin' and fightin' for."

I stared down at the mirrored surface of the counter and considered her words. "What if I'm juggling too many lies to make it out of this in one piece?"

"Does he love you?"

I thought about it for a beat. "I think so."

"Do you love him?"

This time I didn't hesitate. "Yes."

"Then there's always hope."

Even after a year, I hadn't yet figured out why Con kept the tattoo parlor open until ten on Sunday nights. It was almost nine o'clock, and we were dead slow. Which was dangerous. Delilah had gone home after her last appointment of the day, so only Con and I remained.

"Want to add to your sleeve?" Con asked.

That was why it was dangerous for me to be here when it was slow. I started to get the itch.

I couldn't say no. Especially when I already knew what I wanted next. *Fuck it.* "I was thinking my shoulder blade." I described my idea.

Con grinned. Of course, I assumed the grin was because these tattoo sessions usually ended with him getting laid. That part was *not* happening. I was pretty sure he knew it, but I needed to be sure we were both on the same page. "I'm not fucking you after."

His grin faded. "I know, Lee. I still don't like him."

"Why not?"

"Long story. I suppose I need to start getting over it if he's going to keep coming around."

"That's all you're going to give me?"

"That's it." His smile returned. "Are you at least going to take your shirt off so I can get to your whole shoulder?"

I pulled my tank over my head in response as he readjusted the chair and readied his station.

"Bra, too?" He reached out and snapped the strap against my shoulder.

I gave him the evil eye. "Work around it." He slid the strap down, gloved up, and got to work. As soon as I heard the familiar buzz, I relaxed into the seat.

simon

Number one on the list of things I didn't want to see when I walked into Voodoo to pick Charlie up from work: her, shirtless, with the guy she used to fuck.

I've never been the jealous type before, but something about Charlie fueled my most basic instincts. If Con hadn't been holding a tattoo gun, I might've decked him. I started boxing at the Naval Academy, and still made sure I hit a bag or got a workout in at least five days a week. Con might have a couple inches on me, but I could take him. I was pretty sure he'd gone Army, so we might spill some blood before I finished him. I fought to bury my emotions when he lifted the tattoo gun away from her skin and smirked as I crossed the room.

I kept my tone light. "Charlie, sweetheart, why aren't you wearing a shirt?" The answer was obvious, and I was probably being a dick by asking, but I couldn't hold it in.

Charlie twisted to smile at me and then looked over her shoulder at the burst of color that hadn't been there when I'd left her at the Dirty Dog this morning. She looked as relaxed as I'd ever seen her outside of bed.

"Do you like it?" I stepped into the small room and checked out her new tat: vivid fireworks exploding across the creamy skin of her shoulder blade. Blue, red, green, and golden yellow, artfully shaded and incredibly detailed. This time I was the one smiling. She'd marked herself permanently with a memory we'd made together. I leaned down, ignoring Con, and kissed her for all I was worth. I heard his stool roll away but wasn't sure if he'd left the room. Regardless, I wasn't stopping the kiss until I was damn well good and ready.

When I finally pulled away, I kissed the top of her other shoulder. "I love it." Although I wasn't entirely sure what it meant to Charlie—I could never guess what was going on in her head—I was going to take it as a sign that she was committing to this. To us. "Can you get the night of the Fourth of July off? It's a Saturday."

She glanced toward Con where he stood leaning against the doorway. "You've had a lot of Saturday nights off lately," he replied.

I was ready to argue, but he continued, "But I'm always telling you that you work too damn much anyway. So go for it." Con turned to me with a mocking stare. "What's the occasion? Or don't I want to know?"

Hell, I'd hoped to warm Charlie up to the idea gradually, because I didn't want her to say no. I needed her next to me. "Just some festivities."

Charlie stiffened. "Public festivities?" she asked.

"Let's talk about it later, yeah?" I said, hoping we could have this conversation without an audience. Thankfully, she nodded.

"You mind waiting a few more minutes while Con finishes up?"

I leaned down and kissed her shoulder again. "As long as it takes." I shot her a pointed look. She bit her lip at my double meaning. I'd never claimed to be subtle.

I stepped aside for Con to come back in and get settled on his stool. He picked up where he left off, and Charlie slipped back into her relaxed state as soon as the buzz of the tattoo gun filled the room.

Her easy mood lasted about three steps outside Voodoo. "So tell me about Fourth of July."

"It's a holiday celebrating American independence."

She shot me a sidelong look and waited for a serious answer as we walked in the direction of my car. Parking in

New Orleans had never been irritating to me until I met Charlie. She lived and worked in some of the most unparkable places. I opened her door, and she climbed in. I rounded the hood and hopped in the driver's seat.

The silence in the car forced me to explain. "It's an event called Fighting for Freedom that's being held on the Steamboat Orleans. It's put on by two nonprofits focused on serving veterans that I'm partnering with to get my own off the ground. There's a dinner and silent auction before the fireworks." I pulled away from the curb.

"Your own?"

I looked over, realizing I hadn't yet shared it with her. She was quickly becoming the most important person in my life, but every time I saw her, my thoughts were filled with nothing but Charlie. So it was little wonder we hadn't discussed it.

I explained further as I drove. "I'm starting a nonprofit to offer PTSD counseling and alternative therapies to vets who'd prefer not to seek treatment at the VA for whatever reason. My lawyer has already formed the corporation, and we're working on the application for tax-exempt status. There's still a ton of work to be done, but it's all starting to come together. That's why this Fourth of July thing is so important, because there will be a lot of people there who support veteran's causes who I'll need on my side to make The Kingman Project a success."

"Wow. That's ... amazing. If you need help with pro forma financial statements, I'm your girl."

My gaze snapped to hers for a second before refocusing on the road. *What the hell? Pro forma financial statements?*

"Why—" I started to ask her to explain, but she interrupted my question.

"Wait, Kingman—was he the pilot who...?" Her change of subject derailed my thoughts as my stomach dropped, the same way it did every time I relived the explosion in my head. *It should have been me.*

"Yeah. He's the one. The one ... who saved me. His widow will be there too. She's remarried now, to a friend of mine. I'd like you to meet her."

I turned onto her street and snagged a spot not far from Harriet's house. I put the SUV in park and turned to face Charlie. She was frowning and picking at the black nail polish on her thumb. Her body language was all wrong.

She didn't look up when she said, "I'm not sure I can do that."

A cold feeling crept into my chest. "What do you mean you're not sure you can do that?"

"The event. Meet his widow. There'll be press, right? Cameras?"

"Yeah, but it's no big deal. A few photo ops and it's done. It's for a good cause, and it's pretty painless."

"I'm not a photo op kind of girl, Simon. I told you before, and I wasn't kidding." She finally looked at me, and the stubborn set of her jaw pissed me off. I tried one more time to explain how much this event meant to me.

"I need you with me for this, Charlie. It's important to me. I want you there, next to me."

"I should go." She reached for the door handle, and the grip I had on my temper snapped.

"You're not getting out of this car until you tell me what the hell you're hiding from that you can't risk a goddamn picture in the fucking paper. And pro forma financial statements? What the fuck, Charlie? You've gotta give me something here."

She stilled before slowly turning to face me. Her glare was ice, and her walls were up higher than I'd ever seen. "Don't talk to me like that, and don't tell me what to do. It's not going to work out how you think."

I slammed my palms against the steering wheel, helpless to stop this conversation from spiraling out of control. "Goddammit. I just want to understand. I could help you if you'd let me. But you won't give me anything. It's driving me crazy. I've made it pretty fucking clear that I'm in love with you, and I think you love me." I gestured between us. "This isn't going to work unless you let me in. If you can't do that, what's the point in even trying?"

I wanted to take my words back as soon as they escaped my lips, but I couldn't. They needed to be said. The ice in her gaze melted into glossy tears. She blinked them back, not letting them spill. I knew what she was going to say before she spoke. *Don't*, I thought. *Don't say it, Charlie.* She opened her mouth, and I reinforced myself for the blow I knew was coming.

"I guess … there really is no point. We both know I'm no good for you anyway." She opened the door like she hadn't just ripped my heart out of my chest. "Goodbye, Simon."

I swallowed, determined to hold it together. "You said you wouldn't break my heart." The words sounded like they'd been dragged over a gravel road before I ground them out.

She turned back to face me, tears streaking down her face. "No, I didn't. I said I wouldn't do it without shattering mine." She dashed away the tears with the side of her hand. Her voice shook as she said, "I didn't lie about that." She shut the door and crossed the street without looking back. I watched, unable to comprehend what the fuck just happened, as she fumbled with the lock and finally slipped inside the gate. She was gone.

charlie

I buried my face in Huck's fur and let my tears soak into his rough coat as I listened to the continuous buzzing coming from the intercom. I could have written the scene before it happened. It was inevitable. I should have been better prepared for it. But I hadn't factored in just how much it would hurt to walk away from him

When the buzzing finally stopped, I knew Simon was gone.

I sniffled back a sob, and Huck's big brown eyes rested on me. I could only imagine how pitiful I looked.

The raw emotions were too much to handle. I didn't want to think. Didn't want to feel. I needed to be numb, or I might not be able to stop myself from going after him.

I was only a few blocks from Bourbon Street. So I'd go with the obvious solution: get drunk and lose myself in the crowd. Lose myself period. I was good at that. I knew I should call Yve or Delilah, but then I'd have to rehash everything that had happened tonight. And I wasn't ready for that. So I'd go by myself. Because at the end of the day, I was the only person I could rely on anyway.

So, *laissez les bon temps rouler.*

I slammed shot after shot, shaking my ass on the dance floor, shoving away every guy who attempted to get close. Just like I'd shoved Simon away.

My actions were a sadly accurate metaphor for my life.

The lights were hypnotic, and my buzz was rolling into straight up hammered. I stumbled to the bar and slapped down a twenty. "Two more shots. Tequila." The bartender didn't even blink before taking my money and pouring the liquor.

"Lime?"

"No need." I tossed one back and smacked the glass down on the wooden bar before wiping my hand across my mouth. I looked down at my ink-covered skin and smiled sardonically. The good-girl-falling-for-the-bad-boy stories might have happily ever afters, but you never really heard about what happened when the good guy fell for the bad girl.

Apparently *this*.

I lifted the other shot in a silent toast to Simon and tipped it back. He deserved better than me. If things had continued on between us, I would've eventually dragged him into the suspicion and contempt that surrounded the girl I was pretending not to be. I looked at the bartender and pulled out another twenty.

"Two more, please."

Then I'd be done. I'd walk my ass home and pass out. I'd call in hung over tomorrow, and Yve would be knocking on my door and dragging me out of bed. *Love that girl.* The thought cued me in to the fact that I had indeed officially passed buzzed. I downed the last two shots and stumbled my way out of the bar into the mass of humanity on Bourbon. I caught glimpses of tits and ass as I made my way up the street. I spotted Jimmy on the corner. Surprisingly, a hot dog sounded delicious. I hadn't been by to see Jimmy since shortly after Huck's accident when I'd promised Simon I wouldn't walk home alone anymore.

"Jimmy!" I called out as I pushed through the crowd.

"Ms. Charlie, I ain't seen you in weeks." Jimmy snapped his tongs in my direction. "Where you been?

Where's my boy Huck Finn? And what can I get for you this fine evenin'?"

I tried to sort his questions out in my tequila-soaked brain. "Umm … Huck's at home. He got hit by a car … so I haven't been walking home for a while. This guy … he didn't think it was safe for me … by myself." I winced at my disjointed explanation.

Jimmy narrowed his gaze at me. "You done tied one on." It wasn't a question. He looked around. "You by yourself tonight?"

I nodded. "It's cool. You know I'm not far from home." I tried hard to avoid slurring my words. I was like a drunk teenager trying to fool her parents.

"I still don't like it." He handed me my hotdog without me having to order. I handed him the rest of the money I had on me. He tried to refuse, but I stuffed the bills in the pocket of his apron.

"See you tomorrow, Jimmy."

"It's a date, Ms. Charlie."

I wandered a few more steps before I took a bite. I chewed and swallowed. And then gagged. *Bad idea.* Tequila and hotdog were not going to coexist peacefully. But I didn't want to waste it. So I kept walking, on a drunken quest to find one of those homeless pups that wandered the street to pull in money for their owners. If it was good enough for Huck…

I finally spotted one sitting on the corner beyond the barricade that blocked the cars from Bourbon Street. The end of his leash was knotted to a pipe. It looked like his owner had just tied him up and left him. He was brindle like Huck, which made me smile. I staggered forward and offered up the hotdog.

"Here you go, baby. Eat up." He swallowed it down in two head-tossing bites. Just like Huck.

"What the fuck, bitch?"

I spun around and registered a man striding out of the shadows. He wasn't one of the hippy-looking homeless guys. He looked … mean.

"Ummm … sorry. I'll just be going." I looked at the dog and started to turn back toward the crowd only a dozen or so yards away.

"I don't think so." His fingers bit into my bare arm as he swung me around and dragged me down the dark street. I started to scream, but the back of his hand caught my cheek and my head snapped sideways. The air in my lungs evaporated as icy fear rushed in to take its place. Memories of my last close call assailed me. I had no Huck this time. No way to protect myself.

He was patting down my pockets, looking for money, while I just stood there dumbly. "You gotta have something. Fuckin' bitches always got something," he muttered, still gripping my arm. He tossed my cell phone into the gutter.

My drunken haze was ripped away as the reality of my situation solidified. I rammed my knee up into his groin and yanked against his grasp as he doubled over. But his grip was too tight. His dog growled, and I stayed just shy of the snapping teeth that had looked so harmless only moments before. I rotated my arm, trying to twist out of his hold. But he was faster, and I felt a slash of pain across my side. I looked down at the slice in my white tank top as it turned red. He froze, as if realizing what he'd just done, as if the action had been a reflex. In his shock, he dropped the knife, and it clattered to the sidewalk near the dog. I kneed him in the balls again. This time he stumbled and let go of my arm. I ran toward the crowd.

"You better run, bitch," he yelled after me.

I staggered down Bourbon Street, clutching my arm to my side as hot, sticky blood seeped out of the wound. I spotted a cop and started toward him. But then common sense intruded. Cops meant a hospital and questions. I turned away, tripping over the curb and stumbling into a doorway next to a strip club. The doorman glanced over at me. Then did a double take.

"Whoa, sweetheart. You're bleeding. Fuck!" He fumbled for his phone. "I'll call 911."

"No. Don't." I started to sweat and dizziness assailed me. "Could you call someone else for me?"

He held the phone, poised to dial. "Number?"

I rattled off one I knew by heart. The bouncer held the phone out, and I pressed it to my ear.

He picked up on the second ring. "Hello?"

"I need you."

charlie

I woke up wearing nothing but my bra and underwear in a bed that wasn't my own. I stretched and winced at the pain in my side, the pounding in my head, and the throbbing of my cheek. I groaned.

I was a total shit show.

Fragmented memories of last night came flooding back as I surveyed the very familiar room and the man in bed beside me. His blue eyes flicked open, as if he'd just been lying there, waiting for me to wake. He stared at me for a long moment before speaking.

"Scared the shit out of me last night, Lee."

I tried to recall exactly what the hell had happened. It was mostly a drunken blur laced with heart-stopping fear. "I don't remember much after the phone call."

"That's because you didn't fucking make it through the phone call. You passed out, went into shock. Bouncer had to tell me where the fuck you were. I paid him four hundred bucks because you dropped his phone and shattered the screen. Well, that, and he was a stand up guy and used his shirt to stop the bleeding before I got there."

I chanced a glance down at my side. There were no stitches, only an angry red seam. I looked up at Con.

"No hospital?"

His snapping blue eyes turned serious. "Did you really want me to announce your whereabouts to the FBI, Charlotte?"

All of the blood drained from my face. I couldn't move. Couldn't breathe. Fear slithered up my spine.

"How...? How long...?"

"Jesus, give me some credit. You really think I'd hire a woman with no ID, clearly running from something, and just leave it at that?"

"I ... I guess not?" My voice faltered on the words. If he figured it out, that meant that anyone else could too. *Fuck. Me.* The illusion that I had any control over my situation died a tragic death.

He shook his head. "Definitely not. I needed to know what kind of trouble might be following you." He propped himself up on an elbow. "I don't know why you're so surprised. I mean, I was more than just some dumb grunt in the Army. I was Special Forces. I've still got buddies who work intel. All it took was sending a picture of you, calling in a few favors, and misappropriating some government resources."

"But..."

Con interrupted me to continue his explanation. "Before you started in on the tats and found your attitude, you practically screamed 'good girl on the run.' I had to know why. And then there was the fact that I was planning on fucking you pretty much from the minute you walked through my door."

I gave him a dirty look in response to his very Con-like, blunt statement, but my fear started to dissipate. If Con had to pull strings with military intelligence, who'd presumably used sophisticated facial recognition software to identify me, then it was possible I wasn't completely screwed.

I pulled the sheet tighter against me, still trying to process everything. "Why didn't you ever say anything?"

"We've all got our secrets. Yours is just a hell of a lot bigger than most. I can respect the fact that you're not looking to be found. That you wanted to leave it all behind. I'm also damn sure you weren't in on the scheme dear old dad pulled."

My heart thumped against my ribs at his statement. "And how do you know that?"

"You wouldn't accept a raise after we'd slept together because it would make you feel like a whore. That's not the kind of character I'd expect from a girl who helped her dad steal $125 billion."

"Maybe..." I started to speak, but the words stuck in my throat. I had to force them out. "Maybe I didn't want that raise because I already had plenty of money from ... you know."

"You look like you're about to puke just saying that. Unless you straight up tell me you did it, there's no way in hell I'll believe it."

I waited for him to ask. To make me tell him conclusively. But he didn't.

"You're not going to ask me?"

"Told you already. Don't need to."

"I don't deserve friends like you." Tears stung my eyes.

He leaned over and kissed my forehead. "Baby, you deserve a hell of a lot better than you give yourself credit for. And that includes good friends."

"Thank you," I whispered. I shifted and the pinch in my side reminded me of my injury. I pulled the sheet away again to study my first knife wound. *Lovely.* Hopefully it would be my one and only. "How did you ... fix me?"

He peered down. "Superglue. It does a good job under most circumstances. This isn't the first knife wound I've dealt with. And it wasn't all that deep. I was glad you were out when I cleaned it, though. Anyway, you'll be fine." He skimmed a finger across my throbbing cheek. "Gonna have a little shiner, though. I'd love to meet the guy who did this. They'd never find his body."

I looked up at Con's words. A cold, determined mask had settled over his features. Most of the time I forgot that

Con had served in the Army. That undoubtedly he'd killed people. Like me, it could be hard to see past his ink.

"Any other injuries I didn't see last night, Lee?" His jaw was set, as if he was bracing himself for what I might say.

I started to shake my head but stopped when it felt like my brain might fall out. "He didn't … touch me. Well, other than to knife me. Asshole." I looked down at my arms and the finger shaped bruises marking them. I held them out for Con to see. "I guess you can add more bruises and a hangover to the list, but that's all."

"Meant to ask you about that." Con gently tilted my chin up, as if he wanted to make sure he had my attention. "What the fuck were you doing getting hammered, by yourself, and then wandering off into trouble? You're smarter than that. Where the fuck was Duchesne while this was going down?"

I pulled my chin out of his grip and looked down at the sheet.

"I don't know." It was an honest answer. I had no idea where Simon had gone after I'd walked away and hadn't looked back. I still couldn't believe I'd done that. It hadn't been my finest moment.

"What do you mean? He left you there? I'm gonna kick his—"

I laid a hand on Con's arm. "No. It's not his fault. He wasn't there. I guess … well, I guess I broke up with him last night." The last words came out in a single breath.

Con pulled back. "You left here all sunshine and rainbows, high on your new tat, and you're telling me that between then and getting knifed, you *guess* you broke up with the guy you're head over ass in love with?"

I fingered the edge of the sheet. "Yeah."

"Jesus, Lee. Only you. Action-packed night."

"Yeah," I said again.

Con rolled off the bed and headed toward the doorway. "I'll get you some ibuprofen for the hangover and everything else that ails you. You can hang here as long as you want, and you officially have the day off. I've gotta head down and open the shop in a few. I've got an appointment at two."

I scanned the room but didn't see Con's clock. "What time is it?"

He looked down at his watch. "One-thirty."

I bolted upright and my stomach roiled in time with my pounding head. "Shit. I'm supposed to be at work."

"I called Yve. She's cool."

I moved my head slower when I looked over at him. "What did you tell her?"

"That you got drunk last night, needed a place to crash, and were going to be too hung over to make it in. She didn't ask me too many questions, but I'm sure she'll have plenty for you later."

I grimaced. "I'm not looking forward to that conversation."

"Called Harriet, too. She's keeping an eye on Huck."

I rubbed my swollen face. I was racking up debts all over town because of last night.

I carefully swung my legs over the side of the bed and looked around for my jeans. I spotted them crumpled up on the floor in the corner. I stood, wobbling a little, and holding my side. When the superglued seam didn't tear open, and I didn't puke after two steps, I figured I would probably live through the morning. I grabbed my jeans and my bloody, ruined tank top from beneath them. The shirt I tossed in the garbage. I shook out my black skinny jeans and saw several dark, crusty splotches. *Shit.* I thought for a second about tossing them in the trash too, but they were my favorite jeans. I didn't know how to get blood out of denim, but apparently I was about to learn. I crossed to Con's dresser to grab a shirt.

I pulled on a giant gray T-shirt stamped with ARMY across the chest, and flinched at the tug on my wound. My actions last night undoubtedly qualified me as 'too stupid to live.' All of my actions. Getting that drunk alone *and* walking away from Simon.

Why was I giving him up before I absolutely had to? It might have been naïve, but I was still holding out some hope that I could crack the damn code. And provided I could get Simon on board with me staying in the shadows when it came to his public life ... maybe this could still work. For at least a little while longer.

Last night it had seemed like the only answer was walking away before I let myself fall any further. But who was I kidding? I was already too far gone. What was the point in trying to guard my heart now?

But what if Simon gave me another ultimatum? It would be a deal-breaker. I pushed the thoughts aside. I had to try.

Getting knifed in a dark alley gave a girl some perspective. I thought about what Yve had said about some things being worth fighting for. Whatever happened next, I couldn't let it end like this.

Con strode into the room, interrupting my musings. He held out a glass of water, and dropped three ibuprofen into my hand. I swallowed them obediently and drank the entire glass.

"You good?"

I nodded and followed him out of the bedroom.

"I'll walk you down then." He paused as we reached the sofa, and I sat to pull on my Chucks. "Shit, you need a ride home. I can't let you walk. Not like this."

"It's broad daylight. It's no big deal."

"And you got knifed last night." He ran a hand through his shaggy hair. "I'm giving you a ride home."

"No." My tone was firm. "Seriously, I'll be fine. I've got some shit to figure out, and walking helps me think. And it's not like it's even that far."

Con scowled at me and looked down at his watch. "No."

I glared back. "I'm walking. Don't push me." I gestured to my side. "You know what I did to the guy who did this?"

Con's eyes narrowed as he shook his head.

"I kneed his balls up into his esophagus. Twice."

He exhaled a long breath and rubbed a hand across his face. I could see just a glimpse of the weariness left over from his sleepless night. A sleepless night I was responsible for.

I could see that I'd won when he relaxed the stiff set of his shoulders. "Fine. But call me when you get there. Or I'll be beating down your goddamn door."

"It's a deal."

I followed him down into the shop and waited for him to unlock the door. Stepping out onto the sidewalk, I had to shade my eyes against the glare of the midday sun. I looked up at Con. *I didn't deserve friends like him.*

"You saved my ass." I pressed my hands against his chest and leaned up on my tiptoes to kiss his stubbled jaw. "So thank you. For last night. And everything before that, too."

He cupped the left side of my face, thumb brushing lightly across my tender cheekbone. "Any time, Lee. That's what friends are for." He leaned down and pressed a kiss to my forehead, my bruised cheek, and finally a brush across the corner of my mouth. "Take care of yourself, girl. No more close calls. You're too important. Give me a call me when you get home. Don't fucking forget, you hear?"

I nodded. He snagged my hand as I started to pull away, giving it a playful squeeze.

"I'll see you tomorrow, Con."

"Damn right. I'm not giving you another day off this week."

I tugged my hand from his grip and grinned at him before walking in the direction of home. I had a sliver of hope and a hell of a lot to figure out. It was a good thing I had the day off, because it was going to take more than walking nine blocks to do it.

simon

A nightmare woke me around four-thirty on Monday morning. I blinked against the blackness of my room, trying to get the image of Kingman's body being incinerated mid-air out of my head. The dream was almost worse than before, because I'd gone so many nights without having it. It had come back full force, in Technicolor. My mistake and the lethal consequences.

Rather than try to go back to sleep, I changed into work out clothes and wandered down to the kitchen to make coffee. My shoulders, arms, and hands were sore from beating the shit out of my heavy bag last night. Today, I'd try outrunning my anger, since I'd already discovered I couldn't pound it away with my fists.

Bottom line: I was pissed. Pissed at myself. And pissed at Charlie. I shouldn't have pushed her and said what I said, but she shouldn't have walked away. Not so easily. Not over something like that.

Yeah, I was frustrated as shit that she still wouldn't let me in, but I could be patient. Like I'd told her before, I was playing the long game. Somewhere along the line, I'd decided she was it for me. I wasn't even sure it'd been a conscious decision. It just *was*. She was the one.

As I found my stride on the cracked and uneven pavement, I worked out my game plan. I wasn't giving up on her. I wasn't giving up on us. Not without a fight.

Nine hours after my unwelcome wake-up call, I was finally able to escape the City Council building and go after Charlie. I parked across the street from the Dirty Dog and hopped out of the car. Yve was behind the counter, ringing up a sale. I scanned the store. No Charlie. I waited for the customer to leave before I demanded, "Where is she?"

Yve's whiskey-colored eyes narrowed on me. She ignored my question. "Something doesn't make sense here."

"What do you mean?"

"Con called me this morning to tell me Charlie wouldn't be coming in to work today because she was passed out cold at his place. Didn't think she'd be getting up any time soon. And now you're here, looking like a man on a mission. So what the fuck happened last night?"

"*Shit.*" Visions of her walking away from me straight into Con's arms flashed through my brain. *No.* She wouldn't. She'd probably just gotten hammered last night. That's it. That's all. And that had to mean something, right? I pictured the heavy bag I'd demolished. We all had our own way of dealing with shit. I tried to calm myself down. "Where does Con live? You know if she's still there?"

"Don't know, but he lives above Voodoo. Con owns the whole building." She seemed to be expecting shock at her revelation, but I didn't give a fuck about Con. I just wanted to find Charlie.

"Thanks." I turned toward the door, but a nagging question forced its way to the surface. It was none of my business, but suddenly it seemed imperative that I know. I looked back at Yve and asked, "Are you and Con still…?"

She fingered her necklace and looked down at the counter. "Nah. He gets bored fairly quick with just about everyone. Charlie was the exception."

It wasn't the answer I wanted to hear.

I drove down Canal, looking for a spot in front of Voodoo, but they were all full. I parked two blocks away and strode toward the shop, maneuvering through the throngs of people. Marquee in sight, I paused at the intersection and waited for traffic to clear. Dodging a taxi,

I crossed and then stopped dead as soon as I hit the sidewalk. A guy stumbled into me and cursed, but I couldn't hear him over the rushing blood in my ears.

What the fuck?

The too-big man's T-shirt Charlie was wearing hung off her slim shoulder. Her hair was wild, and screamed *just been fucked.*

No.

My brain turned to rationalization mode. She'd sat in my kitchen, in my shirt, with her crazy bedhead that morning, and nothing had happened between us. There was no reason to think…

My justifications unraveled as she pressed against Con and leaned up to kiss his cheek. He cupped her face. I wasn't close enough to see their expressions, but to me and everyone else on the street, it looked like a lover's goodbye.

It wasn't. She wouldn't.

He leaned down to kiss her forehead. Then her cheek. And finally her lips.

He held her hand as she smiled and turned to walk away. I could focus on nothing but where his fingers were laced with hers, their arms outstretched as if loathing letting each other go. His hand didn't release hers until the last possible moment.

The breath in my lungs heaved out like I'd taken a solid jab to the liver. I didn't want to believe it. Didn't want to believe that she'd run back to him only hours after she'd walked away from me. But, *fuck.* I was *seeing* it. I stood for several moments staring at the now empty sidewalk in front of Voodoo. Pedestrians streamed around me. Finally, I straightened and pulled myself together. A familiar numbness settled over me. The same one I'd been forced to adopt every time we'd lost one of the men whose names were tattooed on my back. There wasn't time to stop and grieve in the middle of a mission. And now, it was better to feel nothing than the searing burn of betrayal that bled into my veins as I tried to comprehend what I'd just seen.

I needed to walk away. I wouldn't chase her down and demand an explanation. I was afraid of what I might say. Afraid to give voice to my accusations. But more than that, I was afraid of how she would respond. What she would admit to. Because if what I saw was actually what it looked like, there was no going back for Charlie and me.

I stalked through the reception area and straight back toward my office without stopping to talk to anyone.

"Mr. Duchesne—"

"Not now." I ignored my assistant's concerned look and passed my father's corner office, which sat right next to my own. Out of habit, I scanned the interior and halted. My father was standing by the window, leaning heavily on his cane.

What the hell?

He should be in Maine, having surgery tomorrow, not standing in his office.

Fuck. I didn't have the patience to deal with him, but he glanced over before I could retreat from the doorway.

"There you are. Annette said you'd be back a half-hour ago. I wanted to talk to you about—"

"Why the hell aren't you in Bar Harbor?"

My father's mouth compressed, no doubt due to the lack of deference in my tone and my abrupt question.

"Critchley broke two fingers playing squash over the weekend. Had to cancel my surgery. One of his colleagues is going to fit me in sometime next month. So your mother and I decided to postpone the trip until after the Fourth. But I wanted to talk to you about—"

Annette interrupted him from the doorway. "Mr. Duchesne, I apologize for intruding, but Mr. Jackson is on your line. He says he's returning your phone call, but only has a moment to speak with you."

I didn't wait to hear my father's response. I strode into my office and shut the door. I'd bury myself in work until I could reassess whatever the hell I'd seen on the street today without wanting to hit someone. Preferably Constantine Leahy.

charlie

I made good use of my free afternoon. First, I showered away the nastiness of last night. Which was difficult, considering every time I lifted my arms, my side stretched and tugged uncomfortably. Once I was finally clean, I spent some time with Huck while he wandered around the garden oasis. He was starting to put more weight on his healing leg, and I needed to call Dr. Richelieu to see if that was a good thing. Since he didn't whimper or yelp, I hoped it meant he wasn't pushing himself beyond his limits.

Huck sat awkwardly before laying down on the grass. I sat beside him, and he lifted his head to rest on my outstretched legs. Absently stroking his thick coat, I debated what to do.

I wanted to tell Simon everything.

But I couldn't.

Not yet. Not until I had a handle on cleaning up the mess my father had made.

But I would give him more ... me. I'd drop my walls a few stories and let him at least part of the way in and hope it'd be enough for now.

He'd said he loved me. That meant something. And I was damn sure I loved him. But I'd walked away, and he'd let me. I didn't know what the hell that meant for us. I pushed off the grass and stood. I wasn't going to waste any more time thinking about it. I was going to do something about it.

I settled Huck back into his crate before heading upstairs to my tiny closet. I shoved aside my everyday casual stuff and pulled out a maxi dress. If Simon knew anything about me at all, just wearing this would send a message. I was trying. I slipped into the dress and plaited my hair into a side fishtail braid. It took me forever to get my makeup right and camouflage the bruise. I thought about Yve and wondered how many bruises she'd covered before she'd stood up for herself and left her asshole of an ex. I understood how Con had felt about the guy who'd attacked me. If Yve's ex ever came after her again, I'd be first in line to help bury the body.

I heard the taxi honk from the street. I added gold hoops, slid my feet into espadrille wedge sandals, and threw on a thin shrug to cover my bruised arms. One last glance in the mirror told me that, with the exception of my date with Simon, I looked more put together than I had in the last year.

I'd looked up Southern Cross's address in the ancient phonebook stuffed in my junk drawer and hoped the office hadn't moved since the book hit doorsteps a decade ago. At times like this I longed for a smartphone. I slid into the cab and relayed my destination to the driver.

We pulled up to the guard shack I recognized from Saturday night. The security guy waved us through without question, and we drove between the shipping containers and pulled up in front of a tall steel warehouse. A one-story section jutted out into the parking lot, and a sign that read "Office" hung on the brick façade. My heart rate kicked up a notch when I saw Simon's X5 parked alongside the building. I paid the driver and slid out of the cab, hoping like hell I wouldn't be walking home.

Shouldering my bag, I pulled open the glass door that led into a sophisticated reception area. Twin black leather sofas lined two of the steely gray-blue walls. A modern art sculpture sat encased in glass on a pedestal in the corner between them. It was ugly as hell, and in my experience, that meant it was probably expensive. A woman sat behind a sleek black desk topped with dark granite. I glanced at the closed door just beyond her, knowing I would find

Simon behind it somewhere. She lifted her head and smiled up at me. Her eyes widened as she took in the tattoos peeking out from beneath my shrug.

"Can I help you, ma'am?" Her smile was tight and guarded.

I straightened my posture, infusing myself with the imperious *I own this place* quality my mother had always exuded. "Please tell Simon Duchesne that Charlotte is here to see him." I had no idea why I used my real name. I supposed it fit better with the attitude.

My authoritative tone had the desired effect. She replied with a meek, "Yes, ma'am," and picked up the phone.

"Mr. Duchesne, you have a visitor. She says her name is Charlotte…"

Pause.

"Yes, sir. I'll tell her."

Tell me what? If he refused to see me, I was going to … I had no idea what I would do. I hadn't planned for that contingency.

She hung up the phone and stood. *Fuck.* Was she going to call security and have me thrown out?

Instead, she gestured to one of the sofas. "Mr. Duchesne asked if you would wait. He'll be out directly."

I didn't sit. The nervous energy thrumming through me made it impossible. Rather, I walked toward the sculpture and read the plaque adorning the pedestal. I didn't recognize the artist's name, but that didn't mean anything. I'd never enjoyed modern sculpture.

"Charlotte."

The door must have opened on silent hinges, because when I spun, Simon was standing rigidly in the doorway. My name sounded cold on his lips. His expression was completely closed off.

"Simon." I stepped toward him.

"What are you doing here?"

191

A hushed gasp came from the direction of the receptionist. Apparently she'd never heard Simon use that cutting tone either.

"I wanted to see you."

"You've seen me."

Oh fuck, no. He was not going to shut me out. If this was a taste of my own medicine, it was bitter as hell.

"I'd like a few minutes. In private."

He turned and walked through the open doorway to the inner sanctum. I took that as my cue and followed. I didn't know this Simon. He was cold, withdrawn, and kind of an asshole. I felt the hope I'd been holding on to leech out of me.

He stood in the doorway of an office and gestured for me to enter. I stepped inside, and he shut the thick wooden door. The windows faced the Mississippi, and I could see cranes loading shipping containers onto barges—like the one we'd picnicked on the night before last. I wanted to go back to Saturday and redo everything so I could avoid this confrontation.

Simon sprawled in his leather executive chair, but didn't indicate that I should sit as well. I sat anyway. Given his behavior, I'd be waiting forever for an invitation.

He didn't speak. His hazel eyes drilled into me, chipping away my confident front. His lips pressed into a thin, flat line.

"I'm sorry." My apology was sincere but didn't sound remotely humble. I had come here ready to apologize and explain to *my* Simon, but the man before me wasn't him.

He raised an eyebrow sardonically. "For what exactly?"

My patience ran out. "Are you going to be a dick about this? Because if you are, I'll just go." My nails dug into the leather armrests, and I didn't care if I left marks.

Simon straightened in his fancy ass chair, no longer looking like an indolent jackass. "That's your apology?"

"I had a better one planned, but I didn't realize you'd turn into an asshole over night."

One corner of his mouth tugged upward, but he beat back the beginnings of his smile.

"I've never had someone tell me 'I'm sorry' and make it sound like they were also telling me to go fuck myself."

This time the corner of my mouth tugged upward, but I resisted the impulse as well. It was a standoff. A game of verbal and emotional chicken. For a beat, I had no idea who would swerve first. Then I decided it should be me.

"I'm sorry about last night. I did something … kind of stupid. I would have been here sooner, but…" I hesitated, trying to come up with the right words to explain how I'd gone off by myself, gotten drunk, and gotten knifed.

Before I could continue, his expression morphed into something hard and angry. His next words sucked the air out of my lungs.

"Did you fuck Con last night? Or this morning? Because if that's what you're going to tell me, you should get the hell out of my office."

I shot out of my chair, too pissed to wince at the pain. Simon did the same, his chair toppling over from the force. His eyes blazed with accusation.

"Did you?" he demanded. I had no idea how he knew I'd spent the night at Con's, but that was beside the point. The reason for Simon's personality transplant was now clear.

"It sounds like you don't need an answer from me. You've already decided for yourself exactly what happened."

"Goddammit, Charlie. Answer my fucking question." I almost did tell him to go fuck himself this time, but his voice wavered on the last words, and I studied his posture. His hands were fisted so tightly it looked like his knuckles might pop out of their sockets. He held himself perfectly still, as if expecting to shatter with my answer.

I raised my chin and met his gaze. "No. But you can go to hell for asking." I turned and reached for the door handle, intent on pulling it open. Simon's hand slapped against the wood beside my face. His knuckles were raw and split open, and I wondered what the hell *he'd* done last night. The thought vanished as his body surrounded me. This seemed to be a recurring position with us.

I could feel his heart pounding against my back. The heavy *thud-thud, thud-thud* matched my own. The sound of his harsh breaths echoed in the silence of the room. "Don't you dare walk away from me."

I memorized the wood grain of the door. "Don't tell me what to do. It doesn't work out well for us."

He pressed the entire length of his body against me and spoke directly into my ear. "I can't watch you walk away again. Last night it gutted me. Today, it will break me."

My forehead thumped against the door, and I squeezed my eyes shut as tears threatened to spill over. Once again, his honesty leveled me, demolishing my walls. I turned in the circle of his arms—the place I most wanted to be—and stared up at him. His eyes were closed, as if waiting for the executioner to raise his ax and swing the lethal blow. I didn't know what to say to erase the pain etched on his features. So I went with the simplest truth.

"It would break me too."

Lowering his forehead to mine, his eyes flicked open. *This* was my Simon. "Jesus, Charlie. You don't know what you do to me. You could destroy me." His words trailed off as he cupped the right side of my face and angled his lips to take mine. The kiss was hungry, desperate, and I opened to him as his tongue delved inside. I kissed him back with the same passion, but the entire time, his words echoed in my head. *You could destroy me.* It was true. I was almost thankful for the knock at the door that forced us apart.

I stepped out of the safety of Simon's arms to reach for a tissue out of the box on his desk. Dabbing at my tears, I tried to salvage my makeup. Given the amount of concealer staining the white tissue, I was doing a shit job of it. Simon took several deep breaths before opening the door a crack.

"Simon, what the hell? Open the damned door. I just got off the phone with Arthur Jackson, and he's agreed to head up your campaign. He's pulling the committee documentation together, and this thing will officially be off the ground." Simon let the door swing wide, and an older, gray-haired version of him stepped into the room, leaning on a cane. He clapped a hand on Simon's shoulder. "You're going to do me proud, son."

"Dad, could we discuss this another time?"

Simon's father looked up and then around the room. His posture turned rigid when he saw me. I shifted slightly so my right side dominated his view.

"Well, now. Aren't you going to introduce us, Simon? I'm assuming this is the ... friend your mother mentioned. The one who couldn't join us for supper because she had to work at ... what was it? A tattoo parlor?" He studied me like I was a circus freak. "What was your name again?"

Simon's features hardened to granite. "This is Charlie, Dad. She's my girlfriend." Simon moved to stand next to me. "Charlie, this is my father, Jefferson Duchesne."

I held out a hand, and wondered if he'd deign to shake it. "It's a pleasure to meet you, sir."

He gripped my hand for a moment before dropping it. "We have important matters to discuss. If you're finished with your ... girlfriend ... perhaps we could chat."

Simon pulled me against him, and I winced at the twinge in my side. Looking down at me, he stiffened and said absently to his father, "I'm not actually. We can talk tomorrow."

Confusion darkened Simon's expression. Reaching out a hand, he tilted my face toward him so he could see my bruise more clearly. My thought about doing a shitty job salvaging my makeup was confirmed.

"Simon, this is important," his father insisted.

"Dad. Not now." Simon's tone was implacable. His father spun, leaving the office in a huff, the door banging shut behind him.

Simon exploded. "What the fuck happened? Did someone hit you?" His thumb skimmed my cheekbone.

"I ... I made poor choices last night."

"What kinds of poor choices?" He started to wrap both arms around me, but stopped when I recoiled. "Seriously, Charlie, what the fuck?"

I swallowed. "I kind of ... got knifed?"

All of the color drained from Simon's face, and his eyes flicked over me maniacally. "Where? Jesus Christ! What the hell?" He was roaring now, and I was glad the door was closed.

"In the Quarter, just off Bourbon. I was drunk and by myself."

He looked like he wanted to shake me. He gathered the skirt of my maxi dress and lifted it up.

"Hey—wait."

"Shut up." I would have taken issue with his words if he hadn't dropped to his knees in front of me. He shoved the bunched skirt into my hands. "Hold this." His touch was light as he surveyed the angry red slice.

"I'm fine."

He ignored my words. "Con do this?"

"Of course not!"

"No, I mean, did he glue you up?"

"Oh. Yeah. I was passed out. Don't remember anything after calling him." I hastily filled him in on the other hazy details of the night.

The hurt in his eyes at not being the one I called for help was obvious. "At least you had the sense to call someone." He pressed a kiss to my stomach beside the wound. "I owe Con then."

After a long moment, he stood. I dropped the bunched fabric, once again covering the evidence of my idiocy.

"You got knifed, but still put on a dress to come apologize." He sounded a little awed.

Embarrassment flushing my cheeks, I bit my lip and stared at the ground. "Yeah."

He tilted my chin up again and leaned down to kiss me. Just the barest brush of his lips across mine. And then he kissed my bruise.

When he pulled away, his expression was serious. "For a first fight, that was a doozy."

"So we're good now?" I asked.

Simon nodded. "We're good."

"I guess getting knifed means no makeup sex?" I asked, trying to interject some humor into the intense moment. But my statement knocked another question loose. "Why did you think I had sex with Con?"

"Saw your ... goodbye on the street this afternoon." His jaw tightened. "It was ... pretty friendly."

"That's because Con *is* a friend. I'm not going to apologize for my history with him. You just ... need to get over it."

"Let's just say I'm still working on it." Simon threaded his fingers through mine. "How do you feel about dinner?"

"I could eat."

"Then let's get out of here."

"Don't you need to talk to your dad?"

"No. Whatever he's got to say will keep."

I took a deep breath and chose my words carefully. I was going to let him in. A little. Starting now. "You're lucky, in the same situation, my dad would've gotten very quiet and given you this look that would have shriveled your balls to raisins. And after you'd slunk out of his office, he would've smiled like nothing had happened and continued on with the conversation he intended."

Simon stilled. "You've never talked about your parents before."

I kept my eyes trained on the floor, terrified I was giving too much away. "They're not a part of my life anymore. They're not … the nicest people. Especially my dad. And my mom … well, she only ever really cared about keeping up appearances. We were never close."

He lifted my hand to his lips and pressed a kiss to the inside of my wrist. "Thank you. For telling me that."

I finally met his eyes and shrugged. "I'm trying."

"I know. And that matters. A whole hell of a lot."

I tugged him toward the door. I needed to change the subject before I was tempted to tell him everything. "Feed me."

"Whatever the lady wants."

I smiled, but it felt forced. My confession had unsettled me. And what's more, I couldn't stop thinking about what his dad had said about Simon's campaign getting off the ground. How the hell could I stay out of the spotlight and hold on to Simon at the same time? *You can't,* the realist in my head whispered. The bitch was undoubtedly right. But I wasn't giving up yet.

charlie

Simon was holding out on me, and it was starting to piss me off. Correction: I *was* pissed off.

No sex.

For two weeks.

It wasn't like he and I were engaging in all out Sexual Olympics before I decided to make poor life choices, but now there was nothing. Simon was adamant about me not doing anything too taxing, which apparently included all forms of sexual activity, until he was satisfied that I was fully recovered. I supposed I should be happy that we were, after our first fight, firmly back in the honeymoon phase. Except honeymoons included sex. Well, honeymoons without knife wounds did.

Granted, I had much bigger things to worry about, but focusing on the sexual drought I was experiencing was easier. Safer. And if it made me a coward, I could live with that. For now.

I'd worked tirelessly trying to make progress with the notebook. I'd even considered asking Con for help. But I couldn't do it. It wasn't that I didn't trust him, but the need for secrecy was crushing. People would kill for the information I had. I was pretty damn certain of that.

I also considered telling Simon the truth more times than I could count. But just the thought of admitting to all of my lies had bile rising up in my throat and eating away the words like battery acid.

"If you keep begging, I'm going to make you wait longer."

I glared at him. "I'm fine."

We were sitting on the couch in his den, watching a movie. *A movie*. Like high school freshmen on a handholding-only date.

"You're pretty hot when you're pissed."

"Then you're going to think I'm goddamn gorgeous if you won't fuck me tonight. Why am I the guy in this relationship? Why can't you be as hard up for it as I am?"

Simon's smile turned sinister. "Did you really just call me the girl in this relationship?"

"Hell yes, I did. You're giving me a complex."

He shook his head slowly. "Charlie, you really are something else." He reached behind the sofa and produced a large box. "If I were the girl in this relationship, I think you'd be giving this to me and not the other way around." He set it in my lap.

"What is that?"

"A present."

"But why?"

"Just open it, okay?"

I looked down at the blue box with black lettering. It was from a fabulous boutique specializing in 1950s and rockabilly dresses. Eighteen months ago I could have bought the whole store; now, I could only afford to look.

As excited as I wanted to be about what was probably inside the box, I feared we'd end up at another impasse. Or worse, another fight. "Simon—"

"Just open the damn box, Charlie."

I lifted the lid and handed it to him. I parted the tissue paper to reveal a gorgeous red dress and a black and red-feathered mask. I lifted the dress out. It was one I had drooled over in the window—ruched sweetheart neckline, thick straps and a full skirt. It was fabulous.

My heart sank as I lifted my eyes to Simon's face. He wasn't smiling.

"I'm not giving you an ultimatum. I'm simply extending an invitation. I would love to have you next to me on the Fourth, but if you can't, I'll get over it. What I won't get over is losing you again."

I squeezed my eyes shut against the sting of tears. He lifted the box from my lap and folded the dress and put it back inside. Once again the words of confession bubbled up inside of me. But when Simon pulled me close and tucked me against him, the thud of his heartbeat and my desperate need to savor the moment pushed them back down.

I am a coward. A lying coward who doesn't deserve him.

simon

I stood on the deck of the Steamboat Orleans and sipped my scotch. Derek stood next to me, leaning against the railing. We hadn't seen much of each other since his wedding in May. Between his honeymoon and newlywed status, and my chasing after Charlie, we'd lost touch. But he was here tonight because I'd asked him to come. I was still holding out hope that the other person I'd asked to come would show up. Because of the fireworks, the Orleans was staying docked all evening. There would be no excuse of missing the boat. I'm not sure if that made it better or worse.

"Your dad's in fine form this evening," Derek said. He was scanning the crowd for Mandy. She'd gone off to the ladies room to readjust her mask. Apparently, it was ruining her hairstyle.

I tipped my scotch back, swallowing a healthy swig. "Ain't that the truth."

My father had arranged for Arthur Jackson, his choice for a campaign manager, to attend. They'd cornered me for an interminable fifteen minutes before I could escape to the bar. I was here tonight to support two great causes—and to help gain support for my own. I wasn't here to talk about campaign tactics or fundraising or any other bullshit that my dad threw at me at every opportunity. It wasn't even time to officially kick off the campaign, and I was already sick of it all. The urge to tell my father to forget it was strong and growing stronger every day. Local politics was one thing, but the idea of jetting off to D.C. and kissing every ass on Capitol Hill to accomplish anything left a sour taste in my mouth.

I couldn't hold my tongue when I thought something was bullshit. I called a spade a spade. I didn't know how my father had done it. He had some higher need for intrigue, machinations, and manipulation that I didn't share. I'd entertained the possibility because he was so damn invested in it. I'd never been a disappointment to my father, but in this, I would be. It was time for him to face facts: I was not cut out to be a career politician.

Gut instinct told me it was the right decision. And once I'd made it, I could focus on the things I actually wanted to do: keep running day-to-day operations of Southern Cross, continue improving my hometown on the NOLA City Council, push forward with The Kingman Project, and figure out what a future with Charlie was going to look like.

I tossed back the rest of my scotch. I'd have to tell him tonight before he got any further down the road of campaigning on my behalf.

"Well, holy shit. Would you take a look at that?" Derek said.

I followed his gaze to the dock. A woman was strolling up to the boat wearing a siren red dress and black and red-feathered mask. Waves of black, red, and purple hair bounced with each step.

I dropped my empty glass on the tray of a passing server. "I believe that's my date."

Derek slapped my shoulder. "Better go after her before the sharks start circling."

Several heads had craned in Charlie's direction as she made her way up to the ship. Shit. She looked amazing. I pressed through the crowd to meet her at the railing as she stepped onto the deck.

"You're here."

She nodded. Her aqua eyes stood out even more brilliantly against the feathers of her mask. I bent to kiss her cheek, not wanting to smear her crimson lips.

"You look beautiful."

"Thank you. And I never thanked you properly for the dress. So thank you for that too."

Charlie had fallen asleep in my arms that night without making it to the end of the movie. I'd carried her to my bed and tucked her in beside me. She'd been gone when I awoke, but the dress box had been missing as well. It had given me hope. Between my work schedule and hers, we hadn't managed to see each other again until tonight. We'd spoken briefly last night, but the conversation had been awkward and stilted. Both of us dancing around the subject of tonight, and neither of us having the balls to bring it up. *But she was here.*

"You're very welcome. Can I get you a drink?"

"Open bar?" she asked.

"Cash bar—it's a fundraiser, babe."

"Then you're buying."

"Done."

We ate, mixed, mingled, and bid on silent auction items. Charlie charmed everyone she met. She had a knack for small talk and putting people at ease I'd never noticed before. If I was still considering a life as a politician, I couldn't have picked a better conversationalist. It was like she was born to work a room. But I didn't give a fuck about her ability to make small talk; I was just happy that she seemed to be enjoying the event and had instantly connected with Kingman's widow. Although I guess I should call her Carina. Her husband was another active duty sailor. I gave her credit for taking the same risk again. Not everyone would be quite so brave.

I purposely maneuvered us away from my parents, not because I didn't think Charlie could handle my father, but because I didn't want him to piss me off and ruin the night. I'd say what I needed to say to him tomorrow. It would be soon enough.

Then I saw a familiar head of blond hair in the crowd. *Vanessa.* She had accompanied her father this evening, and I could hear his booming laugh from across the ship. He was a bull of a man who liked to keep everyone and everything under his thumb.

Charlie must have recognized Vanessa bearing down on us, because she said, "Should I be concerned that the claws are going to come out since I stole her man?"

I frowned. "Vanessa's not like that. At all. So sheathe your claws, babe. She's good people. I think you'll like her."

With the mask obscuring her face, I couldn't exactly see Charlie's skeptical expression, but I knew it was there all the same.

My brow creased as I studied Vanessa. She was wobbling on her heels and her cheeks were flushed. She was drunk. Which was completely out of character. I'd never even seen her *tipsy* in public. Ever.

I reached out an arm to steady her. Charlie seemed to pick up on the unusual nature of the situation and held out a hand. "I'm Charlie. It's nice to finally meet you." Her words weren't snide; they were sincere and genuine, and I loved her for that.

"I've heard so much about you, Charlie. I'm so glad to finally meet you too." Vanessa's words slurred as she shook Charlie's hand. "You've found yourself a good man … don't let him get away."

She stumbled, and the clear liquid in her glass sloshed onto the deck, just missing Charlie's shoes. Another thing I'd never seen Vanessa do was drink hard liquor. Something was seriously fucked up.

"What's going on? You seem a little…"

"Drunk?" she finished for me. "Then mission accomplished."

Charlie and I worked as a unit to maneuver her into a corner.

"What the hell is going on, Vanessa?"

She downed the remainder of what smelled like a gin and tonic. She threw the glass over the railing into the river and wiped the back of her hand across her mouth. Her actions were all wrong. "Nothing you need to worry about, Simon."

I opened my mouth to continue questioning her, but Vanessa was looking over my shoulder at Royce Frost as he crossed the deck, presumably heading toward us. She leveled a relatively sober stare on me and said, "I think I've had enough festivities for the evening. It's time for me to go. Especially if you don't want my father to think you're still potential husband material."

Charlie and I exchanged a confused look.

"Let's get you cab then. Unless you want us to see you home," I offered.

"No, a cab is fine." She turned to Charlie and spoke softly. "Treat him right; he's one of the good ones."

Charlie glanced up at me and nodded. "I know."

We helped Vanessa down the gangway, across the private section of dock, and then through the masses of people filling the streets. After Vanessa climbed into the back seat, I paid the driver and gave him directions to take her home.

"I've never seen her like that. Something's definitely off," I said to Charlie, as we turned away from the street.

"Maybe you should check on her tomorrow? See if you can get a better sense of what's going on after she's had a chance to sober up?" Charlie suggested.

I squeezed her hand, happy that she'd not only sheathed her claws, but was concerned about Vanessa, a woman she'd previously considered a threat.

"That sounds like a plan."

We pushed through the crowd, but a fat bastard of a man shoved between us, breaking my hold.

"Charlie!" I spun, looking for her red dress as the mob of people carried her away from me like a riptide. When I finally caught sight of her, she was elbowing her way through the crowd, and her mask was gone.

I made my way toward her, and when I finally reached her, I swung her up in my arms.

"You okay?" I asked.

"Jesus, it's a freaking riot out there. You'd think it was Mardi Gras," she said, sucking in a breath. She gestured to her face. "Lost my mask. The elastic snapped, and I didn't want to risk looking for it. It's not worth getting trampled."

"Good call."

I hoisted her up higher so she had a better vantage point to see over the craziness, and we made our way back to the private dock. When we reached the less crowded space, I set Charlie down, and we both paused to right ourselves. A ginger-haired guy tried to follow us, but was stopped by an Orleans employee at the gate. He gestured wildly, but the security guard wouldn't let him pass. I hoped he wasn't a guest who'd misplaced his ticket. When he backed away and faded into the crowd, I assumed he was just another partier, wanting to get out of the craziness for a minute.

I watched Charlie as she shook her head—black, red, and purple waves falling into her face. She brushed them away as the first barrage of fireworks ripped through the night sky.

My mind veered to the last time we'd watched fireworks. I grabbed her hand and pulled her up the gangway and across the ship. Everyone's attention was on the sky, so no one noticed as I led Charlie down two sets of stairs and into a dark, empty room on the lower deck. Given the relatively small size of the event tonight, only the upper decks were in use.

The glow from the dockside windows streaked through the shadows, creating pockets of light.

"Simon, what the hell? I thought we'd watch—"

"Oh, we are. But I want a repeat of last time."

She spun to face me, her face half in shadow, half in light. "We can't! Not here."

"After all your bitching about no sex, are you really going to shoot me down?" Venturing farther into the room, I picked a dark section between two tables with a view of the river and the fireworks exploding overhead.

"When you put it like that—" Charlie started.

I cupped her face and kissed her bold red lips, stealing her words. She tasted like champagne and sin. Her hands clutched the shoulders of my linen suit, and I wanted her to wrinkle the hell out of it. I skimmed my hands down her back and under the skirt of her dress. Sliding my palms up the backs of her thighs, I gripped her ass and pulled her hard against me.

"You feel that? You ever think I don't want you? You're crazy, babe." She flexed her hips into me. I took that as her assent and tugged at the sides of her lacy panties until they dropped to the floor and she stepped out of them. She bent to grab them and shoved them in my pocket. Her next words told me she was fully on board with my plan.

"I'm hoping I won't be able to remember my name, let alone my panties, after you're done with me."

"Jesus, Charlie." My hard-on pulsed against my suit pants as she dragged me down for another deep, drugging kiss. I pulled her hands away from my face and spun her toward a table. "This time, I'm in charge, sweetheart. After all, you did challenge my manhood."

She shuddered at my words, and I pressed her against the table with a hand to her back. She moaned at the contact. Leaning over her, I whispered in her ear. "You gotta hold those hot little moans in, baby. You think you can do that?"

She only nodded in response. "Good girl."

I pushed up the skirt of her dress and the sight of her gorgeous ass had me struggling to hold in a groan. I wanted to spend the rest of my life memorizing her every curve. She fisted the white tablecloth as I nudged her feet apart. Another whisper into her ear. "That's right, sweetheart. Hold on tight. This is going to be hard and fast."

She arched her back, pushing her ass against me. Urging me on. I could only imagine what she'd be saying if we weren't worried about being discovered. It'd be something filthy, and I'd fucking love it.

I freed myself from my pants and cupped her between her legs to find her hot and slick and ready. She pressed her face into the tablecloth as I slid two fingers inside her. A low moan escaped her lips. My answering groan was strangled in my throat. "Shhh, baby. I'm going take care of you, don't worry."

I fit the head of my cock against her entrance and thrust home. Because that was exactly what Charlie had become for me. Home.

charlie

Simon didn't let his inner caveman out to play often, but when he did, *watch out.*

I loved the heat of his palm against my back, pressing me into the table, the way he handled my body so confidently, as if he had no doubt that he was going to give me exactly what I wanted. What I needed.

And I had no doubt that he would. Simon was everything I needed.

I bit the inside of my mouth to keep from moaning his name when he finally pushed inside me. My fingers curled into the tablecloth, and I tried to hold on to my sanity and keep my silence. Thrust after thrust, hard, soft, slow, fast, shallow, deep. I couldn't keep up with his pace, couldn't latch on to a pattern, just reveled in the sensations overtaking me. I turned my head toward the window where fireworks burst in the air and trails of red, blue, green, and white sparkled and descended to the dark river.

My eyes fluttered shut as my body tensed. Simon reached around me, slipping a hand between my legs. With a press of his thumb to my clit, the orgasm tore through me, and I could see nothing but the bursts of color in my mind as I detonated.

Simon, being the Southern gentleman, produced a handkerchief from his pocket to clean us up, and helped me step back into my underwear. I may not have forgotten my name—I'd tried for months without success—but I'd had an epiphany. He needed to know everything. I owed it to him. And then he could make his choice about whether or not he wanted me in his life. I knew what I wanted. I just needed to get him home and lay it all out.

The party was winding down after the firework display had concluded. We crossed the deck, ready to depart, when Simon's mother flagged us down. She was concerned about his father making his way off the ship by himself. Simon steadied his dad, and we headed down to the private dock where dozens of cameras were flashing just beyond the railing. I reached up to touch my face and froze. No mask. But it wouldn't have mattered anyway. The volley of questions hit me like a slap in the face.

"Charlotte—how long have you been in New Orleans?"

"Charlotte—where's the money?"

"Ms. Agoston—why aren't you cooperating with the FBI?"

It was like I was stumbling down the courthouse steps all over again, determined to outrun the stigma of my name. My stomach knotted, and even in the hot, humid Louisiana night, a cold weight settled over me.

A youngish redheaded man, apparently with balls of steel, jumped the rail and strode toward us. "I knew it was you. I saw you first! I deserve the exclusive."

For destroying my carefully constructed life? He deserved nothing but a stiletto to the groin. Instead of carrying through with my thought, I focused on the obvious. But I couldn't form the right question.

"H … how…? I don't—"

"Out in the crowd earlier. I saw you. I didn't even think it was really you at first, so I followed you back to the boat. I spent weeks watching you and your mother come in and out of the courtroom. And then hours studying you on the stand. I was interning at *The Post*. My boss was covering your dad's trial. He was cool enough to let me tag along for all of it." He paused. "It was your eyes first. And then your face. You just don't forget those Agoston eyes."

"But—"

He continued, "Shouldn't have fucking said anything, but I told my editor I had the story of the year, if he'd let me run with it. Don't know how the rest of these vultures heard. Grapevine, I guess."

"Get the fuck back before I throw you off this dock, boy." Simon's voice was harsh, promising violence. It had the intended effect. The redhead scuttled back and hopped the fence before an Orleans employee could grab him.

Outted by an overzealous intern. It was almost as ridiculous as Al Capone going down for tax evasion.

Simon dropped my hand and stared down at me, assessing my every feature with new intensity. Everyone and everything else—the voices, the flashes—fell away. There was nothing but Simon. There was also nothing I could say to fix this.

He was a stranger again. The one who'd met me at the door to his office. His expression was stony, and his hazel eyes gave nothing away as they stripped me bare.

I straightened, trying to prepare myself for what I knew was coming. My heart was already cracking. But I'd brought this on myself. I could have told him weeks ago. Months ago. But I'd chosen not to.

The muscles in his jaw clenched as he reached for a section of my hair. He shook his head and yanked his hand back without touching me.

"Simon … I—"

"Why?" The quiet word rasped over me and scraped me raw. "Why didn't you just tell me? If you think I would've cared, that it would have made a damn bit of difference, you don't know me at all."

"Can we not do this here?" I begged.

He ignored my plea and continued.

"I would have protected you, hid you away from the world, if that's what you wanted. But you didn't trust me. Not even with something as simple as your goddamn name." He paused, inhaling a harsh breath. "I thought you coming here tonight meant something. Meant that this was finally real. But it was never real, was it?" His lips quirked up in a mockery of a smile. "Can't have love without trust, Charlotte."

His words, punctuated with the use of my real name, were a blade between my ribs. The shaft of pain through my heart stole any response I could muster.

Jefferson Duchesne shoved his way between Simon and me, popping the bubble that had formed around us. He pitched his words low, but they still hit me like an uppercut to the gut. "You can't be seen with her. You need to put as much distance between you and her as you possibly can. She'll ruin everything."

The words ricocheted through my brain.

Ruin everything. Ruin everything. Ruin everything.

And he was right. I owed Simon more than that. Simon turned to his father, and I did what I did best.

I ran.

simon

I flung open the door of Voodoo, eyes searching for the one person I knew I wouldn't find. But I didn't know where else to look.

It all happened so damn fast. The press, their questions, the intern. The truth of who she was slamming into me. *Charlotte Agoston.* Person of interest according to the FBI. Missing former society princess. Daughter of the universally hated Alistair Agoston. All of the questions I'd had for months answered in a single moment. Unfortunately not by Charlie.

Weeks ago I'd point blank asked her if she was in trouble, if she was running from someone. Her answer was something along the lines of 'not exactly.'

It seemed our definitions of trouble were wildly different. But even that, I didn't care about. What I cared about was the fact that while I'd been trying to process what the fuck I'd just learned, and placating my father, I'd turned my back for a moment—and she'd run. *She'd fucking run.* From me.

Maybe my words had been harsh, but *Jesus Christ*, she needed to cut a guy some slack when he'd just been blindsided by the fact that the woman he was in love with was living under a false identity. But before I could get a grip on the situation and tell her, unequivocally, that we'd deal with this together, *she'd run.*

And I already knew she was damn good at that. If she didn't want to be found, she wouldn't be.

As soon as I'd shepherded my parents past the swarm of reporters and gotten them into their car, I'd gone on the hunt.

I didn't give a damn what her name was. Charlie and I weren't done, and I wasn't letting her run from me. From us.

I'd come up empty at Harriet's. No answer to the buzzers I'd pressed at least a hundred times. I vaguely recalled Charlie mentioning Harriet was going to an art festival up north somewhere over the holiday.

I didn't know where Yve lived, so that left Voodoo and Con. I swallowed my pride as I crossed the black and white checkered floor. I slapped my hands down on the graffiti-covered counter, and both tattoo guns stopped buzzing. Con rose, and a deep bark echoed from the back.

Huck.

My heart lodged in my throat, and I headed for the break room; Con blocked the hallway.

"She's not here."

"I don't believe you. Her dog's here."

"He is, but she's not."

"Then where the fuck is she?" I barely restrained myself from grabbing him by the neck and shaking him.

"Gone."

"Where? Just fucking tell me where." My words sounded like a plea. If I had to humble myself to get answers, I would.

"From what I heard, you weren't incredibly understanding when it all shook out."

"And you were?"

"I'm not blind and in love. I knew exactly who she was within a week of laying eyes on her."

"She told you?" The stab of betrayal was swift.

"No. And she didn't know I knew until she got herself knifed."

I squeezed my eyes shut and gripped the back of my neck. The words tasted like ash, but I had to say them. "Please don't jack me around, Con. I need to find her."

"Told you man, she's long gone. Besides, you being with her isn't exactly a winning campaign strategy."

"There's no campaign. I'm not running." It felt good to say the words aloud. The feeling just reinforced that I'd made the right decision.

"Because of her?"

"No, because of me. It might've taken me a while to figure it out, but this is my life. I get one go 'round, and I'm going to fucking live it how I want. And to do that, I need her."

The conversation with my father hadn't been pleasant, but it had been necessary. It was unlikely he'd be speaking to me for a while. Hell, he might even fire me. But all of that, with time, could be salvaged. What I had with Charlie … I needed to find her before she slipped away again, and this time for good.

Con nodded. "You just might do, then. Come on." He strode down the hallway and pushed open the door of the break room. I followed him, because I didn't know what else to do.

Huck stood in his crate and barked as we entered. Just seeing him made my chest ache. It would have killed her to leave him behind, and I could have spared her the pain.

"How'd she get him here?"

"I helped." Con pulled open a desk drawer and produced an envelope. "She left this for you." I ripped it from his hand. "Feel free to hang out while you read it. If you still have any questions after … well, I'll tell you what I know." He headed for the door.

Dropping to my knees beside Huck, I tore open the envelope. Inside was a single sheet of paper with my name scrawled at the top. I devoured her words.

SIMON,

I DON'T DESERVE YOUR FORGIVENESS,
AND I WON'T ASK FOR IT. I'M SURE YOU
SEE NOW THAT BEING WITH ME WOULD
HAVE DESTROYED ANY CHANCE OF THE
FUTURE YOU'VE PLANNED. I HOPE I
DIDN'T DESTROY IT ANYWAY. THAT
WOULD BE EVEN MORE UNFORGIVABLE.

BELIEVE IT OR NOT, I TRIED TO TELL AS
FEW LIES AS POSSIBLE. STILL, THERE
WERE TOO MANY TO COUNT. BUT MY
FEELINGS FOR YOU WERE PROBABLY
THE MOST HONEST THING IN MY LIFE. I
MIGHT NOT HAVE ANY RIGHT TO YOUR
LOVE, AND IT MIGHT BE STOLEN, BUT
IT'S MINE AND IT'S PRECIOUS AND YOU
CAN'T HAVE IT BACK. CONSIDERING I'M
LEAVING MY HEART WITH YOU, I'M
CALLING IT A FAIR TRADE.

YOURS,

CHARLIE

I dropped my head against the metal bars of Huck's crate, grateful I was already on my knees. The words were unapologetically Charlie. After reading it three more times, I pushed to my feet and turned to the door. Con was standing there, watching me. I should have hated him seeing my lowest moment, but I couldn't bring myself to care. Every thought and emotion was focused on Charlie. *Finding her. Bringing her back to me.*

"Where is she?" I would beg if I had to. And if that didn't work, I'd beat it out of him.

"She went to make things right."

218

"What the hell does that mean?"

"It's what she said when she tossed a backpack into my Tahoe and handed me that letter. I assumed she meant she was going back to New York to turn herself over to the FBI."

A solid chunk of ice formed in my gut. "And you let her go?"

"Didn't have a choice. You ever try to stop that woman from doing anything?"

He had a point. I looked at my watch. It was just past one o'clock in the morning. I could get a flight out first thing tomorrow. Or maybe I could charter a private plane and get there sooner…

Con interrupted my thoughts. "Taking a wild guess, but you're thinking about how fast you can get to New York."

I met his stare. "Wouldn't you be?"

"Sure, I'd want to. But what are you really going to be able to do for her? Hold her hand while they slide the cuffs on? You'd be better served sending her a lawyer than going yourself."

Again, he had a point. But I could do both. I wasn't letting her face this by herself. No way in hell.

Then Delilah popped her head around the corner and added her two cents. "I think it's all very white knight of you to want to go rescue her, but did you ever think that maybe this is something she needs to do herself? I mean, you didn't see her when she left. Charlie was *determined*. She's nobody's fool, and she doesn't need anyone holding her purse while she tells the FBI to go to hell."

"I don't care if all I do is stand behind her so she knows she's not alone in this anymore. I'm going."

Con smirked. "Yeah, you just might do, Duchesne."

I threw random shit into my overnight bag and checked my watch. It'd been four hours since I'd last seen Charlie, and it was still four hours until my flight. I'd be in New York by nine.

I didn't care how long I'd have to cool my heels on a bench in front of the FBI field office; I'd be there when she showed up. And then I'd talk some fucking sense into her. She wasn't going within fifty yards of the FBI without a shark of a lawyer at her side and me at her back.

My cell buzzed from its perch on the nightstand. I lunged for it, hoping it was Charlie.

I looked down at the screen as I answered. *Mom?*

I tensed. A phone call at three AM from my mother couldn't mean anything good.

"Mom? Is everything okay?"

It was my father's voice that replied. "I need you to come to the house."

I ran for the stairs.

"What happened?"

There was no answer. He'd already hung up.

I slammed out the door and raced across the lawn. I heard sirens wailing in the distance. They were growing louder and louder.

Oh fuck.

I ripped open the front door and sprinted up the stairs to my parents' bedroom.

My dad was holding my mother against his chest, tears running down his face. He was speaking softly to her unconscious form.

"Maggie, please. You've got to wake up, my love." They were the pleas of a desperate man.

I dropped to my knees beside the bed.

"What happened?"

"I don't know. She woke me up. Her face looked funny. Then she passed out. I think … I think it was a stroke. I called 911. And then you." The words tumbled disjointedly from his lips.

He rocked my mother's still body in his arms. "Maggie … please."

The sirens blared from the street. I didn't want to leave them, but I knew someone had to let the paramedics in.

"I'll be right back. With help."

I clung to the railing as I stumbled down the stairs. The thick, jasmine-scented night air clogged my lungs. I focused on the flashing red and white lights. I opened the gate and gripped the wrought iron with both hands as the ambulance surged up to the front of the house. I pulled myself together, knowing I needed to be my father's strength. I'd never seen him look so lost and broken.

I couldn't lose her, too. Not my mother.

I released my grasp on the metal bars and ran back toward the house to lead the EMTs up the stairs.

One thing was certain: I wasn't going to New York.

charlie

Twenty-four hours was a long time to think about all of the things you could have done differently. *Should've* done differently. By the time I pulled into long-term parking at JFK, I was ready to stop replaying all of the moments I could have spoken up and told Simon the truth. I couldn't take back the choices I'd made, and now I had to live with them.

I left the keys in Con's magnetic case under the back bumper. I wasn't sure if he'd actually come get it or not, but it was the plan we'd agreed on. I would have offered to return it myself, but I think we both knew I might not be coming back. Harriet was holding on to all of my stuff, but I wasn't holding my breath. My lack of progress with the composition book, along with my strong suspicions about what it contained, made me wary of what I was about to do. But I was running out of options. As much as I wanted to consider the possibility, I couldn't run forever.

I worked my way through the busy station to board a train toward Manhattan. Even though I had been a lifelong New Yorker, this was my very first subway ride. Like my first flight in coach—it wasn't something I was proud of. I could only hope this wouldn't be my last new adventure as a free woman.

I made one detour before re-boarding the train toward Federal Plaza. I rubbed my sweaty hands against my jeans as I ran through my plan. After what felt like a million stops, I exited the subway carrying only my real license and a hundred dollars in cash.

It was strange to be back in New York. It smelled different than New Orleans. The people were all rushing around with places to go. No one moved at the leisurely pace to which I'd become accustomed.

I looked down at my outfit. I had dressed up for the occasion: black skinny jeans and Chucks paired with my vintage Black Sabbath Heaven + Hell Tour T-shirt. It reminded me that I'd been duped just like everyone else. It was a subtle proclamation of my innocence.

I walked through the metal detector, ignored the curious stares, and ducked into the elevator. On the twenty-third floor, I stepped out and stared at the glass doors in front of me. Once I stepped through those doors, my choice would be irrevocable. I squeezed my eyes shut and fought the urge to turn around, get back in the elevator, and keep running. I knew how to disappear. I could do it again. I could start over somewhere else.

I pressed a hand against the cool glass. It was time to stop running.

I pushed the door open.

At the reception desk, an older woman with silver streaks in her dark hair perched on a chair. She held up a finger and gestured to her headset. I waited until she transferred the call and looked up again.

"Can I help you?" Her expression was skeptical as she took in my full sleeves and choice of apparel.

"I'd like to see one of the special agents in charge, please." She raised an eyebrow at my request.

"Do you have an appointment?"

"I'm pretty sure I don't need one."

She shifted in her chair, looking like she was five seconds away from calling security.

"Excuse me?"

"My name is Charlotte Agoston. I believe they'd like to speak with me."

I sat in a small, windowless room with the requisite one-way mirror. For a moment I wondered who was behind it, but then decided it didn't matter. I would say only what I intended to say, regardless of the questions asked.

The door opened, and a barrel-chested man in a navy blue suit, white shirt, and red striped tie walked in. A second, taller man in a similar uniform followed. The first man held out his hand.

"Lou Childers, Special Agent in Charge."

I shook his hand and watched his eyes rake over my tattoos.

"Those real?"

I smiled. "As real it gets."

He nodded. "You did a good job staying under the radar. You're a tough woman to find."

"I was just trying to get on with my life."

"So, New Orleans?" he asked.

"It seemed like as good a place as any."

"Never been. But Mardi Gras always looked like a fun time."

"It is."

I put an end to the small talk.

"So, you have questions."

"That we do." His entire demeanor shifted.

He read me my *Miranda* rights, and shit got real.

simon

"What do you mean you can't get in to see her?" I tried to keep my voice low as I paced the hallway of the intensive care wing. A woman in flower print scrubs stared at me as she hurried down the hallway. My attempt at outward calm was failing.

"Mr. Duchesne," Andrew Ivers's tone was cool and professional, "unless Ms. Agoston affirmatively requests an attorney, there's nothing I can do. I have a junior associate sitting in the lobby, waiting to call me the moment we have any indication that she has exercised her right to counsel."

The thought that Charlie hadn't asked for a lawyer made me hope that things weren't as bad as I was imaging. She was smart. I was pretty damn sure if things went sideways, she'd ask for one. Still, Ivers had fucked up my well-orchestrated plan.

"You were supposed to stop her from going in alone." I raked a hand through my already disheveled hair. "I don't understand what the fuck happened."

Ivers paused before speaking, as if choosing his words carefully. "We sincerely apologize. I had another urgent client matter, and the associate I sent over this morning was detained. He was there by nine o'clock, but she must have gotten there first."

I blew out a frustrated breath. "Well, she has to leave sometime, so you better have someone there, waiting. I don't care what your associate has to say to them. He better make it fucking clear to the FBI that your firm represents her, and she's not being questioned again without a lawyer present."

"I'll send a second associate down, just to be certain."

"Just make sure they don't fuck it up again. Hell, after this morning, I'd expect you to go take care of it yourself."

"As I said, you have our sincerest apologies, Mr. Duchesne." He sounded like his teeth were grinding when he added, "I'd be happy to go wait myself. I'll be in touch as soon as we've made contact with Ms. Agoston."

Ending the call, I sagged against the wall. I bent my knees and slid down the plaster until I sat on the industrial gray linoleum. Resting my elbows on my knees, I dropped my head into my hands.

I wasn't sure how much more I could handle.

My mother was down the hall, in a coma, hooked up to too many beeping machines. The doctors had run all sorts of tests and had shared theories and ideas, but the bottom line: all we could do was wait.

I didn't know if I could take another day of sitting across from my father. With each hour that passed without any sign of improvement, he looked more and more like a shell of the man he'd been.

My father had always been larger than life. Confident. In command. But this experience had exposed him as all too human. For two days I'd listened to him speak to my mother's unconscious form while clutching her hand, and I'd come to realize that much of my father's strength stemmed from his love for my mother. And without her standing next to him, he was ... broken.

I pushed up off the floor and started back down the hall. I'd give him another few hours and then I'd try, once again, to convince him to go home, shower, and get some rest. So far, we'd both been terrified to leave her side for more than a few moments at a time, certain that without us there, she'd just slip away.

Settling myself back into my chair at my mother's bedside, I listened to my father launch into another trip down memory lane. This time about how angry Mom had been when Dad had laughed after she'd burned their first dinner as a married couple, and how he'd told her he'd eat charred meatloaf for the rest of his damned life and smile while it crunched. His quiet words washed over me, and I couldn't help but wonder if I'd have a chance to make those kinds of memories with Charlie. I stared down at my phone, willing it to ring.

It didn't.

charlie

There are experiences in life that make you question everything you thought you knew about yourself.

Like watching your father be led away in handcuffs after learning that he *allegedly* committed the largest financial fraud in the history of the world.

Like arriving in a new city, a fake ID in your pocket, and realizing the rest of your life would be built on a lie.

Like meeting someone who made you want more than the half-life you'd thought would be enough.

Like today. Today had made me question everything.

My strength, my fortitude, my intelligence, my sanity.

I sat huddled on a steel bench in "the bin" at Rikers Island, my body shuddering as the adrenaline seeped away. I brought my knees up and wrapped my arms around them. Tears tracked down my aching face to soak into the gray cotton of my jumpsuit. My left eye had already swelled shut.

The last eighteen hours had taken me down the rabbit hole, and I was fairly certain I would never find my way back. And let me tell you, this rabbit hole was fucking scary.

How did I find myself in solitary at Rikers? I'd like to say it's a long story, but it really wasn't. It was the result of the dangerous combination of my own arrogance and ignorance.

I'd been so cocky and self-assured as I'd sat in the interrogation room at the FBI field office, making my demands before I'd deign to speak to them about what I knew. I could only imagine how stupid they'd thought I was.

First lesson learned today: an immunity, or proffer, agreement didn't mean shit. I'd confidently signed my name—my real name—across the bottom and told the FBI the locker number and combination where they could find the notebook, along with my backpack. Nine hours of questioning later, Childers had said we were done. I'd stood to leave, but the door had opened and two of New York's Finest had walked in. When I looked questioningly at Childers, one of the officers had said: "You're under arrest for conspiracy to commit grand larceny in the first degree." He'd followed those chilling words with another recitation of my *Miranda* rights.

Second lesson learned today: if the FBI wasn't done questioning you, but didn't want to let you go because they were afraid you'd run, they'd contact the district attorney and have state law charges filed against you. Childers was kind enough to explain this to me as the cold metal of the handcuffs closed around my wrists.

Third lesson learned today: I didn't deserve Simon. He'd once again proven he was too good for me. As the two NYPD officers were leading me through the lobby, a distinguished-looking man in a pricey tailored suit had stopped them.

"My name is Andrew Ivers," he'd said. "Simon Duchesne has arranged for me to represent you, Ms. Agoston. I apologize for not intercepting you on your way into the building this morning."

I'd wondered if I would have listened to him even if he had stopped me earlier. But it didn't matter. What was done was done.

Ivers had exchanged a few words with Childers and was up to speed within moments. He'd promised to be present at my arraignment.

Yeah.

My arraignment.

It didn't get any more real than that.

After a short ride in the backseat of a police car, the officers hauled me into a precinct where I was booked—fingerprints, mug shot, the works. Then I was shuttled to Central Booking at the New York City Criminal Court for further processing. After being shoved into a holding cell with a dozen other women who, from the looks of them, were primarily hookers and crack addicts, I waited. And waited. A few hours later I was escorted into a courtroom that looked altogether too much like the one I had escaped from over a year before. The difference between then and now? I wasn't leaving this room a free woman.

The arraignment hadn't lasted more than five minutes. Ivers and the prosecutor had spoken rapidly, firing words at the judge. I caught phrases like *one-ninety-fifty* and *remand*. It was yet another code I couldn't crack. All too quickly, I was being led out of the courtroom, and Ivers had followed me into a small room. His explanation of what had just happened, and what was going to happen next, had scared the hell out of me.

I'd been denied bail. Ivers had argued for an astronomical figure, but given the flight risk I presented, the judge had been resolute.

Nothing Ivers could have said would have prepared me for the reality of being chained to the arm of another woman as the bus chugged toward Rikers and then, upon arrival, being stripped of my clothes and my dignity. But three things he'd said stuck with me. First, his phone number, not that I could make calls from the bin. Second, Simon had ordered him to do whatever he could to help me. And third, I only had to endure this hell for 144 hours. Then they either had to indict me or conduct a preliminary hearing in front of a judge. Six days. I could survive anything for six days. I hoped. The second bit of information was all that was holding me together at that moment. The knowledge that even though he knew everything, Simon hadn't given up on me yet. Which meant I wasn't giving up either.

I wanted to smile at the thought of Simon, but my busted lip hurt too much. I rested my chin on my bent knees and tried to block out the woman screaming obscenities at me from where she was locked across the hall. It hadn't taken more than twenty minutes for shit to unravel once I'd been escorted to the large bunkroom-type cell. I could still hear the ripple of whispers as my identity was passed from one inmate to the next. And then Bertha, as I'd dubbed her, had stepped up and told me that no skinny, rich, poser bitch was going to look sideways at her. I was still having a *what the fuck are you talking about* moment when her Mack truck of a fist had connected with my cheekbone. White spots had burst in my vision as she'd tackled me to the floor. The guards had been slow to pull her off me, and my scalp stung where she had ripped out a chunk of my hair. I'd gotten a few elbows in, but there was no question that I'd been the loser in that exchange.

So we'd both been thrown in the bin. While it was considered harsh punishment, I was thankful to be by myself and felt relatively safe within these four gray concrete walls. If I was still in the bunkroom, I would've been afraid to close my eyes, regardless of the fatigue dragging me under. But in here, once I blocked out Bertha's threats, I could let myself drift off to sleep. Only 142 more hours to go…

simon

I stepped out of my mother's hospital room to answer my buzzing phone.

Ivers. I'd been waiting for him to call me all damn day.

"Please tell me you have good news."

He cleared his throat, and my stomach dropped when he hesitated before speaking.

"Mr. Duchesne, I would have called sooner, but I wanted to be able to give you a full picture of what we're dealing with here."

"What does that even mean?"

"Unfortunately, Ms. Agoston has been charged with conspiracy to commit grand larceny in the first degree, and was remanded into custody following her arraignment this evening."

My breath heaved out of my lungs like I'd been sucker-punched. I bent at the waist and tried to comprehend what the fuck Ivers was saying.

"What do you mean, remanded into custody? She's in jail?"

"Yes, Mr. Duchesne. She's at Rikers."

"What the fuck?" My hands shook, and my words echoed off the sterile white walls of the hallway. The charge nurse glared and made a cutting motion across her neck. For the second time today, I sank to the floor, weak-kneed. "Can't you get her out?"

"Mr. Duchesne, I pushed for the judge to set bail—even a ridiculous figure—and he refused. I have a meeting with Special Agent in Charge Childers tomorrow morning to discuss the information Ms. Agoston provided, and I'm hoping we can come to an agreement that will end with the state charges being dropped. We'll do everything we can to get her out, as quickly as possible."

Jesus Christ. What a clusterfuck. I closed my eyes and pictured Charlie in a prison jumpsuit. The dinner I'd choked down in the cafeteria threatened to come back up.

Ivers waited patiently for me to respond.

"Look, call me if anything changes. Day or night. Don't wait next time. I don't care if you don't have the full picture or not. I want to know everything, as it happens."

"Of course."

I ended the call, dropped my head back against the wall, and squeezed my eyes shut. Charlie was in jail, and my mother was in a coma. In a matter of days, my life had morphed into a waking nightmare.

My father shuffled out of my mother's room and jerked his head toward the bench across the hall.

"Sit with me?" he asked.

I pulled myself together and joined him on the teal and yellow flowered cushion.

My brain started firing again, and I thought about the connections my father still had. "Do you know anyone who's close with the governor of New York?"

His eyes widened. "What happened?"

"They arrested her." The words stuck in my throat, but I forced them out. "She's ... in jail. At Rikers. The judge denied bail."

My dad sat back and laced his fingers together on his lap.

"Is there any chance you're going to change your mind about running for my old seat?"

I stared at him, not sure where this was going. "If you tell me that you'll only get her out if I agree to run, then…"

He unlaced his fingers, twisted toward me, and dropped a hand on my shoulder. "No, I wouldn't force a choice like that on you. But the fact that you think I could makes it clear you don't think all that highly of me right now. But that's something for another day. My point is that if there was any chance you were going to change your mind, she would make an already difficult road impassable."

"I'm not changing my mind."

"Okay. So tell me—what are we up against?"

His matter of fact acceptance, even after I'd insulted him, humbled me.

I explained the situation, and once I'd finished, he rubbed a hand across his bristled jaw. "Shit."

"Yeah. I know."

"Do you want to go to New York?"

My eyes snapped to his. "I can't leave Mom. Not now. Not until we know…"

He nodded. "I know. Well, I can't make any calls right now, but I've got some ideas of whom I can contact in the morning. We'll see what we can do to get her out. And barring that, whatever we can do to keep her safe on the inside."

charlie

My six-inch thick steel cell door swung open, and the guard motioned for me to exit. I'd spent three days in segregation, and I was starting to lose my shit. I knew I should be happy that I'd been unmolested, but seventy-two hours by myself gave me too damn much time to think. I mostly thought about all of the places I should have run instead of New York. I'd been so naïve to think I could just show up, wave my magic notebook, and make everything better. Pride goeth and all that.

He led me through the maze of hallways to a guard station. It took me a few minutes but I caught on to the fact that I was being processed for a transfer. Whether this was a good thing or a bad thing, I wasn't certain. I saw the U.S. Marshals waiting for me on the other side of the door; I decided it was a bad thing.

No one bothered to correct my assumption.

We drove back to Manhattan, and my stomach knotted tighter with each mile. When they finally parked in a garage under the U.S. District Court, my dread grew. It multiplied when I was led in front of a federal magistrate judge, and he launched into his spiel.

The list of charges against me was so long, I couldn't keep up as he rattled them off.

Mail fraud, wire fraud, securities fraud, money laundering.

The charges that registered were all too familiar; my father had been convicted of them all. My very own worst-case scenario was playing out in a federal court. *Why hadn't I just kept running?* Because I'd wanted to make things right. And maybe I would. For everyone but myself.

As the magistrate judge rambled on about being appointed counsel if I couldn't afford my own, I knew I needed Ivers. ASAP. I needed someone to explain to me, using idiot-proof words, what the fuck was going to happen to me.

As soon as Ivers's name entered my thoughts, he was pushing through the doors of the courtroom. The judge dismissed me, and Ivers followed the Marshals as they led me out the back. We were escorted to a small room and Ivers shut the door. He pulled out his phone and started barking orders into it. When he ended his call, he sat down next to me.

My voice shook as I asked, "What the hell just happened?"

"In addition to conspiracy, you've been charged with several of the felonies of which your father was convicted."

"But why? I had nothing to do with it."

"Well, the information you turned over to the FBI seems to say differently."

"What are you talking about? I don't understand." My voice rose on the last words; I was barely holding it together.

The door opened.

Shit.

Cold fear snaked down my spine.

Michael Drake, the Assistant U.S. Attorney who'd eviscerated me on cross-examination during my father's trial, had joined the *burn Charlie at the stake* party.

"Well, Ms. Agoston, you're looking a little different than the last time I saw you." If I weren't handcuffed, I would have been tempted to slap the smug smirk off his face.

I didn't know how to respond to his taunting statement other than telling him to go fuck himself, so I kept my mouth shut.

"Let's cut through the BS and get down to why you've bothered to drag my client through this farce when we both know she didn't have anything to do with Agoston's scam."

Drake sat down across from us.

"The accounts in her name say otherwise."

The cold fear spread from my spine to envelop my entire body like an icy straight jacket. "Wh … what are you talking about?"

Drake's smile was triumphant. "So far, we've identified several accounts in your name in the Caymans and in Switzerland, courtesy of the little book you turned over to the FBI."

"How … how is that even possible?" I stammered, between shallow, panting breaths.

"You tell me, Charlotte."

"Cut the crap," Ivers said. "Her father did it. She wasn't involved. You know it, and I know it. Besides, if she was smart enough to pull this off, why the hell would she be dumb enough to put the accounts in her own name and turn over evidence to help the FBI find them?" Ivers sounded so calm and self-assured, but then, his entire life wasn't flashing before his eyes. I thought of the days I'd spent in the bin. *I can't do this. I can't do this.*

Drake's laugh could have been used as a track for an evil movie villain. "Lucky for me, I don't need to answer that question in order to send her to prison for the rest of her life. No jury on Earth is going to let her walk after they see the evidence."

I lunged for the garbage and threw up the rubbery chicken patty I'd been served for lunch. I dropped to my knees, gagging and spitting, resting my arms and handcuffed hands on the edge of the trashcan for support. My head spun, and the urge to pass out was pressing down on me. Part of me welcomed the darkness and the escape it would offer.

"Disgusting." Drake's snide tone pulled me out of my momentary stupor. Awareness rushed back in, along with an untapped inner reserve of strength. I had to get up. I was already ashamed that he'd brought me to my knees.

Ivers crossed the room and opened the door. "Could someone get us some water?"

I pushed up and stumbled to my feet, Ivers catching me by the arm and helping me back to my chair. A few seconds later he pressed a styrofoam cup into my hands. I drank slowly, not wanting to puke again.

I fumbled the cup to the table and took a moment to compose myself. The silence in the room was deafening. Or maybe it was just the blood rushing in my ears.

Finally, Ivers crossed his arms and leaned back in his chair. He continued the conversation with Drake as though nothing remarkable had happened.

"Are all of the accounts you've been able to identify in her name?"

I squeezed my eyes shut, not wanting to hear the answer that would send me running for the garbage can again. My heart thundered so loudly I almost missed Drake's self-satisfied, "Yes."

Tears burned my eyes, but I blinked them back. I was not going to let him see me cry.

"Do you suspect that all of the accounts are in her name?" Ivers asked, his cool tone completely at odds with the damning information he was hearing.

"No," Drake replied. "But it's a clear possibility at this point that dozens of them are." I clenched my hands together to stop the shaking.

"How long do you figure it's going to take you to cut through the red tape with all of these foreign banks and recover the money?"

Drake straightened, and looked down as he spun a cufflink. "It'll take some time, but we'll get there."

Ivers leaned forward, elbows resting on the table. "So the reason you ran down here so damn fast isn't because you want to cut a deal in exchange for Charlotte's help to recover the money? Because we both know if she's the one signing the withdrawal slips and approving the wire transfers, it'll take weeks rather than months or years of the red tape you'll be wading through to get it back."

Drake looked bored as he said, "We might be willing to discuss the possibility."

The icy grip clutching my chest receded a fraction. I reminded myself that with my recent luck, a deal could still mean years in prison. If not decades.

I held completely still, as if afraid any movement from me would derail whatever ground Ivers had just gained.

"Recovery of the funds from the accounts you identify in her name, but only if the subject bank is willing to cooperate, in exchange for full dismissal of the charges with prejudice. And no re-filing any state or federal charges arising out of, or related to, any aspect of Agoston's scheme," Ivers said.

"Full recovery of the funds," Drake shot back.

"With interest, even a partial recovery is going to approach the original amount Agoston took, and she can only get you money from accounts in her name identified by the FBI, and only if the bank cooperates. She can't agree to things that are outside of her control."

Drake leaned back in his chair, taking his time to mull over Ivers's words as if my future wasn't hanging in the balance.

"I don't know…" Drake drawled.

Ivers went in for the kill. "Would you prefer the media know that the DOJ has the ability to recover the money right now, and it's considering throwing that advantage away and taking years to accomplish the same result because it wants to prove a point by locking up one innocent girl?"

Drake's features were carved in stone. I held my breath as Ivers and I waited for his response.

"Let me make a call." Drake rose and left the room.

I sucked in huge breath and looked over at Ivers. "Is this really going to work?"

Ivers didn't hesitate. "Yes."

Sweet relief rushed through me for a beat before another thought struck me.

"Do ... do I have to go back to Rikers? Because ... I don't know if I can handle that."

He bit his bottom lip. The action was decidedly at odds with his expensive suit and air of confidence. After a moment, he shook his head.

"I can't imagine the feds are going to let you out of their sight now that we know you're effectively the key to recovering the money. It's much more likely that they'll stash you somewhere in protective custody. If this gets out, people would kill to get to you. They can't risk that happening."

Then I asked the question that had been reverberating through my head since Drake had dropped the bomb about the accounts being in my name.

"I didn't set up any of those accounts, so how could they possibly be in my name?"

Ivers's expression was sympathetic when he said, "I really think that's a question for your father, Charlotte."

We sat in heavy, awkward silence while we waited for Drake to return.

And waited.

And waited.

Finally, the door to the room swung open, and Drake strode back in, expression unreadable.

He crossed his arms over his chest, and once again, I held my breath.

"You've got a deal."

simon

Three weeks later.

I grabbed the heavy bag to slow its swinging motion. Sweat stung my eyes as I swiped the back of my forearm across my dripping face. Releasing the bag, I reached up with both hands to grip the beam where it hung from the ceiling of my garage. I leaned into the stretch and dragged in a few deep breaths. Exhaustion was the only way I could shut my brain off for a few minutes at a time. And God knew I needed a break.

To say the last three weeks had been brutal would be an understatement.

Prolonged uncertainty took a vicious toll on a person. Physically, mentally, and otherwise. The ability to compartmentalize that I honed in the service was all that was holding me together. My father had tapped into a well of strength I hadn't known he possessed. Even before my mother opened her eyes, he'd seemed to make a decision that his capacity to fight for her was stronger than his fear of losing her. His spine had straightened, he'd cleaned himself up, and his eyes had regained the sharpness I was used to seeing there. I was starting to think he'd brought my mother back from the brink by force of will alone. She'd opened her eyes two days ago with a lopsided smile and whispered, "Jefferson? What happened?"

I'd dropped to my knees beside her bed as my father had pressed her small hand to his lips and thanked every deity known to man for bringing her back to us. A portion of the crushing weight I'd been carrying had lifted. She wasn't out of the woods completely, but it was a hell of an improvement over watching her lay there, motionless, for weeks on end. The doctors had already started discussing moving her to a rehab facility. Today she'd insisted that I go home and get some rest. Take some time to myself.

Which is why I'd spent the last hour pounding the bag until my arms were almost too heavy to lift.

My father had urged me to go to New York, but Ivers had told me unequivocally it would be a wasted trip. The FBI wouldn't let Charlie see anyone except him, and his visits were extremely limited. For ethical reasons, he couldn't tell me anything except she was fine. It was a small consolation.

Since the day Charlie had been discovered, it had seemed like every media outlet in the country had tried to pin me down for an interview. We'd had to beef up security at the hospital, and I'd never been so happy to live behind a gate. It was all I could do to refrain from beating the shit out of the former intern who still waited outside my house, yelling that he deserved an exclusive for being the one to break the story. Every time I saw him, I couldn't help but wonder if Charlie would have ever told me the truth. Because of him, I'd never know, and that fact ate at me, continually dredging up doubt.

The folded up letter in my wallet was all that kept me from losing hope. She'd said she'd left her heart with me. But that wasn't enough. I wanted all of her.

The letter also kept me up at night because of what she didn't include: an assurance that she was coming back.

I'd stopped myself time and again from asking Ivers to give her a message. I would move heaven and Earth to smooth the road ahead of us, but at the end of the day, she needed to decide that she wanted to walk down it with me. Charlie had to be all in for us to have any chance at a future. What would I do if she decided that disappearing again was easier than coming home? The thought sent me back to the bag. If I was too tired to move, hopefully I'd be too tired to think.

charlie

Three more weeks later.

The black Suburban inched through Manhattan's morning rush hour traffic. Today was the first day I'd been permitted to leave the split-level in Staten Island where the FBI had stashed me. And I wouldn't be going back. Because today I was regaining my freedom.

Six weeks in a safe house was certainly no vacation, but given the alternative, I hadn't voiced a single complaint. Instead, I'd signed every piece of paper the feds had put in front of me. With each signature, I felt a sense of justice being served. That I was righting my father's wrongs. And that feeling went a long way toward helping me cope with the boredom. I'd been allowed virtually no contact with the outside world. No internet access, no phone calls and, other than my rotating teams of FBI babysitters and rare appearances by Ivers to ensure the feds were holding up their end of the deal, no visitors. I surmised that my lock-down was to prevent the possibility of any information being leaked about the recovery of the money.

Regardless of the reason, once again I'd had altogether too much time to think. And as you might expect, Simon dominated those thoughts. And how could he not? He was the kind of man you waited your whole life to meet, even though you had no idea you were waiting.

I'd had endless hours to replay the shock, disappointment, and betrayal that had flashed across his features as the press had hurled their questions like daggers, shredding my carefully constructed charade. It didn't matter that I'd finally decided to come clean. All that mattered were all of the times I'd chosen not to.

Simon wasn't the kind of man who deserved to be dragged through the scandal that would always follow me. It wouldn't matter that the funds recovered nearly exceeded what had been originally stolen when you added in the interest that had accrued. You could glue a broken plate back together, but you'd always see the crack. You'd never forget that it'd once been damaged.

In my case, recovering the money wouldn't wash away the fact that I'd always be the infamous daughter of the reviled Alistair Agoston.

The Suburban pulled into an underground parking structure, and we traveled up a freight elevator that opened into a service hallway and the rear entrance of the U.S. Attorney's Office. My escorts led me to a conference room where Drake and Ivers were both waiting.

I took the chair next to Ivers, and Drake slid two documents across the table. My hands shook as I reached for them

"As we agreed," Drake said. I'm not sure if his words were for me or for Ivers, but I didn't care either way. I was too busy staring at the signed and filed orders from a federal judge and a state court judge dismissing all charges against me with prejudice. These documents meant that neither the U.S. government nor the State of New York could come after me again for anything connected with my father's crimes. They were giving me back my freedom. *My future.*

Now that I had them in my hands and no one could take them away, I asked the question that I had been afraid to ask before. "What about the rest of the accounts? The ones that weren't in my name? What about that money?"

"They're our problem, not yours." Drake gave me a brisk nod of acknowledgment and stood. "I believe we're done here. Have a nice life, Ms. Agoston."

I sagged back in my chair. It was really over.

Ivers rose and shook Drake's hand. "Could we have the room for another minute or two? I need to have a few words with my client."

"Take all the time you need."

Drake shut the door as he left the conference room. Ivers reached into the inner pocket of his suit jacket and produced a piece of paper folded into neat thirds. He held it out to me.

"What is it?" I asked.

His lips quirked. It was the first time I'd seen anything approaching a smile on his face.

"Just take it."

I complied and unfolded it. It was a printout of an e-ticket. A flight from JFK to New Orleans. For tomorrow.

I looked up, eyes wide. "What is this?"

"I would think that's obvious."

I blinked down at the e-ticket again. "But … why?"

"I was asked by Mr. Duchesne to make certain you got it. I informed him that the dismissals would be filed this morning. He made the reservation for tomorrow as he thought you might need some time to wrap things up here before heading home."

My heart thudded in my chest.

Home.

I swallowed, continuing to stare at the piece of paper as if the flight information would somehow rearrange itself into a message from Simon.

He wants me to come home.

My mind raced with the possibilities. His motivations. The consequences.

Just being near him, I would tar him with my notoriety. It wasn't like I could keep pretending that I was Charlie Stone—that ship had sailed. Or maybe sank was more accurate. But even if my name wasn't Charlotte Agoston, the tattoos covering my arms ensured that I would never look demure in a dress, standing behind him as he gave a rousing speech to a cheering crowd. I was political cyanide, and there was no doubt in my mind that he'd have to choose between his dream and me.

I fingered the piece of paper in my hand. What the hell was I supposed to do with it? Be selfish or selfless? God knew I wanted to be with him. But how could I really choose to taint his future with the darkness that would always follow me?

"There's also a reservation in your name at the Waldorf for tonight. Everything has been taken care of; all you have to do is check in."

I looked back down at the e-ticket and double-checked the departure time.

Twenty-four hours to decide.

I drew in a deep breath and let it out slowly. No pressure. Just a choice that would dictate the course of the rest of my life. Run to him or run from him?

Ivers stood and offered his hand. I shook it. "Thank you."

He tilted his head slightly and studied me. It was like he was analyzing the chaotic indecision of my thoughts. "You're very welcome, Ms. Agoston. Is there anything you'd like me to tell Mr. Duchesne when I speak with him? Will you be using the ticket?"

There was a knock at the door, and I was saved from having to answer when Drake stuck his head in.

"You have a visitor in the lobby, Ms. Agoston. One that has been very persistent over the last several weeks. Both here and at the FBI field office."

I scrunched my brow, trying to figure out who the hell would be trying to see me. "Who?"

"Your mother."

My mother? My hands flew to my hair, and I began smoothing it into place before I realized that just the thought of facing her had me falling back into old habits. I forced my hands down to my sides. There was nothing about my appearance my mother would find acceptable, so what was the point? I could hope she'd just be happy to see me. *Right*. I wouldn't hold my breath.

Moving slowly to delay the coming confrontation, I folded the e-ticket and dismissal orders and stuck them in my backpack. I hefted the duffle bag that the FBI agents had supplied to hold the extra clothes they'd provided me. More jeans and T-shirts to round out my wardrobe.

"Thank you again for everything," I said to Ivers.

"It was my pleasure. Best of luck to you, Ms. Agoston."

I met Drake at the door. "Lead the way."

The paneled lobby of the U.S. Attorney's Office was empty except for the receptionist and my mother. She was dressed in a linen pantsuit that she'd somehow managed to keep wrinkle free. *No surprise there.* Wrinkles were the enemy. Except it was clear that her current budget didn't allow for regular Botox, because for the first time in my life, my mother had crow's feet and looked very much her actual age. It reminded me that the last year hadn't just been rough on me. My feelings toward her softened when I thought about her staying in New York and braving the gossip and ugly aftermath, while I'd chosen to run and hide. Whatever else she was, she was a strong woman.

"Mother. How are you?"

Her eyes raked me from head to toe, and any softness I felt faded. I could only imagine the flaws she was cataloging. The hair (which desperately needed a fresh dye job), the dozens of interconnected tattoos, the plain black tank and jeans, and my ratty old Chucks (which desperately needed replacing). I braced for her criticism, but it didn't come.

"I've been trying to see you for weeks, but they wouldn't let me." Her tone was aggrieved.

Maybe ... she'd missed me? It was possible that a year had given her some perspective about what was really important. Not money. Not status. Not influence. *People. Family.*

"I'm sorry. I didn't really have any control over that."

She waved off my response with a flip of her golden bob.

"Despite your ... appearance ... you seem to have done well for yourself in New Orleans. You are your mother's daughter after all. Landed on your feet."

What the hell was she talking about?

If she called over a year of lying to everyone and living under a false identity 'doing well for myself' and 'landing on my feet,' then we had very different interpretations of those phrases.

And then her meaning hit me. Her reason for being here became crystal *fucking* clear. A cold rush of disappointment flooded me as her next words confirmed my thoughts.

"The son of a former congressman? I didn't think you had it in you, Charlotte. I was happily surprised when I saw it on the news. It's too bad he's decided not to run. They're blaming it on his mother's condition, and I'm hoping it's not really because of you. It'll be much harder to get him back if that's the case."

His mother's condition? Decided not to run?

"What happened to Mrs. Duchesne?"

"It all hit the papers at the same time. She had a stroke. Spent several weeks in a coma. She's only been out of the hospital and home for a week or so now. I've been following it rather closely, given the circumstances."

I stumbled to a chair and sat.

Oh my God. Simon.

"She's okay, though? She's going to be all right?" I asked, my chest aching for him. For his father. *Jesus Christ.*

"The extent of her recovery is unclear from the papers, and the family has released very little information. I came to bring you some things so you'd be properly attired when you rushed to his side to comfort him during his time of need. It's just unfortunate it's taken so long for the FBI to sort out this ridiculous mess."

Mercenary. Bitch.

She crossed the lobby to retrieve a garment bag from the sofa on the opposite side of the room.

"This is for you."

I eyed the bag like it held hazardous waste. If it contained trappings of my former life, that description wasn't far off in my mind.

"Keep it."

"But Charlotte, you need to—"

I crossed my arms. "Don't tell me what I need to do." I fought to keep my voice steady, but my success was marginal. "You don't know me. You never did."

Her gaze hardened as she straightened her already perfect posture.

"You have a chance to pull us out of the gutter where your father dragged us." She hissed the quiet words from between clenched teeth. "And you will not waste it. Do you hear me, Charlotte? If there's a chance that man will take you back after all of the shameful publicity you've brought on yourself—You. Will. Not. Waste. It." She reached down and grabbed my arm, her nails biting into my skin.

"Let. Me. Go."

She glanced down and released her hold as if she was surprised to find my arm in her grip.

Smoothing her pristine linen suit jacket, she attempted to tuck away the flare of emotion. It was probably the most honest reaction I'd ever seen from her. But she couldn't quite hide the desperate look of a drowning woman. One who thought to use her daughter as a life raft. *Well, Mother,* I thought, *I'm not even sure if I can save myself.* But she needed to know that Simon wasn't going to be her ticket back into the social circles from which she'd fallen. I wouldn't let anyone use him. Not even my own mother.

"My relationship—or lack thereof—with Simon, is none of your business. And it will *never* be any of your business. Please don't come looking for me again until you've decided to act like a decent human being instead of a manipulative bitch. I have to go. Good luck, Mother."

She stayed frozen in place as I stepped around her to make my way to the elevator. As the doors shut, I wondered if it would be the last time I saw her.

Although the papers had referred to it as 'Club Fed,' the razor wire, stony-face guards, and shifty-eyed inmates of FCI Otisville reminded me all too much of Rikers. A chill slid through me at the memory. If not for Ivers's intervention at Simon's direction, I might be spending the rest of my life in a place like this.

I followed one of the guards to a large room filled with chipped, gray formica-covered tables and orange chairs, all bolted to the floor. I studied my surroundings as I waited for the door to open.

My father still walked like a king, a man certain of his superiority to all of those in his domain. Neither prison, nor the khaki-colored jumpsuit, had diminished his air of authority. His silver hair had thinned on top and had lost the perfect style ensured by weekly five hundred dollar haircuts. His eyes widened upon entering the room. Apparently he hadn't seen pictures of the *new* me.

He settled into the chair across from me as the guard backed away.

"You've got twenty minutes, Agoston." My father didn't bother to reply to the guard's statement. His focus had shifted entirely to me.

"Charlotte. Jesus, I've been worried sick about you."

I stilled. Parental concern was the last thing I'd expected from him.

"Excuse me?"

"You disappear for a damn year, no word to anyone, and then you reappear out of the blue and throw yourself on the mercy of the FBI. Which, God knows, they have none. What the hell were you thinking? I thought you were smarter than that. I *know* you're smarter than that."

Seriously? He was going to criticize me? I leaned forward, fingers gripping the edge of the table.

"Apparently I wasn't smart enough to realize that my own father tried to frame me. Who does that to their own kid?"

He blinked in confusion. "What the hell are you talking about?"

"The notebook. The one that was hidden in *my* closet. The one with all of the account numbers and deposits. The one that linked *me* to everything *you* did. I'm lucky I'm not still sitting in a cell because of you. Why would you do that?"

His jaw dropped.

"I never ... It wasn't ... You weren't..." I'd never heard my father stutter before. I'd never heard him speak except with absolute, unwavering confidence. He cleared his throat, seemed to pull himself together, and leaned forward to whisper, "I was taking care of my family. You were supposed to use that damn brain of yours and get the hell out of the country. I knew your mother would never figure it out, but I knew you could. I left the book in your room so you'd have the means to get your hands on resources to look after yourself and your mother when everything fell apart."

This time my jaw dropped. My grip on the table tightened almost to the point of pain. Of all of the motives I'd attributed to my father over the last weeks, this one had never crossed my mind.

"Holy shit." I hadn't meant to speak the words aloud.

"Indeed. But you blew that plan out of the water. I thought … for over a year, I thought that you were being taken care of. That you'd managed to figure everything out. But then I find out you were scraping by, living hand-to-mouth, and then you go to the FBI?" He shook his head in disgust. "You're a smart girl, Charlotte. I expected more from you."

"You expected more from me? I expected more from you!" My temper flared hot and fierce. "You ruined thousands of lives—including mine—and you expected more from me?"

"Keep your voice down." His tone snapped with impatience.

I shook my head in disbelief. "I can't believe you." I had the answers I came for. They weren't the ones I expected to get, but I had them all the same. "I almost ended up in prison for the rest of my life because of your goddamn contingency plan. So don't expect me to thank you for doing me any favors."

"None of that would have happened if you'd just used your brain, found the money, and kept your head down. But you had to try to *fix* things. You should've just left well enough alone. Frankly, I'm disappointed in you. You're not the daughter I thought I knew."

I pushed up from the table. Once again, I was done.

"Well, thank God for that. Goodbye, Dad."

charlie

I studied the outline left by the stylized *A* that used to grace the marble exterior of the Agoston Investments building on Madison Avenue. Eighteen months ago I'd thought that this place would be the center of my world. Standing on the sidewalk after my emotional rollercoaster of a day, I could see how cold and empty that existence would have been. Countless hours spent worshipping at the altar of the almighty dollar. Superficial friendships based on social capital and influence. And probably a loveless marriage born of parental and societal pressure. Now, just the thought made me shudder.

I'd lied to my father earlier about one thing: he hadn't ruined my life. He'd *saved* it. His actions had forced me out of my comfort zone and taught me to *live*.

I deeply regretted the hardships his victims had faced, but his insatiable greed had flung open my cage door. When I'd left New York, I might have been trying to get lost, but I'd found myself instead.

My eyes pricked with sneaky tears at the thought of my life in New Orleans. Part of me wished I could return and have everything be the same as it had been before I left. But then I'd still be living a lie.

How could I go back now? The city I'd fallen in love with would never be the same for me again. Charlotte Agoston wouldn't be allowed to have the simple life of Charlie Stone.

"Charlotte, sweetheart. Is that really you?"

The familiar voice chased away my warring thoughts. I turned away from the building—away from my past and the future I'd escaped.

Juanita's dark hair was threaded with more silver than it had been the day I'd left New York, but to me she'd never looked better. She looked happy. Tears tracked down her cheeks as she pulled me into her arms.

"God, I've missed you, girl." She squeezed me tighter before stepping back to examine me. "Look at you."

Unlike my mother's inspection, Juanita's didn't have me ready to haul out my armor.

"You look beautiful. Like … you're finally comfortable in your own skin."

As always, she was perceptive as hell.

"I missed you. I'm sorry I didn't keep in touch. I was afraid that if you knew where I was…"

"Don't even try to apologize. As far as I was concerned, no news was good news. Now, let's get off the street and get a cup of coffee. I want to hear everything that's happened since you walked out of my kitchen." Juanita looped her arm through mine and pulled me across the street to the café where we had agreed to meet.

A thought occurred to me. "How did you know where I was just now?" I should have been waiting in the café, but I'd been unwillingly drawn to the symbol of my past rising high in the Manhattan skyline.

"You stand out like a sore thumb in this part of town, Charlotte. I saw the rubberneckers from across the street. Wasn't hard to figure out."

Fair enough.

We settled into a back booth with steaming mugs in front of us, and Juanita wasted no time getting down to business.

"Tell me everything. But first, tell me about this Southern gentlemen you were photographed with when everything hit the papers."

I squeezed my eyes shut for a beat as guilt battered me. Those pictures had probably killed any possibility of Simon having a future in politics.

But there was a chance that if I stayed away, and he decided to run after his mother was well again, the buzz around him would die down, and he'd eventually have a fighting chance of being elected. But if I went back ... well, suffice it to say that between my name and my colorful appearance, Simon's political career would stay dead.

"Charlotte?"

I looked up, realizing that Juanita had been waiting for me to answer her question.

I tried levity to deflect. "Jeez. Why can't you start with something easier? Like, why the heck I decided to cover my perfectly good arms with tattoos."

My attempt at deflection failed. Juanita just raised a brow. "So, he *was* someone important. Duchesne, was it?" I didn't like that she was speaking in the past tense.

"His name is Simon Duchesne."

She eyed me shrewdly. "And he was important?"

I swallowed. "He *is* important."

"And you love him."

That one wasn't a question, but I answered anyway. "Yes."

"So now what?"

"I don't know." I stared down into the steam rising off my mug. I gave myself permission to be honest. "I want to go back, but if I were a better person, I wouldn't even consider it. I should run as far and as fast as I can in the opposite direction. And I hate myself for not being strong enough to do it. That's just one more reason he deserves better."

"So you've decided to be your own judge, jury, and executioner? I didn't realize you'd become a martyr."

I bristled. "How is that being a martyr? Aren't you supposed to put the people you love before yourself?

She ignored my question and countered with another of her own. "What would your Simon have to say if he were here listening to this?"

I pictured Simon's strong features, flashing hazel eyes, and tousled dark hair. What *would* he say? I thought of the plane ticket. That was as clear of a message as he could send. "Probably something along the lines of 'get the hell home where you belong'."

"Then there's your answer."

"It's not that simple."

"Why does it have to be complicated?"

"Because he's better off without me. Even if he doesn't want to admit it."

Juanita covered my fidgeting hand with hers. "And you? Are you better off without him? Isn't that the real question you should be trying to answer?"

"I'm not worried about me—"

"Why not? Don't you deserve the same consideration?" Her tone was no-nonsense. "You have to stop treating yourself as somehow being less because of what your father did. I've told you before, but clearly it didn't make an impression. Your father's actions are no reflection of your character, Charlotte. You need to quit thinking they are, or you're going to spend the rest of your life running from something you can never escape."

"But—"

"But nothing. Simon's a grown man. You should let him make his own decision. If you love him, then he deserves that much. Anything else is a disservice to both of you." Her dark eyes pinned me. "You're not a stupid girl, Charlotte. So stop acting like you are. What other plan do you have? Keep running?"

I bowed my head, letting my hair fall into my face. "I'm still figuring that out."

"My advice would be not to take too long to decide. Life only gives us so many chances at happiness. You'd do well not to waste this one."

simon

I watched the same two pieces of unclaimed luggage go around and around the baggage carousel. One was a hard case of golf clubs, and other was a tapestry-patterned bag that looked like something a grandmother would carry. My suspicion was confirmed when an airport employee loaded the flower-covered bag on a cart pushed by an older woman in tan orthopedic shoes. A man on a cell phone hauled the golf clubs away.

My hopes were sinking, but I refused to give up on her. She traveled light. No luggage didn't mean no Charlie. But from my bench, I had a perfect view of all of the arriving travelers, and she hadn't been among them. The gate agent had been able to confirm that the flight out of New York had been delayed, but the passengers aboard probably had enough time to make the New Orleans connection. Even at my most charming, the woman had refused to tell me one way or another whether Charlie had boarded either flight. Her murmured apologies about policies and data privacy didn't calm the knots in my stomach. My call to Ivers didn't give me anything either. He had no idea what Charlie had done after he'd left her at the U.S. Attorney's Office. When I'd booked the flight, I'd once again debated whether to include a message for Ivers to pass along. But something had held me back. The conversation Charlie and I needed to have couldn't take place through an intermediary. I was banking on the fact that the plane ticket would speak for itself.

How much clearer could I make it that I wanted her to come home? That I didn't care who she was?

But I *did* care that she hadn't trusted me. I hated knowing that she'd made a conscious decision to withhold the truth, even though I'd made it pretty damn clear that it didn't matter what she was hiding. Well, as long as it wasn't three husbands and a string of serial murders. I tried to put myself in her position, but even then, it sucked to know she hadn't felt like she could trust me.

So I sat on my bench and waited.

And waited.

And waited.

When I finally rose, feeling like the metal slats had imprinted themselves on my ass, I had to face facts: I'd been waiting for a lot longer than four hours. I'd been waiting for months—even before she'd run. All I'd wanted from her was a sign that she was in this with me. A sign that we had a chance at something real together. And I'd gotten nothing.

I'd waited for nothing.

I left the airport wondering how much longer I could wait for this woman.

Derek met me at the bar.

"I take it she wasn't on the plane."

"No." My tone was clipped. I really didn't want to talk about it. About her. I wanted to get drunk. "Maker's. Neat," I told the bartender.

"Yes, sir."

"So what are you going to do? You going up there?"

I turned to Derek. "Can we just drink?"

"Come on, man. You gotta have a plan. I know you. You *always* have a plan."

He was right. Except, for the first time in my life, I didn't. "Charlie has a habit of blowing all of my fucking plans to pieces." The bartender set the bourbon in front of me, and I picked it up and took a healthy swig. "You want to know what my plan was for today? I was going to pick her up at the airport, and it was going to be romantic as hell. Instead, I watched luggage go round and round the baggage claim for four fucking hours, and she never came. Killed my sense of romance." I tipped back the rest of my drink and smacked the glass down on the bar. "So now, I just want to get drunk enough so I can stop thinking about everything for a few hours. How's that sound?"

Derek studied me with all too knowing eyes. "How long are you going to chase this girl before you finally give up on her?"

The thing that sucked about having a best friend who'd known you since childhood was that he wasn't afraid to ask a question you weren't ready to answer. I wasn't ready to give up on Charlie yet, but I was nearing the edge of my fortitude.

I gestured to the bartender to pour me another. Derek stayed silent, clearly waiting for a response. Refilled drink in hand, I turned back to him. "What? How the fuck do you expect me to answer that?"

He shrugged and sipped his drink. "With the truth, I guess."

"The truth is, I don't know. If you were in my shoes, would you have stopped chasing Mandy?"

He swirled the liquor in his glass. "No. But still, there comes a point when she's gotta push all her chips into the middle too. You've both gotta be all in."

"You think I don't know that?" My frustration ratcheted up a few more notches.

"I don't know what to say, man. I guess, if I were you, I'd give it a few more days, and then I'd start asking myself some tough questions. Because with her history of running, you might have to face the possibility that she might never be coming back."

I downed the rest of my bourbon. I waved the bartender over. "Can you just leave us the bottle?"

Derek looked sideways at me. "Getting hammered ain't exactly gonna help."

I sloshed liquor into my glass. "Sure ain't gonna hurt."

charlie

After one delayed flight due to mechanical problems, one missed connection because I'd misread my boarding pass, and one uncomfortable night of no sleep on a bench in the Atlanta airport, the plane touched down in New Orleans at eleven AM. I waited impatiently for the passengers ahead of me to grab their luggage and disembark. The saying, 'a day late and a dollar short' kept running through my head.

As the cab approached the familiar iron gates, topped with intricate fleur de lis, I struggled to piece together what the hell I was going to say.

I'm sorry seemed so ... inadequate.

I paid the driver and climbed out. I faced the fence that separated me from Simon. The irony wasn't lost on me. Just like before, there was more than metal between us. There were the lies, the truth, and everything else. I wondered if we could really overcome it. I reached for the button on the intercom, but paused when I spotted Simon through the vine-covered bars.

He was holding a leash.

Connected to my big mutt.

Huck's head jerked up, and a series of deep barks ripped through the stillness of the late morning. His huge body lunged forward, tugging the leash from Simon's hand.

Simon turned and froze.

He looked like hell. Tired. Ragged around the edges. He was barefoot, wearing khaki cargo shorts and a black T-shirt. His hair was shaggy, curling around his ears in a way that suggested he'd had more important things to worry about than making time for a barber. Several days' worth of beard covered his jaw. He was still gorgeous, but once again, I was faced with a different Simon than I'd ever seen before. His expression gave nothing away. And it certainly didn't fill me with hope.

Huck trotted—without limping—toward the fence. He whined and pawed and licked my hand through the bars.

I scratched behind his ear, and he leaned into my touch. "Missed you, too, baby," I whispered.

Simon took his time crossing the lawn. When he finally came close enough, I could see the dark circles under his eyes.

"Hi." It was the lamest opening line, but I didn't know what else to say.

Simon stopped in front of the gate and watched me. He didn't reply.

I'm not sure how long we stood, just staring and trying to guess what the other was thinking. The seconds ticked by in almost painful silence.

I remembered the last time we'd played emotional chicken. It seemed I'd have to swerve first this time, too. "I—"

He spoke at the exact same moment. "I waited at the airport yesterday. For four hours. When you didn't show up, I thought you'd decided to keep running."

I swallowed. The time had finally come for absolute honesty. "I thought about it." A flash of anguish arced across his features, but I pushed on. "I probably should have. It probably would have been better for you in the long run never to see me again."

He laughed humorlessly and gripped the back of his neck with one hand. He looked skyward. "Don't do me any favors, Charlie."

"Trust me, I'm not. I don't see the upside for you in this. I pretty much see nothing but downsides on your end. Being with me is a bad deal. The secret's out, and unless I run and hide and become someone else again, everyone will know who I am—the daughter of a thief, and a liar in my own right. That's who I'm going to be for the rest of my life. Anyone who stands by me is going to be ruined by it." I took a deep breath and cut to the heart of the matter. "But it turns out I'm not strong enough to walk away from you again. This time, you're going to have to tell me to go. Because otherwise, I'm not leaving."

At some point during my speech, Simon had moved closer to the gate. He gripped one bar in a white-knuckle hold. The muscle in his jaw ticked, and I braced myself, hoping like hell I hadn't said too much. Hoping like hell I hadn't finally convinced him that I wasn't worth it.

"I've spent all day trying to figure out what I was going to do if you'd decided to run. How I was going to deal with the fact you might not be coming back."

A shaft of pain lanced through me. *Had he already started trying to figure out how to cut me out of his life?* "Simon—"

"No. You've said your piece. It's my turn." He reached a hand through the fence and toyed with a lock of my hair. "Because there's still one thing you don't seem to get: I don't care who you are. I don't care if you're Charlie or Charlotte or Lee, or anyone else. Because all that matters is that you're *mine*. I wasn't going to let you go without a fight. If you'd run, I would've chased you. Just like I have since the beginning."

"But—"

He cupped my face with his hand and ran his thumb over my lips to silence me. "If you're going to tell me one more time how bad you are for me, I don't want to hear it. The only thing I want to hear coming out of your mouth is you telling me that you love me."

His thumb moved away from my lips, and the words tumbled out. "I love you."

Simon leaned against the fence and squeezed his eyes shut for a moment. A smile stretched across his face, and his eyes met mine.

"Welcome home, Charlie. I missed you."

He pulled his hand back through the bars and reached for a button to open the gate. As soon as there was enough room, I left my bags on the sidewalk, slid through the gap, and launched myself at him.

Simon's strong arms caught me and lifted me off my feet. I wrapped myself around him. This man was mine, and I was never letting him go again. He pressed his lips to my hair, and whispered, "Missed you so fucking much. Not letting you out of my sight for a goddamn year." My only response was to hold on tighter.

When he finally set me down, the lightheartedness left me, and my expression turned serious. "How's your mom? Is she going to be okay?"

Simon's smile didn't fade. "She's going to be fine. A lot of therapy, but she's going to be just fine."

"And your decision not to campaign ... was that because of me? Because I—"

Simon cut me off. "No. I'd already decided that before the Fourth of July. You just didn't stick around long enough for me to tell you about it."

Heat flared up my cheeks. "I knew if I wanted a chance with you, I had to make things right." I looked down at the ground and the toes of my ratty Chucks. "It just didn't exactly work out like I'd planned."

"If Ivers had gotten to you before—"

This time I cut him off. "It wouldn't have made a difference. It needed to happen this way. I definitely could have lived without setting foot in Rikers, but at least people are getting back what they lost."

Simon scowled. "Like I said. Not letting you out of my sight."

The front door swung open, and we both turned toward the sound.

Simon's father stood behind his mother's wheelchair. She smiled, her face still slightly askew, but she lifted a hand and waved. Mr. Duchesne called out, "Welcome home, Charlie. Maggie would like to invite you to lunch. Nothing fancy. Just family."

I smiled as a lump rose in my throat. *Just family.* Their easy acceptance humbled me. And I knew I was truly home.

"I'd love to."

Simon pressed another kiss to my hair, and whispered, "I love you."

I threaded my fingers through his, and we walked hand in hand toward the house.

simon

I parked across the street from Harriet's and turned to
Charlie.

"When I said I wasn't letting you out of my sight, I
wasn't kidding. If this is where you want to stay tonight,
you'd better be ready for some company." I hoped she
realized how serious I was. After more than six weeks
apart with nothing but questions and unknowns between
us, I wanted us on the same page when it came to our
future. I knew what I wanted—Charlie in my bed every
night, with my ring on her finger. My store of patience had
run dry. After facing the possibility of losing her, I wasn't
going to rest until I'd locked down forever with this
woman.

She looked up from beneath her dark lashes and shot
me a saucy smirk. "Since I wasn't planning on letting you
leave, that works for me."

I reached for my door handle, but Charlie was already
out of the car and crossing the street. What the hell was
her hurry?

Impatience or anxiety or something else I couldn't
quite identify had been rolling off her since she'd asked
me to bring her back to the apartment after dinner. As
much as I'd wanted to tuck her into my bed, I hadn't
argued. Strangely enough, she'd suggested leaving Huck
curled up at my mother's feet. Something was up, but I
had no idea what. With Charlie, it could be anything.

When I climbed out of the car, she was already
shoving her key into the ancient lock. "Excited to see
Harriet?" I asked.

She smiled and held open the gate. "You first."

"What's going on here?"

She bit her lip, unsuccessfully holding back a laugh. "Just roll with it, Simon."

I leaned down and brushed a kiss across her hair. "Only for you."

I walked through the narrow passageway into Charlie's garden oasis and stopped dead. Dozens of fat, white pillar candles sat on the table, the edge of the fountain and koi pond, on the ledges of the brick walls, and around the splash pool. The yellow flames flickered in the evening breeze.

I spun in a slow circle, taking it all in. A romantic gesture from Charlie. I liked where this was headed.

"How did you manage to pull this off?" I asked, finishing my circle just as she tugged her black T-shirt over her head and dropped it on the ground. The best sort of déjà vu rushed through me.

"Harriet. And she was kind enough to give us some privacy." She reached behind her back and unclasped her bra. It dangled from her fingertips for a moment before it landed on her shirt. She was so goddamn beautiful she stole any other thoughts straight out of my head.

I watched with pure male appreciation as she toed off her Chucks and reached for the zipper on her jeans. She shimmied them off as she said, "Last time I tried this, you told me to let you know when I was ready for more than a quick fuck."

She exposed the pale, white skin of her legs as she kicked her jeans and panties aside, and I fought to follow her line of conversation. "I remember saying something like that."

"This is me telling you, without a single reservation, that I want more. A whole hell of a lot more, Simon. I want it all. With you."

My heart hammered at her words and the sight of her before me. Naked in every way. No walls. No masks. No secrets. No lies. Just Charlie. My inked, pierced, beautiful Charlie.

My already wide smile stretched further. "That's convenient, because I wasn't going to take no for an answer."

She tilted her head. "An answer to what?"

I stuck my hand in my pocket and felt the ring that I'd been carrying around since yesterday morning. After my grand airport reunion plan had been derailed, I told myself I was going to wait. That I wasn't going to do this tonight. That I was going to let her settle in for a few more days before I brought it up. But for some reason, I'd kept the ring in my pocket anyway. And I was glad as hell, because I couldn't let this moment pass without asking.

I dropped to one knee on the concrete in front of her, pulled the ring out, and held it up.

She slapped a hand over her mouth. "Are you serious? Now? You're doing this now? While I'm fucking naked? Seriously?"

I grinned. Now was the perfect time. I reached for her left hand.

"Charlotte Agoston, I love you. Every goddamn piece of you, including your past, because it made you who you are, and it brought you to me. I want to spend the rest of my life with you by my side. I want to stand up in front of God and everyone and make you mine. Will you marry me?"

She squeezed her eyes shut. "Why do you never do what I think you're going to?"

I lifted her hand to my lips and kissed it. "That's not the answer I was hoping for, baby."

"Jesus, Simon. You realize we can never tell this story to anyone. Because if you tell anyone we got engaged while I was naked..."

I stood and drew her against me. "Is that a yes?"

She reached up to wrap her arms around my neck. Just before she pressed her lips to mine, she whispered, "Of course, it's a yes."

The kiss started sweet, but I couldn't stop myself from taking over. I would never get enough of her. *Never.* When we finally separated, I remembered the ring, which I'd managed not to drop. I reached for her left hand again, and stared into her shimmering aqua eyes as I slid it onto her finger.

She glanced down at it for a moment before twining her fingers in mine. The diamond flashed in the candlelight as Charlie led me toward the edge of the pool. Releasing my hand, she stepped down the stairs and sank into the water.

With her hair floating around her on the surface, she looked like a pagan goddess. *Thank God Derek got drunk enough to want Mandy's name tattooed on his ass.*

"You coming in?" she asked.

I tugged off my T-shirt and stripped off my shorts and boxer briefs in no time.

"Wherever you are is where I want to be."

A soft smile stretched across her face, and I knew that if I could make her smile like that every day for the rest of my life, I'd be a damn lucky man.

I descended into the pool and followed her as she floated backward. Trapping her against the concrete edge, I ducked my head to kiss her shoulder, her neck, and then her jaw. "So you say you're ready for a whole hell of a lot more…"

She threaded her fingers through my hair and met my eyes. "I'm ready for anything, as long as it's with you."

"Not just anything, Charlie. *Everything.*"

EPILOGUE
charlie

The early afternoon sunshine heated my skin; I closed my eyes and soaked it up. A crowd of people poured from the arched doorways of St. Louis Cathedral. Simon pressed a kiss to my shoulder.

"You look incredible. And I'm the luckiest bastard on the planet."

My vintage Dior dress had cost me almost two months' worth of pay from my very beloved job—Director of Finance of The Kingman Project. It was perhaps the most indulgent purchase I'd ever made, but seeing the look on Simon's face as I walked down the rose petal strewn aisle on his father's arm was worth every penny. The strapless, champagne-colored bodice faded into a thinly layered tulle skirt of the same color. It was encrusted with hundreds of scattered crystals that glittered like diamonds in the sun.

My eyes devoured Simon. He was, as always, devastatingly handsome in a tux. "You don't look so bad yourself." I tilted my face up for a kiss. "Guess that makes me one lucky girl."

And I was lucky. My father might not have given me away, and my mother might not have looked on with tears in her eyes as her daughter married the man she loved, but today—everyday—I was surrounded by people who accepted me for who I was. They'd welcomed me without question when I'd had no past, and embraced me unconditionally even after my secrets had been revealed. They'd shown me what true family was supposed to be.

Simon brushed his lips across mine before straightening as Con approached, Huck at his side.

Handing off the leash to Simon, Con said, "Better treat her right, Duchesne. Or you'll answer to me." While his words carried a warning, the tone wasn't harsh. Simon and Con had, after a few fits and starts, formed a solid friendship of their own.

The men shook hands. "You have my permission to kick my ass if I don't."

Con released Simon's hand and focused on me. Leaning down, he pressed a kiss to my cheek. "Happy looks good on you, Lee. Give 'im hell."

"Thank you. For everything," I whispered.

Con nodded and slipped away to find his date.

"He's right; happy looks beautiful on you." I turned toward the familiar voice to see Juanita dabbing at her eyes with a delicate handkerchief.

I stepped away from Simon to wrap my arms around her.

"Thank you for being here."

"I wouldn't miss it for the world." She squeezed me tightly for a long moment before releasing me.

"Don't forget this, girly," Yve said, holding out a feathered parasol. "It's almost time."

I accepted it from her, along with a hug.

"Thank you. Both of you." The smile that stretched across my face was so wide it made my cheeks ache. It had been that way for days. Blinking back sentimental tears, I twirled the parasol, making the feathers bounce.

Simon returned to my side and accepted hugs from both Yve and Juanita. Then he held out his free hand. "Are you ready, Mrs. Duchesne?"

I laced my fingers through his and smiled up at him. "I am now."

The bandleader called off a beat, and the sound of jazz filled the air as the wedding party, followed by all of our guests, moved en masse toward the streets of the French Quarter.

The End

How do you feel about sexy, tatted-up bad boys? Con's story is next! *Beneath This Ink* is coming this winter. Want special sneak peeks and insider info? Sign up for my newsletter:

http://www.meghanmarch.com/#!newsletter/c1uhp

acknowledgments

I owe thanks to so many people who helped bring *Beneath This Mask* to life. To my husband, for listening to me babble about some crazy plot as I dragged him through the streets of the French Quarter and the Garden District, and then proceeded to ignore him for the next several months while I chained myself to my keyboard. To my family, for your unending support and patience. To my beta readers—Angela Smith, Serena Knautz, and Megan Simpson—thank you for your time, your thoughts, your friendship, and for loving Charlie and Simon as hard as I do. You ladies are amazing. This book wouldn't be what it is without your input. To MCL, for helping with the technical twists. Any errors that remain are my own. To my editor, Madison Seidler—you answer my zillion questions and provide invaluable, no bullshit feedback. I'm so glad I found you! To Katie Spillner-Goodale for polishing it until it shone. To Sarah Hansen of Okay Creations for creating the gorgeous cover. To Jovana Shirley of Unforeseen Editing for the beautiful formatting. To Christine Estevez of Shh Moms Reading for arranging the promo, and all of the book bloggers who took a chance and gave it a read. And finally, my biggest thanks goes out to all of the readers who plunked down their hard-earned money to buy a story that grew out of a fleeting thought at 30,000 feet on a flight to New Orleans. I hope you enjoyed the ride, and I can't thank you enough for joining me on it. Con's story is next! Stay tuned for *Beneath This Ink*!

Come find me!

WEBSITE:
HTTP://WWW.MEGHANMARCH.COM

FACEBOOK:
HTTP://WWW.FACEBOOK.COM/MEGHANMARCHAUTHOR

TWITTER:
HTTP://WWW.TWITTER.COM/MEGHAN_MARCH

PINTEREST:
HTTP://WWW.PINTEREST.COM/MEGHANMARCH1

INSTAGRAM:
HTTP://WWW.INSTAGRAM.COM/MEGHANMARCH

GOODREADS:
HTTPS://WWW.GOODREADS.COM/AUTHOR/SHOW/
8184875.MEGHAN_MARCH

CPSIA information can be obtained
at www.ICGtesting.com
Printed in the USA
LVHW041340040820
662378LV00002B/239